KILLING ROCK

KILLING ROCK

A Sullivan and Broderick Murder Mystery

ROBERT DAWS

This edition published in Great Britain in 2020

by Hobeck Books Limited, Unit 14, Sugnall Business Centre, Sugnall, Stafford, Staffordshire, ST21 6NF

www.hobeck.net

A CIP catalogue for this book is available from the British Library.

ISBN 978-1-913-793-00-5 (pbk)

ISBN 978-1-913-793-01-2 (ebook)

Cover design by Jayne Mapp Design

Map by Josh Collins

Printed and bound in Great Britain

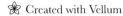 Created with Vellum

Are you a thriller seeker?

Hobeck Books is an independent publisher of crime, thrillers and suspense fiction and we have one aim – to bring you the books you want to read.

For more details about our books, our authors and our plans, plus the chance to download free novellas, sign up for our newsletter at www.hobeck.net.

If you would like us to keep in touch with you, please do sign up to our newsletter via www.hobeck.net for regular updates on our publishing programme, our future plans and our news and a free copy of *Echo Rock*, a Rock ghost story. You can also find us on Twitter @hobeckbooks or on Facebook www.facebook.com/hobeckbooks10.

For Simon, for Paul

'Did you know that the word "trauma" comes from the Greek for "wound"? Hm? And what is the German word for "dream"? Traum. Ein Traum. *Wounds can create monsters, and you, you are wounded, Marshal. And wouldn't you agree, when you see a monster, you ... you must stop it?'*

Dr Jeremiah Naehring, *Shutter Island*

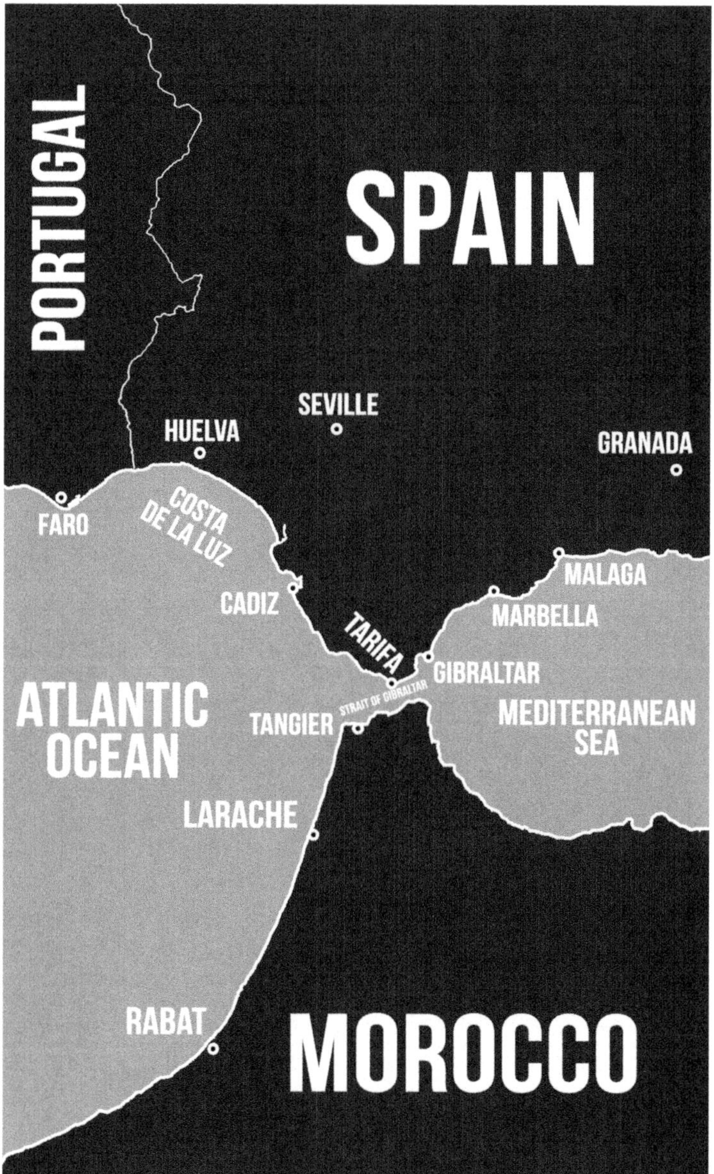
PORTUGAL
SPAIN
SEVILLE
HUELVA
GRANADA
FARO
COSTA
DE LA LUZ
CADIZ
MALAGA
MARBELLA
TARIFA
GIBRALTAR
STRAIT OF GIBRALTAR
ATLANTIC
OCEAN
TANGIER
MEDITERRANEAN
SEA
LARACHE
RABAT
MOROCCO

Costa de la Luz, Spain
SUMMER 2005

The cry of seagulls quickened her heartbeat.

Stepping from the dirt path, her sandalled feet hitting the tarmac of the main coast road at Tarifa, the woman turned once more to check that the track behind was clear. It was a gesture that had become a nervous tic over the two hours she'd been travelling and would not cease until safety had been reached. Nobody was behind her, but she knew she had to move faster. Fear was in her heart, and death, she was certain, was close behind. She had been fortunate to hitch the lift on the orange grower's truck for most of the twenty-kilometre journey from the depths of the country to the sea. With five kilometres still to go, the old farmer had apologised for dropping her an hour's walk from the coast. He could see the desperation in the Englishwoman's eyes but knew better than to interrogate his passenger.

'It will take not long. Straight to sea,' he had told her, pointing to the track. And as a concerned afterthought, '*Buena suerte, señora.*'

At first, the early evening sun shone fiercely as the

woman hiked through the open countryside. Buzzards gliding on thermals above had given way to the sight and sound of ocean-going gulls. Her throat was sore from dust and thirst, a problem secondary to the need to keep moving and reach her destination. The Rock of Gibraltar was some forty kilometres east of where she stood, and she'd be safe there. Gus would make sure of that. She knew he would.

Around her, twilight engulfed the landscape, and the artificial light from passing car headlamps and a roadside neon sign was fast replacing the last embers of sunset. Turning left, the woman crossed the road, which was busy with local traffic and articulated lorries heading westward to Cádiz or in the other direction to Algeciras and the Costa del Sol beyond. Metres to her right, the legendary white sands of Tarifa beach spread for many kilometres in both directions. The surf-loving wind created waves of stature and beauty as they rolled in from the Strait of Gibraltar and the mighty Atlantic Ocean. This southern-most part of Spain, with the Rif Mountains of North Africa seemingly within touching distance, had long been a mecca for surfers and travellers in search of alternative lifestyles. Passing several of the shabby chic hotels and hostels fringing the beach, the woman walked on, her left hand raised, signalling the need to hitch a ride out of town.

The panic was still within her. She wasn't safe. Not here. She'd not felt safe for days. Ever since Yvonne had told her the *secret*. At first it had seemed quite ordinary. Yvonne told of how she'd first met the father of her son the year after the *Summer of Love*. How this small guy with incredible eyes had started talking to her as she stood beside the dance floor of a club on Sunset Boulevard. They were surrounded by the rich and famous of Tinsel Town, all crammed within the hip night spot that everyone in the late nineteen-sixties craved to be *seen* at.

We only spoke a few words, but I just knew he was different. Special. I was only seventeen and shouldn't have even been there – my parents would've killed me if they'd found out – but I knew, I just knew, that this person would be the only man I would ever want.

Yvonne said it was love. The deepest she'd ever known. But the truth of that love was a secret, and now she had to share it. What Yvonne told her next scared the woman. Scared her half to death.

Struggling with these thoughts and the tiredness of her aching limbs, an urgent voice within her screamed, '*Move fast! Don't stop! You'll die!*' The thoughts that now filled her mind were about herself and herself only. *What if I'd remained obedient? What if I'd stayed?* The answer turned her stomach.

A large black van pulled off the main road a short distance ahead, its driver leaning from the window and waving the hitchhiker towards him.

Sitting beside her ramshackle vegetable stall on the other side of the *autopista*, an old woman, her face leathered and furrowed from the Andalusian sun, looked on as the attractive blonde lady in the floral T-shirt was driven off towards the oncoming darkness.

Chapter 1
ROYAL GIBRALTAR POLICE HQ, THE ROCK, LATE SUMMER, 2015

DETECTIVE SERGEANT TAMARA SULLIVAN sat beneath the low-hanging fronds of a palm tree in the central courtyard of the Royal Gibraltar Police HQ on New Mole Parade. The courtyard was a bustling oasis at the heart of the police building, and she looked on as uniformed officers went about their business, crossing the shaded open space from one side of the HQ to the other. Her watch read 3.20 p.m. and opening the Marks & Spencer prawn salad she was about to eat marked the start of her lunch break. Later than usual, but in harmony with Mediterranean siesta hours. Not that meal times were timetabled in the Force. You grabbed food as and when you could. A busy copper was a good copper, or so the unwritten code observed. So it was with some guilt that Sullivan savoured the first mouthful of seafood and marie rose sauce – a favourite since she had first tasted it on a childhood holiday in Blackpool.

It had been a quiet day so far. In fact, it had been a quiet week. Her boss, Chief Inspector Gus Broderick, had been grouchier than usual, faced with yet another tobacco-smuggling investigation and dealing with a shoplifting spree by a group of Eastern Europeans on Main Street. It was important police work, but it bored the veteran cop to tears, an emotion that Broderick didn't hide from either his colleagues or his superior officer, Chief Superintendent Harriet Massetti. Things had been busy over the summer months: two murder investigations completed and adrenalin levels on a seemingly permanent high. That these events corresponded with Sullivan's arrival on a three-month secondment from London's Metropolitan Police Service had also attracted comment.

'We had a bloody easy life over here till you turned up,' Detective Constable John Calbot had teased her. Although that was far from the truth, the two recent cases had pushed the Force to its limits and attracted international attention.

'The press might think you're a star, Sullivan,' Massetti had warned her, 'but you'll notice that I'm not asking for your autograph.'

What Massetti did ask the visiting detective sergeant was whether she wanted to stay on with the RGP permanently. This offer had surprised Sullivan on two counts: first, that the offer had been made at all, and second, that she had accepted it. The realisation that she had fallen for life on the Rock – its people, its climate, its lifestyle – had come to her slowly. But now, as she shaded herself from the baking September sun, she could not deny the excitement she felt at making Gibraltar her home.

The practicalities of taking up this 'new' job meant that, from the following day, she would have to take a month's leave before returning to her position as a DS with

the Royal Gibraltar Police CID. The break was an adminis-
trative requirement – to deal with the paperwork involved
in leaving one force for another, finding new and affordable
accommodation and so on – but it provided welcome time
off, for which Sullivan already had plans.

Finishing her lunch and taking a gulp of mineral water
from a plastic bottle, she stretched her long legs and
allowed the rays of the baking afternoon sun, filtering
through the palm fronds above, to play on her face. *This is
nice*, she thought. *Beats a wet afternoon in Muswell Hill.*

'All right for some, Detective Sergeant.'

The voice of Chief Inspector Gus Broderick broke
Sullivan's reverie. He was walking across the courtyard
from the custody suite, heading for the front gates, and was
clearly expecting Sullivan to follow him. The forty-eight-
year-old police officer was wearing his usual rumpled suit
and loosened tie. Sullivan also noted that he must have had
a haircut during the lunch break. A little too brutal with
the clippers at the back, perhaps, but neater than Broderick's usual unkempt styling.

Dumping her half-eaten salad in the bin, Sullivan ran
to catch up with her boss as he passed through the iron
gates of the HQ and headed out towards New Mole
Parade and his ancient Mercedes estate car. A view of the
busy waters of the Bay of Gibraltar spread westward from
the front of the police building, a glorious sight under-
scored by the noise of the repairs being carried out on the
ships in the dry docks below the low wall that lined the
opposite side of the road.

'Given any thought to Ric's offer of house-sitting for
him?' Broderick asked as he reached his driver's door.

'I have,' Sullivan replied.

Ric Danaher was an old friend of Broderick's; he was a retired London copper who now lived in a small Spanish *finca* that hung grimly onto the side of a hill near the white-washed Andalusian town of Gaucín. As a part-time private investigator, he had helped out Broderick – in an unofficial capacity – with a recent murder inquiry on the Rock.

'And?' Broderick asked.

'I'm going over to see him this evening. To check it out.'

'Nice views from up there and only three goats, some chickens and a dog to look after while he's away. Right up your street I'd have thought, Sullivan.'

'I'll let you know, Guv. Where are we going?'

'Someone's found a body out near Eastern Beach. Thought you might be interested.'

Sullivan opened the car door and got into the passenger seat. Broderick was right. She was very interested.

The body was like none Sullivan had ever seen before. She could only liken it to a zombie created for a horror film or a *Thriller*-type Michael Jackson video. Matted hair, once blonde, covered the top and sides of the skull. What once had been a face was now just bone and teeth and had dark, hollowed eye sockets. Although rotten in places, the remains of clothing – a T-shirt, jeans, sandals – still clung to the body like a macabre costume. Beneath lay a mix of smooth mummified skin and brittle bone – a covering that still allowed some parts of the skeletal framework to show beneath it. Sullivan had assumed that these remains were those of a woman, but now it wasn't obvious that the dehumanised relics had once been female.

'Shit,' Broderick had muttered at first sight. 'The full Halloween.'

They had driven out from Gibraltar Town, heading east along Devil's Tower Road. To their left, they passed the War Memorial and the cemetery with its war graves, and then the airport runway built across the northern end of the isthmus. To their right was the towering northern end of the colossus of limestone that was the Rock. Their destination was a warehouse complex, now demolished, next to Eastern Beach. The land on which it had stood was soon to be redeveloped into a billion-euro super-marina with luxury flats, shops and restaurants. As a prestigious landmark, it would be a 'Jewel in the Rock' when seen by passengers arriving at or flying from Gibraltar airport. Right now it was just a demolition site bordering the sea.

Temporary wire fencing cordoned off the flattened area, within which stood a prefabricated hut and a lone portable toilet. A large tractor, a construction lorry and an RGP patrol car were parked in the centre of the plot. Officers Borrell and Williams were standing beside their vehicle, next to site manager Karl Goosen. Borrell had introduced Goosen to Broderick and Sullivan and then led them all across to a large, shallow excavation nearby. After putting on their shoe and hand protectors, the new arrivals had peered into the hole. The trench had revealed an underground conduit about one metre in diameter and many metres long, which had once run beneath the warehouses. It was a simple ventilation duct, containing no wiring or other structural items. Sullivan observed that several small ants' nests lined its dry, sandy bottom and that hundreds of ants were moving around their defiled world. At the far end of the open trench lay the remains of the body.

In his broad South African accent, Karl Goosen was the first to explain the scene.

'The tractor fell into the hole this morning. Bit by bit the rest of the surface caved in, you know? That's when we found this. Bloody mess, *ja*?'

Officer Borrell looked towards Broderick.

'Do I send for the team, sir?'

Broderick nodded.

'Doesn't look much like an accident, Borrell. Get the crime scene wagon out here and alert Portillo and Kemp. Sullivan and I will have a word with Mr Goosen here.'

Officer Borrell headed back to the patrol car as Broderick turned to the site manager, who was looking alarmed.

'Look, man, I don't know nothing more about this, you know?' said Goosen. 'Surprised the hell out of me.'

'I'm sure it did,' Broderick replied, taking a handkerchief from his pocket and wiping the sweat from his brow. 'Anyone else here when it happened? Were you driving the tractor?'

'No, no. I don't do that stuff. It was Danny on the tractor – Danny Mates. Scared the shit out of him. The whole thing toppled over, you know? He could've been crushed.'

'So where is he now?' Sullivan enquired.

'At the hospital. I think he broke his wrist or something. He was in big pain. I had to let him go, man.'

'How'd he get to the hospital?' Sullivan asked.

'Jayden took him in the van.'

Sullivan and Broderick shared a look.

Goosen continued. 'Yeah, man. Jayden, Danny and me. There's just the three of us here finishing up, you know. Tomorrow we clear this site. Job done. Drive back to base in Rotterdam.'

'You'll have to delay that journey until we get results on this body, Mr Goosen,' Broderick informed him.

'You think *we* had something to do with that?' Goosen said uneasily, pointing at the trench.

'We don't know, Mr Goosen,' Sullivan replied. 'But we may need to ask you and your colleagues a few questions. Just standard procedure, you understand?'

'Yeah, yeah. Okay.'

'Just give your details to the officers over there, please.'

'Sure. Whatever.' Goosen shrugged his shoulders and headed to the patrol car. 'Boy, I need a beer.'

'You're not the only one,' Broderick muttered under his breath.

Sullivan glanced down at the remains once more.

'I think it's a woman.'

'Maybe,' Broderick said. 'Just skin and bone now. Once possessed a name, though, and it's our job to discover it. Or at least it's my job. You're off for the next month.'

Sullivan had not factored that into her thinking. 'I can't just head off and leave you to it.'

Broderick gave her a cold stare.

'You were happy enough to bugger off and leave Calbot and me on tobacco-smuggling duties, as I recall.'

'But this is a game changer. I can't walk away from this.'

'Not my decision, Detective Sergeant. Massetti's the one to convince. Mind you, perhaps your observational skills won't be such a great loss to us over the next few weeks. You didn't even spot I'd had a haircut this lunchtime.'

'Oh, I spotted it, Guv,' Sullivan said, looking her boss straight in the eye. 'It's just that some gruesome discoveries are best left unmentioned.'

Chapter 2

BY LATE AFTERNOON, the site of the demolished warehouses was swarming with activity. The main gates were guarded by uniformed police, allowing access to authorised vehicles and personnel only. Several RGP vehicles were parked beside the prefabricated hut, and the crime scene investigation van – a white Suzuki – stood close to the open trench where the body lay. Having erected a small tent over the remains, the Forensics team now moved around the scene wearing white paper overalls, protective masks and nitrile gloves. All the activity threw up clouds of dust and sand, which stuck in the throat and added to the general discomfort of working under the harsh afternoon sun. Police Surgeon Hannah Portillo, the RGP's Forensic Medical Examiner, exited the crime scene tent and walked over to Broderick and Sullivan.

'Seen nothing quite like this,' she began. 'Virtual mummification from the chest down. Rats or some such may have got to the head, but the rest dried out. Perfect conditions down there for preservation, mind you. Heat and dryness. Ants might have helped in the early stages.'

'Ants?' Sullivan asked.

'Yes. Gobbled up all the insect eggs and maggots before they could get a full hold and hasten decomposition. Just a thought. I'll know more later—'

'And the sex?' Broderick interrupted.

'Female,' Portillo replied, with a look that suggested this was obvious.

'Cause of death?' Sullivan asked, admiring Portillo's style and efficiency.

'There's a large fracture to the back of the skull. Probably the most likely cause, I'd say. Only the post mortem will tell us definitely.'

Broderick checked his phone.

'Got a text here from HQ giving the warehouses' construction date as May/June 2005.'

'Uh-huh,' Portillo replied, removing her nitrile gloves. 'The body could have been preserved indefinitely down there if the conditions had remained unchanged. We have plenty to go on, though, so we should get a fairly accurate date of death after a full examination.'

'Thank you, Hannah.' Broderick smiled. 'Much appreciated.'

'You're most welcome.' Portillo smiled back.

Sullivan indulged in a mischievous thought: *What a good couple they'd make*. Her fantasy was interrupted by a police car being waved through the main roadside gates.

'Looks as if the top brass are coming out to play,' Portillo observed.

Broderick viewed the approaching vehicle grim-faced.

'The Chief Super's on to us early doors. That'll slow things down a good bit.'

The police car pulled up a few yards away from where the officers stood, and Chief Superintendent Harriet Massetti got out from the back seat. Broderick and Sullivan moved across to meet her. At barely regulation height for a police officer, the tough-minded and able Massetti often punched well above her weight within the Royal Gibraltar Police. Her short dark hair framed a delicate bone structure that was Genoese–Gibraltarian by descent. Massetti was a high achiever whose abundant charm disguised an iron will and shrewd professional acumen. A future role for her as the commissioner of police was considered a given by many.

Massetti launched straight in.

'DC Calbot is at the hospital with Jayden Krupps and Danny Mates. What you have here will dictate whether we bring in all three of the demolition employees for questioning.'

'There's no chance of them having anything to do with this, ma'am,' Broderick said. 'Looks like murder. Historic by a decade, we think. Once we've searched here, it'll be a question of looking for the people who put up the warehouses in 2005.'

'Press and media aren't onto this yet,' Massetti said. 'Let's hope it stays that way for a while. A body found on land that's about to be turned into a billion-euro flagship development is not the kind of publicity Gib needs right now. I'm sure you'll agree.'

'Not thinking that far ahead, ma'am.'

'Well, start!' she snapped back, heading for the crime scene tent. 'In the meantime, bring me up to speed here.'

Sullivan hurried after her.

'May I have a quick word, ma'am?'

'Speak.'

'I'd like to request that I stay on this. I know I'm supposed to be off for the month, but I think I might be useful.'

Massetti stopped just short of the tent.

'I'm sure you would, Sullivan, but no can do. Up till now, you've been on secondment. The London Met's baby. You don't start on our payroll until October. That's the process, I'm afraid. I'd have you working for free, but that won't hack it with the admin guys here at the RGP.'

'Any chance of a fast forward, ma'am?'

'None. Red tape is red tape, and that's the long and short of it. See you in October, Detective Sergeant.'

With that, Massetti ducked into the tent. Broderick followed, addressing Sullivan over his shoulder.

'Do yourself a favour. Clock off early and enjoy your break. Just don't forget to send us all a postcard.'

As both her superiors descended into the trench, Sullivan kicked the ground in frustration. What had made her think she was indispensable? She had been a police officer long enough to know she was just a cog, part of a machine that trundled on regardless of the individual. Massetti's reminder of that fact had smarted, though.

The sun was leaving the eastern slopes of Gibraltar, and behind her the limestone Rock, at four hundred metres plus, now appeared dark and cold. Perhaps it was time for a break. A month in Spain might just be what she needed. With a sigh, Sullivan turned and walked towards the waiting patrol cars.

Hasta la vista, baby.

Chapter 3

Two hours later, Sullivan opened the throttle of her Kawasaki Ninja 250R and thrilled to the sudden burst of acceleration. The bike had been both a treat for herself and a superb way of navigating the narrow 'car unfriendly' streets and passageways of Gibraltar. The trip ahead was the first time she had taken the motorbike off-Rock, and she had to admit to feeling excited about the prospect.

Once over the border and into Spain, Sullivan took the scenic route to the Andalusian town of Gaucín, skirting the Parque Natural Los Alcornocales and passing through the towns of Jimena de la Frontera and San Pablo de Buceite. As she had told Broderick earlier, she was meeting Ric Danaher at his old farmhouse in the hills to discuss the house-sitting.

As she flew past the beautiful Spanish countryside along the A-405, she was excited by the prospect of some peaceful isolation in the extraordinary Andalusian landscape. Just before San Pablo the road inclined steeply, and Sullivan cut her speed to concentrate on the increasing curves of the road as it climbed into the hills above. Nearing the town of Gaucín, she almost missed the small sign pointing to the narrow dirt track that would take her two kilometres off-road to the isolated *finca*.

Her second-hand Kawasaki seemed unimpressed by the new demands placed on it by the rough ground and copious stray rocks that littered its path. Climbing the hillside, which was covered with olive trees interspersed with dry vegetation and outcrops of dark grey rock, Sullivan soon spied the old farmhouse on a small plateau-like ridge about thirty metres below the summit. It comprised two single-storey whitewashed buildings – one much larger than the other and both with renovated terracotta-tiled rooves.

Long before Sullivan pulled into the yard at the front of the buildings, the sound of a dog barking had prepared her for the sight of the large golden Labrador that stood guard at its centre.

'All right, Leggo, all right!' came a cry from within the main house as Sullivan brought her motorbike to a stop and dismounted. Seconds later, a man appeared at the door with a broad smile on his face. He walked towards Sullivan, waving his arms in welcome.

'Don't mind the dog. Leggo wouldn't harm a flea, not that I broadcast that fact to all and sundry. I'm Ric. Nice to meet you, Tamara.' The well-built, ruddy-cheeked Englishman reached over and shook Sullivan's hand vigorously.

'Hi,' Sullivan said, a little taken aback by the heartiness of the welcome. 'I'm early. Hope you don't mind?'

'We don't clock-watch up here. Sun comes up. Sun goes down. Everything in between just happens.'

Before she could respond, Sullivan noticed a woman in the *finca*'s doorway. She had golden blonde hair and a pretty face that wore a gentle smile. Ric turned his head to follow Sullivan's gaze.

'Ah! And this is my daughter, Consuela.' Taking Sullivan by the arm, he led her across the yard. 'She's a copper just like you, only with this lot over here – the Cuerpo Nacional de Policía in Málaga. Homicide. Just made inspector, at only twenty-seven, if you please. Not bad going for a little sprog.'

Consuela was now close enough to slap her father's arm.

'Papa, enough!' she said, her Andalusian accent taking Sullivan slightly by surprise. 'I am sorry, Tamara, but my father is too boastful.'

'Not at all. Inspector, eh?' Sullivan said, fighting an unexpected pang of jealousy.

'It's not all it seems,' Consuela replied. 'It's a new fast track initiative. There's been political pressure to get more women into top jobs in the force. This is one way they are trying to achieve it.'

'That's brilliant.' Sullivan said, attempting a smile.

'It is. But it's not very popular in some areas, as I'm sure you can imagine.'

'With certain male officers, you mean?'

'The men call us "*Learner Inspectors*" and joke about us needing to have a green L-plate on our backs.'

'Some things may never change. I'm envious, though. I'm older than you and still a DS.'

'Not for long,' Ric said, 'if the RGP have any sense.'

'It's complicated.' Sullivan replied, reaching out to

shake Consuela's hand. 'Congratulations, Inspector. Well done.'

Consuela Danaher smiled.

'Thank you.'

Appearing to sense an unexpected tension in the air, Ric jumped in quickly.

'Now come on in, Tamara, and we'll get you a drink. Then you can have a look round. See if you fancy staying up here while I bugger off back to Blighty for a month.'

━━━

The decision to take up the offer of a bed for the night had gone hand in hand with Sullivan's acceptance of a second delicious Mojito.

'I've just completed the annexe across the yard. You will be the first to sleep there,' Ric said. 'Besides, staying overnight will give you a better idea of what you might be taking on.'

Alcohol, combined with a guided tour of the farm-house and the promise of home-cooked food, persuaded Sullivan to accept. The views of the Parque Natural to the west and Gibraltar and the African coast to the south made her fall in love with the place.

The meal was sumptuous. A delightful glass of gazpacho was followed by *coquina* clams from the Cádiz coast. These were served with garlic, parsley and white wine plus a hunk of the most delicious bread Sullivan could ever remember enjoying. Aromas from the kitchen had sent her senses spinning, and the taste and textures that followed gave her no excuse but to surrender to their pleasures. Wine replaced the cocktails, and talk turned to police work or, in Ric's case, the lack of it. Taking early retirement from the Met to come to Spain and be near Consuela had been the best decision of his life, he told Sullivan with pride. She also learned how Consuela's Spanish-born mother and Ric had met and married in London, but separated three years later.

'An ambitious copper's life is not conducive to happy relationships, I'm afraid,' Ric said.

'Tell me about it,' Sullivan replied.

After Consuela had moved to Málaga to be with her mother, Ric had visited Spain whenever he could.

'Which wasn't often in the early days,' he added. 'Now, Consuela is the busy police officer with no time on her hands and I sit up here with the goats and old Leggo.'

'Sounds perfect,' Sullivan replied, feeling a little room-spin from the alcohol. 'By the way, why did you name your dog after plastic toy bricks?'

'I didn't. Leggo's name comes from his youthful antics. When he was little more than a pup, he used to put it about a bit ...'

Consuela slapped her father on the arm again. 'Papa!'

'It's the truth. I adopted Leggo seven years ago from an ex-pat couple in Benalmádena. The woman – who worked as a Dolly Parton tribute act – needed a double hip replacement, so she was packing up and moving back to the UK. She told me about the dog's reputation, so I nicknamed him Leggo. It's short for "leg overs".'

Sullivan nearly fell off her chair with laughter. Consuela looked on with mock disapproval.

'How are things with you on the Rock?' Ric swiftly changed the subject. 'Gus Broderick is a good man. One of the best.'

'I like him,' Sullivan replied. 'Not that I'd want him to know.'

'He says you're good at your job. That's praise coming from him.'

'The Guv expects all of us to do our best. Nobody wants to let him down,' Sullivan said, the heightened colour of her cheeks betraying how flattered she had felt to hear the compliment.

'You've been kept busy by the sound of things,' Ric continued.

'Right up to the last minute. A body turned up over there just before I left this afternoon.'

'Same for Consuela this week. Three of them. Dead in a pool!'

Consuela turned to her father. 'That is not fully out yet. I told you in confidence.'

'You never said.'

'I did not think I had to!' Consuela reprimanded him before turning back to Sullivan. 'I am sorry. I do not mean to be rude, Tamara.'

'I shouldn't have mentioned my one either,' Sullivan replied. 'A little too much wine loosens the tongue.'

'Well, here's a pretty situation,' Ric observed. 'Two murder detectives with two new murder investigations and neither of them out and about trying to solve them. What's going on with police business these days?'

'No money,' Consuela answered. 'The economy is on the floor, and that means little overtime. You have to do what you can in your *own* time. *Fin.*'

'So, everything slows down, and murderers have a better chance of getting away with it,' Ric said. 'In my day, you got stuck in, and they didn't let you stop till you'd finished. Mind you, we all had good overtime then. The only way I managed to get enough to pay for this place.'

'Austerity.' Consuela sighed again. 'It can kill in many ways.'

Ric stretched his arms and yawned.

'Excuse me, but I think it's time for me to turn in. I'll leave you two youngsters to it.'

After he'd gone, the two women sat in silence for a few moments. At last, Consuela spoke.

'I hope you don't mind my asking, Tamara, but what's made you stay on in Gib? I'd have thought you would want to get back after your secondment. You have a good career with the Met, no?'

'No.' Sullivan replied. 'No career there at all, really.'

Consuela looked puzzled, and it occurred to Sullivan that maybe Ric hadn't told her the full story. 'Do you think my secondment was a choice for me? Something I wanted to do?'

'Well, yes. Of course. Why not?'

Sullivan sighed. 'Your father didn't mention that my secondment was a form of punishment, then?'

Consuela looked genuinely surprised. 'No. No, he did not.'

'I disobeyed an order, Consuela.' Sullivan said, resenting the need to tell of her shame yet again. 'I broke the golden rule and fell from grace. Or in professional terms, I ignored a senior officer during a dangerous hostage situation – a psychotic father holding his young daughter at gunpoint – and went my own way. I talked the father down, and it ended safely, but my actions had other consequences. The Met didn't want the bad publicity – "Woman Cop, Cops It!" etc. So, they sent me to the RGP to *"enhance relationship and liaison mechanisms"*, hoping the whole thing would blow over by the time I got back.'

'But you're not going back,' Consuela said, her eyes showing no judgement.

'What for? There'll be no chance of me ever making inspector there any more. The fast track is over for *me*, Consuela.' Sullivan was shocked by the bitterness in her own voice. 'I'm sorry, I didn't mean that to sound ...'

'It didn't,' Consuela interrupted. 'It just sounded unfair. But the RGP think well of you, so the future is bright. *Si?*'

Sullivan smiled. 'I hope so. We'll see. A second bite at the cherry, eh?'

Consuela reached for the wine bottle and filled Sullivan's glass.

'Let's drink to that.'

'I've an idea, Consuela.' Sullivan leaned forward, her manner softened by wine and kindness. 'Sod protocol. I'll tell you about *my* murder investigation if you tell me about *yours*.'

Consuela paused for a moment before replying. Although this conversation was most unusual, she had to admit that it was proving fascinating.

'Okay,' she said at last. 'But you first, Tamara. You first.'

Chapter 4
PUERTO BANÚS, COSTA DEL SOL, MONDAY

THE YOUNG COUPLE fell out of each other's arms, the gleam of sweat shimmering on their naked, tanned bodies. Chests heaving in unison, they gasped for air as they lay exhausted on the rumpled silk sheets. Izi Bernard had never before reached the levels of pleasure she had discovered during the last twenty-four hours. This guy was in a different league. No doubt about it. She had known Rudi Janson for less than two days, but the tall, good looking American was something else. She had found herself lost in a frenzy of desire and satisfaction.

Half an hour later, the couple had showered and dressed and were holding hands at a table outside one of the best restaurants on Muelle Ribera, the promenade running the length of the opulent Costa del Sol marina of Puerto Banús. It was lunchtime and they were hungry.

Around them, shoppers, holidaymakers and well-heeled locals jostled cheek by jowl along the harbour-side. Long known as the 'Jag and Gin' centre of the Costa, Puerto Banús still clasped some of the world's richest and more hedonistic individuals to its luxurious breast. The names Versace, Christian Dior and Bulgari graced its shopfronts. Multi-million-pound yachts lounged in the marina, over-looked by expensive blocks of stunning hi-tech apartments. Clubs, casinos, boutiques, car dealerships and sex shops all found their place under the pleasure dome of excess that the Puerto offered.

Izi reached for her glass of chilled *aqua* and made a mental note to get herself some new underwear. Rudi had ripped hers to shreds. Not that she was complaining. Behind streets that led to its prestigious marina frontage, the flagship department store El Corte Inglés stood like a grand Atlantic cruiser on Plaza Antonio Banderas. It was one of Izi's favourite pastimes to roam its floors with her black credit card at the ready.

'Cheers,' Rudi mouthed, raising his glass to meet hers.

'*Prost.*'

'Thank you for a wonderful time.'

'It's not over yet.'

'I hope not.'

'In that case, what next?' Izi asked, arching an eyebrow.

'Anything you want. Anything at all.'

'Well … I would like to swim, sit in the sun and then … and then …'

Izi glided her bare foot under the table and placed it between Rudi's thighs. The American beamed at the beautiful blonde woman sitting opposite him.

'Any ideas where?' he asked.

'I have,' she replied. 'After we've eaten, I'm taking you for a drive.'

The scarlet Alfa Romeo 4C Spider purred out of the subterranean car park and onto Avenida Julio Iglesias. The flash two-seater received not a glance from the pedestrians on the street – high-end vehicles were two-a-euro in the crowded avenues and cut-throughs of Puerto Banús. Not even the glamour of its beautiful driver turned heads. Izi Bernard headed down the street before taking a right onto Avenida José Banús. Here, along the pavements of the main artery out of town, tourists stopped on the Bulevar de la Fama – *'Boulevard of Fame'* – to look at the many starfish-shaped tributes to famous and wealthy local stars and bene-factors.

Stopping at traffic lights, Izi reached for her mobile and took a quick selfie; her social media presence had to be fed at happy times like this.

A minute later, the car reached the main Autovía del Mediterráneo. Taking the westbound lane, Izi squeezed the accelerator and let the power explode from the car's 237 HP engine to reach a speed of 100 kph in well under six seconds. Izi let out a cry of joy as a blast of air hit her face, and the car raced faster. Rudi had no idea where he was going, and Izi had no intention of telling him.

Izi glanced across to her passenger. She had only just met him, and yet he seemed so familiar to her: his dark hair blowing in the wind, his long muscular limbs and perfect tan. The casual, yet studied tailoring of his clothes and his immaculate grooming were to be expected in her circles. His sense of humour and sensitivity were attributes she'd found harder to find in those she'd previously dated. Izi was young, rich and beautiful. 'A hell of a catch,' her father would often tell her, adding, 'Just don't let them catch you, my angel.' It was advice she had found easy to take. Izi enjoyed a good time – she was only twenty-three, for God's sake! – but anything deeper? Avoiding love had never been a problem.

It was less than forty-eight hours since she had first seen Rudi, standing alone at the rooftop bar of her favourite club, Pangea. Their eyes had met, held for a second too long and then, horror of horrors, Izi had crossed the floor to buy the man a drink. He was thirty-one and an investment banker, he told her, in Spain for some meetings and then taking a vacation.

'An older man and a banker, eh?' Izi teased.

'Mature, but good with figures,' Rudi replied, brushing Izi's hand seemingly by accident.

The sudden rush of emotion she had felt at this first touch ensured that she stayed by his side the whole evening. Over the music, she babbled out her history to him:

She was born in Germany, but had lived on the Costa del Sol since a child. Mummy and Daddy were filthy rich, but nice. Very nice. They'd given her the apartment she now lived in overlooking the marina. A good investment dressed up as a present. She'd travelled the world but come back to Marbella to live. She was thinking of maybe starting a fashion label or something further down the road. Something creative anyhow. And she was single. Lots of friends, of course, but nothing serious. Just fun.

At last, intoxicated and danced off her feet, she had whispered into Rudi's ear, 'I will make you a nice cup of tea back at my place if you want.'

'Ah, I kinda have to be up in two hours. I've got an Abu Dhabi emir wanting to discuss the wisdom of continued investment in the USA. Sorry. Could I … see you tomorrow, maybe?'

Izi had blanched, unused to refusal; unused to having to ask for anything.

'I'll give you my number,' she had replied.

Now the couple drove across the parched Río Guadaiza and left the Autovía to head north. Making no concession to speed restrictions, Izi hit the new road hard, following it to the southern slopes of the Serranía de Ronda mountains and her mystery destination.

As they left the Marbella coast and sea behind, Rudi could not help noticing how the view improved the further away from the shore they drove. *Hardly like work at all*, he thought to himself, reaching over and caressing Izi's naked thigh. Izi responded with a playful slap and a filthy laugh.

Eight kilometres on, the road twisting and turning as it climbed hundreds of metres above sea level, Izi turned off it and onto a partly surfaced winding track.

'For a terrible moment, I thought you were taking me to Ronda,' Rudi said.

'Too far.' Izi laughed. 'I'd never last that long.'

For the next five minutes, they drove up through lush cork and pine-tree woodlands, grateful for the occasional canopy of leaves that shaded them as they made their way. At last, they came to a halt before a set of iron gates. Izi pressed a button on her key ring, and with a heavy grinding sound, they opened slowly, in almost ceremonial fashion.

Continuing up a long, winding driveway, through parkland featuring similar trees and shrubbery to those along the approach road but here more manicured, they came to a high wall in the centre of which stood huge wooden double doors of Indian design and origin. Slowing to a stop and pressing her key ring once more, the doors swung open to allow the car into the large inner courtyard beyond.

All Rudi could think to say was, 'Wow.'

Tropical plants and an ornate marble fountain filled some of the space before them. Behind these stood a pale pink house of palatial dimensions, rising to three storeys, its Byzantine-styled windows adorned with flowers hanging down from a roof terrace high above.

To Rudi's surprise, Izi kept driving, crossing the courtyard and exiting on the far side to arrive at the lush gardens at the rear of the house. The view across the garden and down the sloping mountainsides to the coast was enough to take the American's breath away – again.

'And this is …?' Rudi asked.

'The family home. But do not worry. Nobody is here. My parents are away.'

'Right.'

'Which means you can relax and—'

'Who needs to relax?' Rudi interrupted, winking.

Reaching the end of the drive, Izi parked and leaped from the car. Running across the lawn towards the steps of the enormous terrace at the back of the house, she yelled back to Rudi, 'You are going to have to move faster than that!' Tearing off her top, she taunted, 'What you waiting for, Rudi-doody?'

Springing from the car, Rudi began the chase, watching Izi slipping off more of her clothes until she was completely naked. Metres ahead, she raced up the steps at the end of the lawn to reach the side of a calm and glistening swimming pool. Waiting a few moments for him to reach the terrace, she gave him a coy little wave, then turned and executed a perfect dive into the azure water.

As Rudi struggled to remove his clothes, his young lover glided beneath the surface of the pool, its fresh and cooling waters thrilling her senses. Pushing out with her arms and legs, she decided to swim to the far side without rising for air.

Then, mid-glide, Izi was thrust to one side as she collided with something. Her arms flailing as she looked for protection, she opened her eyes to see what the obstacle could be. A swollen, dead face met her gaze, the body lolling as if it were a puppet's, arms hanging by its sides. Izi opened her mouth to scream, an action stifled by water hitting the back of her throat and choking her. Panic and fear propelled her into immediate flight to the surface of the pool. Bursting through the still water above, she gasped for breath and attempted a desperate scream. At the other side of the pool, Rudi looked up in concern.

'Izi?' he called, running alongside the pool to get nearer.

Unable to answer, Izi thrust herself forward to swim to the side, but her limbs would not respond. It was all she could do to remain afloat. Below was the most awful sight she had ever seen, and now she could not escape it. She froze once more – beneath her, something had brushed her foot. The extra adrenalin that shot through her body at this touch gave her voice. As Rudi dived into the water to help her, Izi Bernard finally released a scream of real pain.

━━

Neither the helpless Izi nor her new boyfriend noticed the flash of reflected sunlight on the hillside above: its source, the lenses of a pair of raised binoculars. An upward glance would not have distracted them from the grisly scene they had just discovered. The tunnelled vision of their intense and horrified concentration denied them the larger picture.

On higher ground, the magnified images of the lovers made their observer smile. The man felt good. Things had gone well, despite nearly being discovered at the murder scene below. Fortunately, the engine of Izi's car had been heard long before it had turned into the garden. The escape back through the perimeter fence had been affected only just in time, avoiding the approaching vehicle by seconds. The arrival of the Bernard daughter was something the man had not factored into his plan. The discovery of the bodies in the pool was to have been made by Kurt Bernard alone, returning that evening from his business trip to Paris.

This upset had agitated the man at first. It was an important part of his modus operandi that he be the one to report to the local police by making an anonymous call. He had expected not to have do this until Kurt Bernard had arrived home. That plan had now changed. So it was that upon reaching the higher ground, the man had phoned the local Guardia Civil to announce the murders and their location. Using a handkerchief to cover the receiver, he had talked in a monotone through gritted teeth to disguise his voice. Despite the knowledge that this performance would guarantee a quick response by the Spanish police, the man calmly raised his binoculars to his eyes and proceeded to relish the horrific drama unravelling below.

Standing on the spot where he had observed the Bernard household for days, the man held the naked Izi in his sights. As she was pulled screaming and flailing from the water, he could not help but increase the detail of focus on his binoculars. At this point, a second element of surprise kicked in. He was excited by what he saw. He'd imagined that the carnage – wrought so splendidly upon the three drowned victims – would be the climax of this episode. Now, alongside the pleasure of the day's work and his lethal ambitions for the future, rose another familiar feeling. Lust.

'Time to go,' the man said at last, turning his back on the scene and heading down the rough path towards the track on the far side of the hill. Obedient as ever, his companion followed, her light red hair blowing in the gentle Sierra breeze.

Chapter 5

THE LOCAL GUARDIA CIVIL – two police officers in a jeep, both carrying machine guns and side pistols – had arrived just ten minutes after the anonymous call; so quickly, in fact, that Rudi had not been able to leave the traumatised Izi and make a call himself. Once inside the grounds of the mansion, the officers took in the horrific sight beneath the swimming pool's surface. A flustered call to the Homicidios department of the Cuerpo Nacional de Policía in Málaga swiftly followed. Dealing with the hysterical young woman who had discovered the macabre scene also proved beyond their powers of counselling and control.

By the time the two homicide officers – Acting Inspector Consuela Danaher and Detective Ramón de Galvez – arrived to take charge, Izi and Rudi had been taken into the house to await questioning. Back in Málaga, Consuela had smiled when told that De Galvez was the only officer available to accompany her. He was bright and didn't bore her with terrible jokes like Sergeant Cortés. The middle-aged Cortés also often failed to hide his disdain for

Consuela who, at only twenty-seven, was his superior officer.

From the beginning of her police career, at eighteen years of age, Consuela had been considered a potential high flyer. She'd made sergeant at only twenty-three and now had become the youngest inspector on the force. From the start, Consuela had learned to ignore the sexist attitudes of some of her male colleagues and the barely disguised envy of some of her female ones. De Galvez had always been supportive of her. He also drove well, which meant she had arrived at the mansion in a calmer state than usual.

Greeted by a Guardia officer in the front drive, they were led to the pool area at the rear, both detectives producing plastic shoe protectors from their pockets and pausing to put them on, before moving to the deep end of the pool to take in the morbid scene beneath the water line.

'There's three of them, sir,' the Guardia officer informed them.

'I can count, thank you,' Consuela answered.

'The couple who discovered this are inside. The daughter of the house and her boyfriend. They're in a bad way.'

'I can imagine,' she said, looking down with a professional detachment at the bodies at the bottom of the pool. All were tied, gagged and weighted down to stop them floating to the surface. They seemed to be kneeling on the floor of the pool, their heads lolling from side to side.

'Is this pool sea water?' Consuela asked. 'Salt?'

'*Sí*. Better than chlorine, they say. If you've money, you can have what you want, I guess.'

'Apart from a long and happy life,' she observed,

nodding towards the body nearest to her. 'Do we have names?'

'Bernard. The surname of the owners. German.' The guard looked once more at the pool. 'Señora Ingrid Bernard, her gardener José Guido and María Moralez, the housekeeper. The daughter indoors identified them. She became hysterical. We had to carry her away. Horrible, no?'

The question required no answer.

'The *científicos* will be here soon,' De Galvez said, then turned to the Guardia. 'Go to the front of the house and guide them down when they arrive.'

Nodding, the police officer strode back towards the house as Consuela crouched down by the pool.

'Whoever did this took time to lay things out to their liking,' she observed, brushing a wayward strand of hair from her face.

'Two of these victims are employees. Suggests an intruder.'

'Maybe, De Galvez. When Forensics get here, we'll check the house. See if anything is missing. In the meantime, I'll contact Málaga Centro. This is big. We need to keep it from the press for as long as we can.'

'I didn't mean that kind of intruder. l meant it could be organised.'

'Hit job?'

'All the signs.'

Consuela nodded. '*Sí*. All the signs.'

Chapter 6
THURSDAY, 6 A.M.

SULLIVAN HAD RISEN early and left a thank-you note on the large pine table in Ric Danaher's rustic kitchen.

Thanks for the wonderful hospitality. I'll be returning. Be warned!

Outside, the early morning sun was already hot on her face, and the view from the *finca* down towards the distant Mediterranean was as perfect as the air Sullivan breathed was fresh. Her head was surprisingly clear as she climbed onto her motorbike, started the engine and headed down the hillside towards the main road to Gibraltar. She needed to get back on the Rock. It was going to be a busy day.

Fifty minutes later, Sullivan crossed the border, with its freely flowing queues of travellers from both sides, and arrived at the simple, two-storey Police HQ building on New Mole Parade. The ride through Gibraltar Town had also been easy. A few early birds had passed her as they headed to work, but things would not get busy until the start of rush hour. Later still, the town would heave with human activity as the cruise ships and hotels emptied their inquisitive and excited guests onto the myriad streets, squares and ancient passageways that made up the centre of old Gibraltar Town.

As it was early, Sullivan had hoped to have time alone to clear her desk before departing the building with as little fuss as possible. Thoughts of this vanished with the appearance of Calbot at the HQ's gates. The young officer's eyes glinted as he affected a look of mock surprise.

'Can't keep away from us, eh, Sarge?' Calbot teased. 'I thought we'd lost you to Spanish beaches and suntan oil for a month.'

'Actually, I'm not officially off the clock until midday, Calbot. Thought I'd pop in and make your life hell for a few hours.'

'No need for that. Old Nefertiti is keeping us all busy.'

'What?'

'The mummy from the East Beach warehouse.'

'Oh, that's nice,' she said, moving on through the gates towards the inner courtyard. 'Good to see such a healthy respect for the dead, Calbot.'

'More than they give us,' he replied, following her to the HQ's entrance doors. 'I was supposed to be off today, but instead, I'm in early. Broderick's got me doing the paperwork on those Dutch guys' statements and then it's all hands to the pump setting up the Incident Room.'

Sullivan felt a sharp pang of envy. 'You should count yourself lucky. While you're in the thick of it, I'll be stuck over the border looking after goats and chickens.'

'And a very good job you'll make of it, Sarge.'

Sullivan raised a middle finger in reply to the smiling Calbot and disappeared through double doors into the shady interior of the building.

Calbot watched her go. The uncomfortable thought struck him that he would miss Sullivan. So would the new investigation. With these revelations proving too much to handle so early in the day, the young officer moved towards the canteen for his customary Danish pastry and hit of black espresso.

Life goes on, he thought, the challenges of the day ahead wiping all worries about DS Tamara Sullivan from his mind.

Chapter 7
9.15 A.M.

'THE NAME of the ship was HMS *Pickle* and its voyage from Gibraltar to Falmouth in Cornwall took nine days.'

The fourteen-year-old girl, having just delivered her last line at the school's special morning assembly, smiled and waved to her family seated at the back of the small hall. Gus Broderick, his elder daughter Penny and his sister Cath waved back. All three had rehearsed the lines with Daisy many times during the previous weeks and they knew how important it had been for her to get them right. The theme of the morning assembly had been the Battle of Trafalgar in 1805, and Daisy's part was the section that described how news of the British naval victory and the death of Vice Admiral Horatio Nelson had been carried to England by the captain of the schooner HMS *Pickle*.

Broderick remembered that Nelson's dead body had been preserved in a barrel of brandy after the battle – *A pickling of sorts*, he thought to himself – although this had been omitted from the school's version of the story, out of sensitivity to teenage squeamishness, he presumed. Not that Daisy would have minded. She loved all facts and her command of historical ones was very impressive. She had blossomed at this small school in the centre of Gibraltar Town, and her father would be forever grateful to its teachers and carers.

Born with the extra chromosome of a Down syndrome baby, Daisy had struggled in her early years. The disappearance of her mother, when she was just two and her elder sister six, had shaken them all. Gus Broderick's decision to move them to Gibraltar – the birth place of his mother – and live with his widowed sister Cath had resulted in a miraculous turn in the family's happiness and security. Cath had made a wonderful home for her nieces and brother, and Broderick had transferred successfully from the Metropolitan Police Service in London to the Royal Gibraltar Police. Despite an extensive search by the Met, Broderick's wife Helen had never been found, and all hope of her returning to the family had died many years before. Nevertheless, the girls had thrived during their years on the Rock and Gus Broderick's pride in them knew no bounds. Her teachers were also full of praise. Ms Buhagia, Daisy's music teacher, and Mrs Robba, her art tutor, were particularly fond of their student and her blossoming talents.

Watching Daisy and her class leave the hall, Gus felt a moment's guilt. He had forgotten all about the assembly that morning, his mind full of his new investigation. As he had opened the front door to head off to work, Cath had just managed to stop him and remind him of his school commitment. It had not been one of Broderick's finest moments and his sister had lost no time in telling him that. Now, as the three of them filed out of the school, Cath squeezed her brother's arm.

'Well done, Gus.' She smiled. 'You can go get the baddies now.'

Chapter 8
10.50 A.M.

THE GREY, hollow skull that had once supported a human face was pinned to the evidence board in the Incident Room – known almost universally as the 'IR' – in photographic form. The eyes, nose and mouth, all long gone, had once given identity, expression and form to the living person they had been a part of. What remained was now brutal and horrific to behold.

'Jane Doe,' Broderick announced, turning to the room full of fellow RGP detectives. 'Anyone like to suggest a respectful substitute name until we discover her true moniker?'

'Darth Vader?' Calbot offered, not getting the laughs he had expected.

'Just can't help yourself, can you, Calbot?' Broderick said. '"Respectful", I said, and a bit more gender-specific perhaps.'

'We've been calling her Nefertiti, sir,' DI Moreno added. 'The body was mummified, right? Like an Egyptian mummy. Quite a good fit. Yeah?'

'Nerfetiti was indeed an Egyptian queen, Moreno. In fact, there's a limestone bust of her in a museum in Berlin. Alas, her mummy has never been found, so we can only assume that she became one – and you all know how I feel about making assumptions. Also, adopting a name based on the body's present condition is lacking in the old respect department, don't you think?'

At the far end of the room, Sullivan was at her desk and out of view. Peering around her desktop screen, she raised her arm and called, 'Guv?'

Broderick turned. 'Sullivan. Didn't know you were still there. Thought you'd gone.'

'On my way, Guv.'

'Got a name?'

'How about Eleanor?'

'Sounds good. Any reason?'

'As in "Eleanor Rigby", sir – "All the lonely people", et cetera.'

'Most affecting, Sullivan, thank you. Eleanor she is then.' Broderick turned back to the main body of the room. 'Not a name she'll need for long, though, because we'll find out exactly who she was and who saw fit to leave her in such a grotesque manner. Somebody killed Eleanor and hid her beneath that warehouse floor. Apart from the remains of her clothing, there were no other belongings alongside the body. The only useful thing we have is a letter found in the back pocket of the jeans she was wearing. What do we have on that, Moreno?'

'Not in great shape, I'm afraid. Writing's very faded and the paper half eaten by insects. Forensics are on it. Hopefully, they'll come up with something.'

Broderick smiled briefly. 'Yes, hopefully. Calbot? Statements?'

'As expected, Guv. Goosen, Krupps and Mates have nothing to offer. No connection with the original building work or warehouse business back then. They found the body by accident. End of.'

'Checking out the building contractors and warehouse employees at that time?'

'We're on it, sir,' Moreno replied.

'Whoever did this thinks they got away with it. But they haven't. Somewhere along the line, they'll have dropped a bollock—'

'Only if the killer was a man, Guv,' Sullivan interrupted as she headed to the door with her box of personals.

'Yes, indeed, Sullivan. Pardon the assumption. Have a good break, won't you?'

'I'll try, Guv.'

Arriving on the pavement outside the HQ, Sullivan approached her parked motorcycle. Only now did she begin to realise how difficult leaving her colleagues back in the IR had been. Her affected casualness had hidden an inner truth: it had taken a huge effort to prise herself away from them. It was not the loss of their individual companionship and talents that bothered her. Well, certainly not in Calbot's case. It was more the need she had to be part of the team. To be together working a new murder inquiry. To feel and use the adrenalin and the pressure it generated to perform well and get results. Leaving that behind hurt. It hurt a lot.

Chapter 9
SOTOGRANDE, SPAIN, 11.A.M.

A MEAL OF SCRAMBLED EGGS, smoked salmon and a double espresso was a special market day treat for Frankie DuPont. Leaving his top-floor home in one of the brightly painted apartment buildings surrounding the Sotogrande Marina, the forty-six-year-old Frenchman ventured down to the quayside plaza and across to the famous KE Bar. With its central position overlooking the main marina, the café restaurant had always been the place for the smart set to be seen in the heart of Spain's most opulent private resort.

Frankie would often visit the bar for a drink or snack with friends, but a Thursday morning solo visit during the summer months had become a ritual. It was the day of the Sotogrande night market and Frankie liked to set himself up with a hearty breakfast before preparing his market stall and stock for the evening's opening. A hobby for several years now, Frankie's little New Age shop had become a popular attraction at the heart of both Sotogrande's night and Sunday markets, offering herbal remedies, crystals, dream catchers, books on spirituality and other such mystical paraphernalia. He would even give tarot card readings if the mood took him, and it often did. As a colourful and eccentric member of the elite resort's community, Frankie's hippy style and mystic ways were happily accepted by most. His wild hair and ethnic clothing set him apart from the _über_ fashion-conscious polo, golf and sailing sets that populated this urban jewel on the Andalusian coast. Frankie stood out from the crowd and he liked it that way.

Now it was eleven in the morning and he was starving. His table in the far corner of the KE Bar was reserved and waiting for him. Greeted by staff and customers alike, Frankie crossed the restaurant floor and took his usual seat. The outside tables of the café, bordering the marina promenade, were packed with customers, but inside all was calm and cool. Frankie found much to comfort him in these familiar surroundings. The KE Bar's trademark model train was in action, as usual, travelling in a continuous loop along a curving length of track suspended above the large central bar. Children and adults alike loved the novelty and so it remained a special feature.

Getting out a pad and pencil, Frankie wrote a 'to do' list for the day. A new stock of rose quartz crystals had arrived the day before and they needed to be sorted and priced. So, too, did the beautiful new incense burners that had been delivered from India. A trip to the bank for a cash float had to be made before lunch, along with a stroll across the plaza to Pelo's Hairdresser's for a quick trim. Even by his own carefree standards, Frankie had been forced to admit that his unkempt hair needed professional care and attention. All in all, it was going to be a busy day and evening.

'Your breakfast, Frankie,' the waiter announced, placing a large plate of delicious-looking eggs, salmon and toast in front of him. 'Your coffee also.'

'Thank you, Rafael. I'm so hungry I could eat this table.'

Reaching for his knife and fork, Frankie smiled the smile of the contented. A happy moment to begin the last fourteen hours of his life.

Chapter 10

CONSUELA DANAHER LEFT the police station in Estepona and crossed the street. Her head had been aching for most of the morning and, with the build-up of pressure in it, the offices and corridors of the building behind her had felt increasingly claustrophobic. The fourth day of the Bernard murder investigation was already proving as frustrating as the previous three. The Costa del Sol had experienced a rise in murders over the summer and the police were grossly under-resourced.

Much to her surprise, Consuela had received an email on the way to work from the *Comisario Principal* in Málaga. 'I can't assign an *inspector jefe* till next week. The *Grupo de Homicidios* is stretched to breaking point. Blanco can join you on Monday. *Maybe.* I'd hoped Hernández would be free, but he's taken leave – his wife has inconveniently been committed to a mental hospital. The way things are going, I may well join her. Bottom line is, you will have to keep things going for the next few days. The media has been low key, *gracias a Dios*. Too busy covering the bombing in

45

Grenada. But it won't be long before the jackals from the *prensa rosa* sniff around in earnest. I'll do what I can on that. You and your team will have to do the rest. Sorry, but it's just the way things are.'

Arriving at work, Consuela quickly realised that the news from Málaga had already circulated, and from the look on her colleagues' faces, it was not going down well. Things were hardly helped by the cramped conditions the team was experiencing. With no space for them in Málaga Centro or even Fuengirola, the investigation had been forced to take over some rooms at the Policía Nacional building on Calle Valle Inclan in the back streets of Estepona. They had been made welcome, but everyone knew it was not the ideal facility for a major murder inquiry. Set back beyond the old town, its easy access to the main coastal motorway was the only real positive. But in the high morning temperatures of late summer, the cooling sea breeze from the Mediterranean struggled to make its presence felt that far into town and Consuela and the other new officers suffered the consequences. A faulty air con system had only increased the discomfort in the workplace that morning, which was why Consuela was taking her work across the street from the three-storey whitewashed municipal building to the Café Mar y Sierra and the shade offered by its outside canopy. She needed to take stock and focus her mind.

Ordering a *café cortado* and a small bottle of *aqua sin gas*, she looked up at the tall, brightly painted apartment building that neighboured the small bar café. But for that, Consuela would have had an uninterrupted view of the Sierras rising above Estepona. To make up for the loss of such a vista, a giant mural had been painted on the side of the building. Its artistic depiction of an archway through which the mountains could be seen in the distance was impressive, but no substitute for the real thing.

Turning her attention to her laptop, the detective once again looked at the investigation's findings thus far. Meagre pickings. Forensics had spent the best part of the last few days examining and re-examining the murder scene at the Bernards' villa in the hills above Puerto Banús. Consuela and De Galvez had also filled long hours at the site attempting to recreate all the scenarios and processes that could have led to the killings. One thing had become clear – the killings could not have been carried out by one person alone. The process that had led to the murders could at this stage only be imagined. The tying up and weighing down of the fully clothed victims, together with their careful positioning on the floor of the pool, suggested that at least two people had had Ingrid Bernard and her servants under their control.

Consuela had articulated this point several times during the briefing earlier that morning. 'As I suggested yesterday, I believe there to have been at least two perpetrators at the scene, if not more,' she had told the team of detectives, all squashed and overheated in the office on the second floor of the police building. Two new detectives had joined the investigation, so Consuela was at pains to bring them up to speed. A particular talent of his inspector, De Galvez noted, was making eye contact with everyone she addressed. This kept minds from wandering and briefings focused.

Consuela continued. 'We are still waiting on the *médico forense* for further details. As most of you know, the preliminary examinations have revealed nothing of any real use.

Hopefully, that will change. Pathology has confirmed that the victims drowned, all three having been thrown into the water alive.'

This news was greeted around the room with nervous comments and shaken heads.

'There was no evidence of sexual assault on any of the bodies. No bruising or anything to indicate a struggle. Only wrist and ankle abrasions, consistent with the tight binding of the plastic ties used to restrain Ingrid Bernard, as well as her gardener and housekeeper, José Guido and María Moralez.'

Consuela took out a handkerchief and patted her neck before continuing. 'As we know, there were no signs of a break-in at the villa and all the security cameras had been switched off – most probably by the killers. Did they just walk in and take control or were they invited in as guests? My instinct is to favour the former. This would suggest a prior knowledge of the villa and its grounds and, therefore, a period of surveillance. Ingrid Bernard had been due to travel to Paris with her husband at the beginning of the week but, at the last moment, had decided to stay at home. Her daughter had no idea of her change of plan – she thought the villa would be empty – but whoever killed Ingrid Bernard knew what was going on. Both Izi Bernard and Rudi Janson's statements have been confirmed as regards their whereabouts prior to their discovery of the bodies. Both were in Banús, mostly at her apartment. They'd only just met and were ... were ...'

Consuela paused for a moment, uncomfortable with what she was about to say. De Galvez took this as a cue to come to her aid. 'Getting to know each other?'

'Indeed, De Galvez. Thank you.'

Consuela could talk with ease about the anatomy and pathology of grisly murder cases, but references to intimate personal relations always caused her some embarrassment.

'I gave Izi Bernard and Rudi Janson my mobile number, in case they suddenly remember something new,' said Consuela. 'He's here on business, isn't he?'

'Works for an investment bank in California,' De Galvez said. 'Janson flew into Madrid five days ago and then down to Malaga, meeting Izi at the Pangea nightclub in Marbella that evening. His plan had been to stay on the Costa for some business meetings this week and then cross over to Morocco for a vacation.'

'And now?'

'Much the same, I guess. We have his statement, which checks out, so he can go. Not sure how Izi will take that. Not that it's on top of her list of worries. Her father's condition is her main concern at the moment.'

'Has the hospital updated us?'

Ingrid Bernard and her two servants had not been the only victims. On the night of the murders, Izi's father Kurt had returned to the villa from his business trip to Paris. On hearing news of the deaths, he had suffered a heart attack and been rushed to hospital in the back of a Guardia Civil patrol jeep. Izi herself had subsequently collapsed. She was now under a doctor's care and heavily sedated to help her deal with the tragedy. It was a horrible mess, and every one of the police officers gathered in the room felt nothing but sorrow for the family.

Detective Diaz spoke from his position by the open window. The middle-aged, overweight detective was feeling the heat more than most and was seeking cooler air. 'Señor

Bernard is still in *crítico*, but his doctors say they expect him to pull through. Just.'

'At last some more positive news,' Consuela said, reaching for the glass of water at her side and taking a sip. 'Our initial suspicions were that this was the work of professionals. So far nothing suggests that we change that interpretation. The anonymous tip-off is a little unusual. However, the manner of the deaths and the elaborate staging of the murder scene indicate that a message was being sent and a very clear point was being made. The sort of thing we have come to expect from organised crime along the Costa.'

Several detectives nodded in agreement.

'The tape of the anonymous call is being analysed. It's poor quality. Might throw up something, but whoever it was clearly went to some lengths to disguise his voice. Either that or we're dealing with an alien life force.'

Alone in the room, De Galvez laughed politely at Consuela's little joke.

'We know Kurt Bernard is a successful businessman with financial interests in many different areas, both abroad and here in Andalusia,' she went on. 'With such a large business empire, it's likely that he's made enemies some-where along the line, the most obvious possibility being his connection to the bankrupt casino and resort development at Manilva two years back. You'll remember that that whole enterprise fell apart, leaving thousands of residential buyers and business investors high and dry. Millions of euros lost and a half-built site left rotting on the hills above Dequesa.'

'Roaming packs of wild dogs are about the only things

living up there now,' Diaz added from his position by the window.

'Kurt Bernard escaped that scandal unscathed,' Consuela continued. 'He claimed the fault lay with other parties. It's not beyond the realm of possibility that criminal elements were associated with the whole thing. If so, we need to find out if any of them have now come after Bernard to exact some kind of revenge. Check your contacts and see what they've got.'

Several pens hit notepads as the group of officers scribbled down the information for later enquiries.

'*Café cortado. Aqua sin gas,*' a young waiter said, placing the hot coffee and water on the table in front of Consuela. The café was a welcome relief from the heat of the police building, the outside canopy blocking the full force of the blistering late morning sun.

'*Gracias,*' she said, her gaze not leaving the screen of her laptop.

Calls she had made to two of her criminal contacts during the morning had already produced one response. Carlos Estrada, a nightclub manager in Málaga, had called Consuela on a safe phone – 'You never know who's listening, *sí?*' – and left a message. Estrada had been useful to her father on gangster-related enquiries in the past and had a nose for what was going on in the illicit underworld. He had been particularly helpful because of his connections with the Italian Camorra, which in recent years had made their presence felt along the Costa del Sol. Drugs, prostitution and extortion remained their main areas of racketeering, but gambling and dodgy property development were noticeably on the rise. If organised crime was behind the villa murders, Consuela's hunch was that investigative roads could easily lead them to the Camorra.

'There's nothing out on this Kurt Bernard guy that I've heard about,' Estrada told Consuela when she rang him back. 'Doesn't mean that someone out there didn't want to cause him pain, but I've heard nothing about it. You know how these things are, Consuela. If a hit's made, there's always someone wanting to boast about it. They can't help it. Big mouths. Ends up with those same mouths getting shut up permanently down a dark alley. Evil karma, eh?'

'But what if this was a professional hit? Not just one of the mob hands being sent in.'

'You still get to hear about it. Just takes more time when they go for a pro.'

'Okay, thanks. Let me know. Pro or not.'

Consuela quit the call and sipped her *cortado*. She needed the buzz. The immense workload expected in this case meant that caffeine would become her special friend in the weeks and months ahead. For a moment, she stretched her legs and leaned her face into the sunshine. 'In your job, you have to take your pleasures where you can,' Ric had often told her.

However, this morning Consuela was not alone in her fleeting pursuit. Nobody in the café or out and about on the busy Calle Valle Inclan took much notice of the parked motorcyclist across the street. Behind the visor of a black safety helmet, the rider's eyes lingered on the young woman detective sitting in the shaded Café Mar y Sierra.

Chapter 11
11.55 P.M.

THE LAST NIGHT market of the summer had been a huge success, attracting hundreds of people to the many stalls, food trucks and attractions along the promenade of the Ribera del Marlin, or La Marina as it was locally called. Situated along one of the main Venice-inspired waterways of Sotogrande Marina and surrounded by brightly painted luxury apartments and villas, the Mercado de Levante had proved a massive summer draw for residents and visitors alike. On one side, the shopping promenade consisted of a line of permanent shops and restaurants – the women's fashion shop Itsomi, the Bokana restaurant and Panaderia Jan Staels, a café and ice cream parlour, all proving to be particular favourites for regular visitors. On the other side of the promenade was the wide canal, full of moored yachts, its surface reflecting the surrounding lights and hiding the many grey mullet greedily feeding below.

Seb and Tristan, Frankie's closest friends, had come over from their villa in San Martin del Tesorillo to help out that evening. The couple's presence had allowed Frankie to accommodate more tarot-reading customers than usual. Demand was high and people had been willing to wait some time for their appointments.

Frankie had enjoyed all of the readings, except one. An intense young woman with bright auburn hair had proved very unsettling. She had been his last reading, but Frankie had noticed her much earlier in the evening, sitting in the café opposite his stall, drinking coffee. She had stayed there for over an hour, her gaze permanently fixed on the stall and, somewhat unnervingly, on Frankie himself. It had even crossed his mind to go over and ask her if she was okay. But then she had disappeared and Frankie had forgotten all about her.

Just after 11 p.m., as Frankie decided to take down the board advertising his readings and call it a night, the woman appeared from out of the crowd and, in an insistent voice heavily tinged with some kind of eastern European accent, demanded a reading. Against his better judgement, Frankie had agreed – a decision he regretted almost immediately. The reading had been disquieting. The first spread of tarot cards revealed a rare and disturbing set of images. Death, destruction and evil were presented in a pattern he had never seen before. As he attempted to hide his surprise, Frankie had looked at the woman to see if she had spotted his response. Only a cold stare met his eyes.

In Frankie's experience, new customers only ever wanted a positive interpretation of the cards. Happy readings led to happy *and* returning customers. In areas of romance, health, wealth and happiness, only good news would do. Even in card spreads containing more negative aspects, Frankie knew his job: to accentuate the positive and eliminate the negative. However, the cards in front of him gave little legitimate leeway for happy endings. Taking a few moments to consider this, Frankie finally decided to ignore their message and lie his psychic's head off. At the end of the reading, the woman nodded, paid the required forty euros and disappeared into the crowd once more. Frankie was relieved to see her go, but there was no doubt that her presence had cast a dark pall over the evening.

Although the market was still busy considering the lateness of the hour, the three friends decided to get ahead of the game and be packed away by closing time at midnight. Doing his best to hide his dampened spirits from Seb and Tristan, Frankie set about helping them clear and dismantle the stall and its red-and-green-striped canopy. Being the last night market of the season, a party had been arranged for stall holders at a bar over in the main marina. Seb and Tristan were heading home, but insisted that Frankie leave early – they would put the stall away in one of the archway units used by the market traders for storage.

'Get yourself out of here and party, sweetheart,' Seb urged. 'You deserve a good time.'

Frankie put up little argument to their urging. After all, that's what friends were for.

The party had been in full swing for over an hour and Frankie had drunk a lot of vodka and very quickly at that. The bar was heaving and many people were having difficulty finding enough room to throw their shapes to the beat as the voice of Bruno Mars sang out against an upbeat funk.

Not that Frankie was interested in elbowing his way onto the improvised dance floor. He had had his eye on a rather beautiful young man who had accompanied the owners of the market's collectables stall. As the tall, fair-haired stranger moved to the bar to get some drinks, Frankie had orchestrated a very unsubtle accidental collision.

'Ooops. What am I like?'

'No probs. Tight squeeze in here,' the young man replied in a strong Australian accent.

'You're Australian,' Frankie said, cursing his unoriginality.

'Yeah. Perth. The land of sunshine, dolphins and boredom.'

'Surely not.'

'For my age group, mate. Don't get me wrong. It's God's own country back home, but in your twenties you want to see the world, right?'

Frankie blanched as the implications of the statement sank in, but he continued anyway. 'If you're going to the bar, I'm buying. Least I can do.'

'Aww, no mate. That's cool. I'm on a round.'

'I insist. Fate has brought us together. Believe me, I'm psychic.'

Bewildered by the bravura, the Australian simply shrugged his shoulders.

'As long as you didn't come on a broomstick, mate, mine's a San Miguel.'

Buying an entire round and continuing his one-sided flirtation, Frankie gradually became aware that he was struggling to stand up. It was not long before he found himself sitting alone in a corner, trying to get the room to stop spinning, which threatened to end his evening of tipsy fun and thwarted sexual advances. A large, balding man approached from the bar.

'Hey, I hear you read palms,' he said with a heavy New York accent as he thrust his massive hands towards Frankie's face. 'What do you reckon to these two?'

Frankie was quite unable to answer. Brushing the man's hands to one side and pushing himself up from his seat, he aimed himself towards the doors to the outside. Thrusting himself forward and stumbling across the room, he exited the party just in time to throw up on the steps outside.

Home was now the only thing on Frankie's mind. The entrance to his apartment building was less than thirty metres away, in the adjoining plaza. Gathering his energy, he once more aimed his body in the necessary direction, took a deep breath, and hurtled forward at a speed that both surprised and frightened him. Somehow managing to zig-zag his way to the other side of the plaza, Frankie paused for breath before moving into the dark passageway that led to the next square and the promise of sanctuary.

Halfway along the cut-through, he was forced to come to a halt. Someone was standing in the middle of the path, someone Frankie recognised immediately. The young woman with the bright auburn hair stood alone and unmoving. Her large vacant eyes and sullen face gave her the look of a zombie, Frankie thought. Not that his own appearance suggested anything much better. Attempting a smile of recognition, he moved to pass the woman on her left side. She immediately stepped sideways to block his way. Taken aback by this, he tried to move past her on the other side. Once again, the woman crossed to block his progress.

It was then that she smiled at Frankie and fear entered his heart. He knew at once that the person in front of him wished him harm. Death. Destruction. Evil. That was what her cards had shown and that was what Frankie now saw in her face. His stomach cramped as his pulse quickened to an alarming rate. Sweat was now pouring down his body and his mouth had gone dry and taken on a metallic taste. Trying to speak, he found to his horror that no words would come. The stunning blow to the back of his head was hard and unexpected. With knees buckling and his body falling to the floor, Frankie's mind was engulfed by darkness.

Chapter 12
FRIDAY

A SUDDEN BURST of cold water hit the back of Tamara Sullivan's neck and shoulders. It was all part of her early morning routine: a freezing shower to shake off her slumbering state and get the blood racing round her body. A three-kilometre jog and two mugs of coffee would then do the rest, but not today. Having spent most of the previous afternoon and evening packing up her apartment, Sullivan had decided to give the jog a miss and cut straight to the caffeine. She had enough challenges ahead for one day, and sadly they were all domestic.

Stepping out of the shower and reaching for a towel, she moved swiftly into the sitting room to look out of the window and across to the adjacent dry dock. Gazing at the sky above the ships and loading cranes, she soaked up the panoramic vista. This would be the last time she would enjoy the view from her apartment – the sun lighting up the Spanish port of Algeciras across the Bay of Gibraltar. It was one of the many things she had grown to love about Gibraltar: almost anywhere you looked, a rewarding sight greeted your eye. None more so than the views of the gigantic limestone Rock itself, towering hundreds of metres above the town, a mighty sentinel guarding the entrance to the Mediterranean. Its position between sea and ocean and between the two mighty continents of Europe and Africa had been fought over many times through the centuries. Even today, its loyalty to the British Crown was the cause of a dispute between the UK and Spain, a situation that triggered heated diplomatic discussions and frequent border delays. Gibraltarians were in no doubt where their continued loyalties lay. Ninety-nine per cent of them were more than happy for Gibraltar to remain a British Overseas Territory.

A large seagull landed on the sill outside Sullivan's window. It cockily strutted up and down the ledge. For some reason it reminded her of Calbot. She smiled.

She had enjoyed her brief stay in this small apartment just along the road from Police HQ, but now she had to depart and she felt a slight melancholy. Allowing herself a gentle sigh, Sullivan dried herself quickly and moved to her bedroom to put on the clothes she had carefully laid out for the day. Beside the bed were several cases and a number of boxes containing her other clothes and her possessions.

In this area of operations, Sullivan had seriously miscalculated. She had thought the amount of stuff she would have to clear out and take across to Spain would easily fit into a couple of small suitcases. Attaching them to her motorbike would have caused the journey to become a bit of a balancing act, but the task of getting all her things over to Ric Danaher's *finca* would have been entirely achievable.

How the hell have I accumulated so much shit? she had asked herself as the cases had filled up and cardboard boxes were brought in to accommodate the rest. Attempts to throw away non-essentials had resulted in only two objects landing in the rubbish bin: a Super Girl onesie and a pint glass with the message 'Drink like there's no one watching' printed on its side.

Now dressed and sipping coffee, Sullivan sat at the breakfast bar in the kitchen and once again contemplated the challenge ahead. Her mobile rang. It was Ric.

'Sorry to bother you so early, but I've got to pop across to Gib this morning and I was wondering if there was anything I could do to help with your move.'

Thanks, Dad! Sullivan thought, putting her hands together in the act of prayer. Her beloved father had been dead for some years, but Sullivan always thanked him when something good turned up out of the blue.

'Well, as a matter of fact, there is something you could do to help ...'

And the day's itinerary was hatched. Ric would pick up Sullivan in his ancient Mitsubishi Shogun, chuck her stuff in the back, along with her motorbike, and then drive back to Gaucín. In return, the plan was that Sullivan would drive Ric to Málaga airport in the early evening for his flight to London and then carry on using the Mitsubishi for the rest of her stay at *finca* Danaher.

'Sounds like a plan,' Sullivan said.

'Don't it just, Detective Sergeant.'

Chapter 13

THE FORENSIC SCHEME LABORATORY was a place Gus Broderick disliked visiting. His feelings were not due to any distrust of the science; on the contrary, the wonders of modern-day forensic science had always been something Broderick was quick to praise and unhesitatingly to use. Good forensics had come to the rescue at many a hopeless moment in his police investigations. No, the problem with forensics lay very much in the chief inspector's personal zone. Simply put, he thought the head of the Forensics team, Professor Richard Kemp, was a complete arsehole. The commandingly tall, scholarly and meticulous scientist had always managed to rub Broderick up the wrong way. The reasons for this remained a mystery to many and even, at times, to Broderick himself.

'You just hate posh clever dicks,' Sullivan had once told him. 'Even when they're perfectly pleasant posh clever dicks.'

Broderick knew that his DS had a point, but her reasoning still could not fully explain his strong aversion to the man. Perhaps it was because Kemp reminded him of his old Physics teacher, a sadistic ghoul of a man named Rawlings, whose covert yet generous use of corporal punishment had blighted several years of Broderick's secondary education. It was a good theory, but Broderick still dismissed it in favour of his belief that Kemp was simply an arsehole.

'I don't want to push you on the results of your examination of Eleanor's letter—' Broderick began as Kemp showed him into the lab.

'But you're going to anyway, right, Chief Inspector?' the professor interrupted. 'I took it for granted that was the happy reason for your visit.'

Taking a position behind a long bench, Kemp began to analyse a tray of fibre samples, an action guaranteed to get up Broderick's nose.

'Well?'

'Well what, Chief Inspector?' Kemp's mock innocent expression was designed to infuriate Broderick.

'Have you got the sodding results or not?'

A slight smile played around Kemp's thin lips. 'It's "or not", I'm afraid. I understood this to be a cold case, Chief Inspector. May I enquire as to the need for rush?'

'Not "rush", Kemp. Just getting on with my job. I've got a whole team up and running and I'd like them to crack on with their enquiries ASAP. You may class this case as cold, but I'm here to tell you that I'm warming it up. Understood?'

'Gosh, yes. Very well put. In that case, I'm happy to inform you that initial DNA findings should be through at any moment.'

Broderick half-rolled his neck to release tension before continuing. 'Okay. Anything on the letter?'

'I'm sure you'll be delighted to hear that my assistant, William, has been working on it non-stop. The actual letter is proving a little stubborn in revealing its contents, but the postmark and the name of the addressee on the envelope are looking more hopeful. So, those "sodding results" are likely to arrive sometime this afternoon. No promises, of course.'

'Oh, of course. Thanks, Kemp. A pleasure, as always.'

Broderick turned to leave.

'By the way, Chief Inspector. How's the very marvellous DS Sullivan? Not returned home, has she? I'd rather got used to her being by your side.'

'On leave. Back next month with a permanent posting.'

Kemp smiled, revealing a perfect set of newly implanted white teeth. 'Splendid news. In fact, I think I'll nip next door and tell William. He'll be as pleased as I am to hear that news.'

'Good,' Broderick said, heading for the door. 'Nice teeth by the way. A bit too Liberace for my taste, but each to his own, eh?'

Chapter 14

INSPECTOR CONSUELA DANAHER was coming to the end of a frustrating day. It was 8 p.m. and she had left Estepona and was now driving to Málaga. The day had produced no real results and she was feeling the pressure.

Not that she had felt any friction from the team. They had been unexpectedly supportive, but she was not at all certain that this would remain the case. After all, she was young and newly promoted, and everyone thought that she was really too inexperienced to take command. She might get by for a few days, but any longer and her fellow officers would most likely have a change of heart. These doubts in her ability were foremost in her mind as she drove along the major toll road. She was hoping to call into Police HQ and check out the situation in person before going to her small apartment in Málaga Old Town. Passing the seaside town of Torremolinos on her right, her mobile rang. Clicking to handless, Consuela took the call. It was her landlady.

'Consuela? It's me, Julianna. Bad news. The top floor

has been flooded and, I'm sorry to say, the water has come down into your apartment. A real mess. Better get over here as soon as you can, but there's no way you can stay here till it's all fixed. I'm so sorry. What can I say?'

The answer to that question was, 'Nothing.' Not usually given to profanity, Consuela now swore out loud. Not only did she feel at sea in the investigation, she was now stranded without a bed for the night. Maybe several nights. Maybe more. Having no choice but to abandon her visit to Police HQ, Consuela decided to head home and sort things out. In the meantime, she would finish her commute by taking stock of the day's work.

Unfortunately, none of her underworld contacts had had anything to say about the Bernard killings. Like Carlos Estrada's, their answers to Consuela's questions seemed genuine to her. She had not sensed anyone covering up or attempting to misdirect her. If the Camorra or any other underworld organisation had ordered a hit on Ingrid Bernard for revenge purposes, they were not talking about it.

Results from Forensics had also drawn a blank. Whoever had carried out the murders had been knowledgeable enough to take precautions against contaminating the site. Not a spot of unaccountable DNA in either the house, the pool or on the bodies themselves.

The plastic ties used by the killers on the wrists and ankles of the victims were a common commercial product, available from a host of retail and wholesale outlets. Enquiries were still being made, despite it being very much the 'needle in a haystack' part of the investigation. But that was police work – you just did not know where your next lead would spring from.

There had been some movement on the killers' likely route in and out of the Bernards' villa on the day of the murders. Access had been achieved by cutting a hole in the wire fence on the northern side of the grounds. Once inside, they proceeded to the house and gained entry to the small security room inside the main dwelling, shutting down the surveillance cameras that covered most of the building. Despite their apparent professionalism, they had not disabled one of the security cameras covering the main driveway of the property. A review of the tapes found no visiting vehicles on the day, save the scarlet Alfa Romeo 4C Spider that Izi and her boyfriend had arrived in that afternoon.

Scouring the surrounding countryside had led to the discovery of a dirt track – the type traditionally used by goatherds – that ran from a single-lane hillside road, some two kilometres away, to within a few hundred metres of the Bernards' residence. Faint signs of motorcycle tyre tracks had been found on the dirt track and were currently being analysed. However, the lack of any municipal CCTV cameras up in the hills had hindered the search for the escaping murderers. Police were stopping and questioning regular users of the roads above Puerto Banús, but no one had recalled seeing motorcyclists during the previous Monday afternoon.

Arriving in Málaga, Consuela found a parking spot a few doors down from her apartment. She had finally consoled herself with the thought that, even if an *inspector jefe* – a chief inspector – had been running the investigation, it was unlikely that they would be any further along.

Once inside, all possibility for consolation evaporated. The place was a disaster zone. The water flooding from above had brought the entire ceiling down in her bedroom, and buckets and pans were still collecting dripping water in both the bathroom and kitchen. It was clear that any future habitation of the apartment was going to be a long way off. Weeks or, more likely, months would pass before she would be able to occupy it again. As Consuela salvaged what clothes and possessions she could, she realised that any alternative accommodation would have to last some time and be available straight away.

Feeling uncharacteristically sorry for herself, Consuela sat on the arm of her small, but dry, IKEA sofa and contemplated her next move.

Chapter 15

DRIVING up the sharply steepening roads to Gaucín from the coast, Sullivan felt a strange freedom. She simply could not remember the last time she had experienced such an unburdening of care. It was quite remarkable, considering the early evening journey had turned out to be quite challenging. Having accompanied Ric Danaher to Málaga airport for his flight to London, she had spent some time adjusting to the specific requirements involved in driving the ageing Japanese Mitsubishi. It seemed to have a mind of its own, not helped by the fact that its power steering had failed to operate many years before.

'I've been meaning to get it fixed,' Ric had told her. 'It's a bit of a bugger on the hillside roads, but you'll get used to it.'

That this comment was a massive understatement became alarmingly clear within minutes of Sullivan driving off. The giant, oil-smelling tin-can-on-wheels was proving to be a 'bit of a bugger' on the flat, straight roads leading away from the airport as well. Achieving a tenuous state of driving proficiency had taken up most of the journey home. With aching arms and a splitting headache, Sullivan was relieved to finally turn off the main road and climb the hillside track towards her temporary country home. Parking outside the *finca*'s annexe, Sullivan stepped away from the car, looked west towards the last glimmers of the fading sunset and breathed in the fresh night air. At the end of a hard day, this was a fitting reward.

Ric had picked her up from Gibraltar just after lunch and they had arrived at the *finca* at three o'clock on the dot. Sullivan had spent the next few hours unpacking and acclimatising to her new surroundings. The newly converted annexe was perfect. A little kitchen and sitting room gave way to a large bedroom and en suite bathroom. There was even a small air conditioning unit, but Sullivan decided to make do with the large ceiling fans instead. With the baking afternoon sun beating down on the hillside from the bluest of skies, Sullivan had even found a few moments to kick off her shoes and enjoy a good, old-fashioned siesta. This was another world, far from the pressures and stress of police work. Far from the pressures and stress of almost everything, in fact.

Now, with night falling, Sullivan lit some candles, poured herself a large glass of red wine and gently stroked the sleeping dog by her side. Leggo had not reacted badly to the first moments of regime change on the hillside and had then stuck close to his new mistress as if they had been an item for years. As the first sip of the Marqués de Cáceres *rioja* passed over her taste buds and slipped down her throat, Sullivan smiled contentedly. *A month of peace and quiet will do very nicely*, she thought.

It was then she heard a car approaching.

Looking down from the annexe, Sullivan could see the vehicle's headlamps spraying the hillside with light as it wove up the steep and winding track. To her surprise, she realised that she felt a little on edge. She had not for a moment considered the isolation of the place and the possible vulnerability that it could present. She considered it now, though, and quickly.

Reaching for her mobile, she placed Consuela's number on standby, just in case the occupant or occupants of the approaching vehicle turned out to be a little unsavoury. Sullivan could handle herself well enough, but it was always better to be safe than sorry. Leggo had begun barking at the first sound of the distant engine, so she swiftly let him out of the door to go about his trained business of guard dog. Peering from a window, she looked on as the car came to a halt outside the main farmhouse across the way. To Sullivan's surprise – and relief – Consuela Danaher got out of the driver's seat and began to walk towards the annexe. Sullivan's new Spanish friend looked pale and rather shaken.

'Hi. Are you okay?' Sullivan asked on opening the door.

'It is a long story,' Consuela said. 'I need a drink first.'

And it was soon very apparent that she did. The first glass of *rioja* hardly touched the sides. It was only after Sullivan filled her a second glass that Consuela became relaxed enough to tell her tale. First off was an explanation of the loosely dressed bandage that now adorned her right hand.

'I got this from an electric shock after turning on a light switch in my newly flooded apartment.'

'Bloody hell,' Sullivan said. 'Great way to start a story.'

'It is, is it not? Could have killed myself, I suppose, but luckily it is just a burn. Hurts like hell, though, and driving from Málaga was not exactly easy.'

'Oh, I can imagine,' Sullivan said.

'Luckily, my landlady is a nurse and went to great lengths to make sure that I was all right. Probably just terrified I will sue her, but saved me a visit to the hospital, I guess.'

'Dear God, you poor thing. Can I get you anything else? Some food maybe?'

'No, I am cool. Even if my hand is still hot.'

Both women smiled, experts in the art of black humour.

'I thought of checking into a hotel for the night, but that is just grim. Do you mind if I stay here till things get sorted?'

'Do I mind? This is your dad's place, for heaven's sake. Of course I don't mind. Be happy for a little bit of company, as it happens. I was only just thinking how remote it is up here.'

'That's very good of you, Tamara. I will not be around that much, not with the investigation I am dealing with.'

'How's that been going?'

'If you've got a few hours to spare, I will tell you.'

Sullivan almost rubbed her hands with glee. 'Get to it then, girlfriend. I'm all ears.'

For the second night that week, the new friends talked police work and murder.

Chapter 16
SATURDAY

AN ANONYMOUS PHONE call to the local Guardia Civil was received at 7.55 a.m. the following morning. The message received had sent a petrol jeep speeding towards Guadiaro Old Town. The caller had reported a body in the River Guadiaro, apparently trapped in the overgrown, trailing tree branches on the southern bank of the river, near the bend in the road where Calle Transito and Calle del Sabio met. When asked, the caller had refused to give a name and the line had gone dead.

It would be another two hours before this news would reach Consuela Danaher. She and Sullivan had talked till nearly dawn, with Consuela finally drifting off to sleep mid-conversation. Not wishing to disturb her, Sullivan had covered her with a blanket and tiptoed into the bedroom. As it was the weekend, the Bernard investigation would continue with only a skeleton team until Monday morning, with De Galvez in charge in the morning and Consuela in the afternoon and evening. Consuela had been frustrated by the enforced work restriction, but at the same time had felt some relief in the light of her current circumstances.

Still fast asleep on the little sofa in the sitting-room of the annexe, she was woken by the buzz of her mobile, as was Sullivan in the bedroom next door. As beams of sunlight entered the *finca* through half-closed slits in the window blinds, she attempted to focus both her eyes and her mind. Locating her mobile in the pocket of her jeans, Consuela answered the call with her unbandaged left hand.

'Danaher.'

De Galvez was on the other end of the line. 'Have I woken you, Inspector?'

'No, no, no,' Consuela lied. 'What's up?'

'I know you're not supposed to be in till midday, but this is urgent.'

'What is?'

'There's been an anonymous tip-off about a body in the River Guadiaro.'

'Can't Algeciras Cuerpo take it? That's Cádiz province, not Málaga. We've got enough on our plate.'

'Ordinarily, yes, but the voice on the phone is clearly the same as the Bernard caller.'

Consuela sat up straight. 'That's odd, don't you agree, De Galvez?'

'Certainly intriguing.'

'Okay. Where am I going?'

As De Galvez gave his boss directions, Sullivan appeared at the bedroom door. The expression on Consuella's face suggested that it was unlikely to be a gentle start to the day.

Twenty minutes later, Sullivan and Consuela were on their way to Guadiaro. It would have been sooner had the two women not disagreed about the best form of transport to take. The fact was, the Spanish detective's hand was in a delicate state and, upon examination, clearly needed some further medical attention.

'I don't know how the hell you managed to drive here last night,' Sullivan said, as the two women left the annexe, both momentarily shielding their eyes from the sun. 'You obviously changed gears with your fingertips. Not the safest way to drive a car, not to mention the pain it must have caused you.'

'I will be fine,' Consuela said. 'It is just a half-hour drive and then someone else can drive me around.'

'How about I drive you to Guadiaro in the Mitsubishi?' Sullivan said. 'I can even pick you up later from Estepona. Nothing more pressing on my agenda.'

Consuela hesitated for a moment. Sullivan was right. The pain in her hand was agonising and she was clearly not up to the job of driving her manual police vehicle. If she could just get to Guadiaro, De Galvez could take over and drive her around. If she was lucky, she might even get to see a doctor later, although that was not a priority at the moment. Giving in to pragmatism, Consuela conceded that she had no choice but to take up Sullivan's offer.

The two women got into the Mitsubishi and Sullivan turned on the ignition. Immediately another problem presented itself.

'It's out of petrol' Sullivan said. 'I don't believe it.'

'Dad never thinks to check. Sorry.'

'I didn't check either. Oh well, looks like I'm going to have to drive your car.'

'Not a good idea, Tamara. For one, you are not insured. Plus, if anything happened I would have a hell of a time explaining why a Gibraltarian police officer was driving a Cuerpo police car, even with my injured hand as an excuse. I am just going to have to get a patrol car to come and pick me up.'

To Consuela's surprise, the look of frustration on Sullivan's face slowly turned into a large smile.

'Not necessarily,' Sullivan said. 'Not necessarily at all.'

'Well, that's the roughest bit over and done with,' Sullivan called out over her shoulder to her passenger behind. 'It's plain sailing from here on.'

Opening the Kawasaki's throttle, Sullivan steered her motorbike away from the hillside track and hit the main road to the coast. With arms stretched around Sullivan's waist and an over-large crash helmet on her head, Consuela hung on for dear life. *It isn't going to be the most elegant way to turn up to work*, she thought, *but right now I'll happily settle for just getting there in one piece.*

Chapter 17

THE VILLAGE of Guadiaro stands on the banks of the river from which it gains its name. From this old centre, the newer Pueblo Nuevo de Guadiaro developed on its eastern edge – closer to the busy main coast road and a short distance from Sotogrande and the sea. The villages were busy, typically Spanish communities where the shops, restaurants and cafés served mostly locals. The polo fields, designer shops, international golf courses and millionaire mansions that lay just on the other side of the E-15 motorway might just as well have been a thousand kilometres away.

Winding their way through the narrow residential streets of the old village, Sullivan and Consuela soon found themselves on Calle Tránsito. As they approached the end of the street, they spotted a heavy police presence. The street turned left, and immediately opposite, in a gap between the houses, the riverbank could be seen with the waters of the Guadiaro flowing fast beyond. Alongside the police vehicles, a small crowd had gathered, villagers keen to find out what was happening in their neck of the woods. Parking the bike on the *calle*, Sullivan and Consuela dismounted and approached the riverbank. Both were pleased to see that it had already been taped off and that Guardia Civil officers were stationed to stop any inquisitive citizens from proceeding further.

Flashing her warrant card at one of the officers, Consuela nodded towards Sullivan. 'She's with me.'

Dipping under the tape and moving towards the tent that had been erected in the small clearing by the bank, Consuela looked at Sullivan. 'I know I do not have to ask you to be discreet,' she said. 'If you could stay back a bit, I will introduce you when I can. Is that okay?'

'Sure. Absolutely,' Sullivan said, stopping almost at once. As Consuela headed towards the tent and her fellow officers, Sullivan considered how strange it felt not to be joining her. It had simply not occurred to her that she could not and should not proceed, so familiar were the circumstances and procedures she was witnessing.

Get a grip, Tamara, she thought to herself. *You're not a Spanish police officer, no matter how much you'd like to be one at the moment.* Consuela had been courteous enough to let Sullivan come within the police cordon, but there was no way she was going to let her foreign counterpart any nearer. *And I'd do exactly the same.*

Approaching the water, Consuela could see De Galvez with two other detectives from the team. With them stood a *medico forenze*, two paramedics and three scene-of-crime Forensic officers. The river was unseasonably high and the current strong. Torrential rainfalls near the river's source in the Grazalema Sierra had led to this, and some flash flooding had been reported in other areas of the Costa. On the bank, all were looking upstream to where dense trees and shrubbery reached out over and into the river. Ten metres along, a diver appeared and gave an 'Okay' signal. Almost immediately, another diver appeared from around the bend with a body floating between his arms. Moving towards his colleague, the first diver reached out to help, and both were now slowly edging the corpse towards dry land and the waiting police team.

While this was underway, Sullivan had managed to manoeuvre herself into a good position within the trees and bushes. From here she could see the body being brought in by the wet team. As soon as the corpse had been landed, it was moved to the tent. The journey took a few seconds but it was easily long enough for Sullivan to have a clear sighting of the dead person.

Two things were clear: first, the corpse was male, and second, he had been murdered, the second conclusion being based on the impossibility of the man being able to tie his own ankles together, place a tape across his mouth, secure his hands behind his back and then – in a macabre finale – throw himself into deep flowing water. From where Sullivan was standing, 'death by misadventure' this was not.

How she had first spotted it, Sullivan would never be able to say, but despite her concentration on the body's retrieval, a sudden flash of light made her look up and out across the river. It was true that her eyesight was exceptional and her ability to take in information from several sources at once was well above that of the average person. Even so, what Sullivan saw next was quite remarkable. Although a good fifty metres across the water, something out of the ordinary had caught her eye in the thick green blanket of foliage that edged the bank of the river. Staring intently at the mass of trees and bushes, she could now see nothing untoward. However, having always held her instincts dear, she still sensed 'a glitch in the matrix'. She needed to focus better.

Leaving her hiding place, she walked towards one of the police officers guarding the site and entered into a ridiculous mime. 'My *español* is not good, *sí?* You have bin-oc-u-lars? *Sí?*' As she spoke, she rounded her hands and raised them to her eyes.

The bemused policeman looked at her for a few seconds before replying in good English, 'You want binoculars, yes?'

'Er, yeah. Yes, please. *Por favor.*'

Calmly, the officer moved to his parked jeep, opened the driver's door and reached in to take out a medium-sized pair of binoculars. Moments later, Sullivan was back in her position between the trees and shrubs and was scanning the opposite bank of the river. She was frustrated to see nothing unusual. Not that she had any idea what it was she was actually looking for. The vegetation was very dense on the other side, and after several negative passes along the opposite riverbank, she was beginning to feel a little foolish. And then she saw it. The flash of reflected sunlight came from a spot where ash and willow trees were particularly clustered. Focusing the binoculars as sharply as she could, Sullivan finally hit pay dirt. Someone was hidden in the thicket. He or she was wearing a black motorcycle helmet and leather top, and like Sullivan they were holding a pair of binoculars to their eyes. Fortunately they were not looking straight back at her but were focused on the Forensics tent several metres to her right.

'Are you okay?'

The voice belonged to Consuela. She had left the tent and was making her way towards Sullivan, whose eyes remained glued to the watcher across the river.

'You're being spied on from the opposite bank,' Sullivan said. 'Someone in a crash helmet is hidden over there watching what's going on through binoculars.'

Consuela turned to look. 'Where?'

'To your left a bit, by the big willows. You won't see them without these glasses.' Sullivan handed the binoculars to Consuela.

'I cannot see anything.'

'Keep looking. Someone's there.'

'I cannot …' Consuela stopped. 'I have got him. Dear God, I think he is looking straight back at me.'

'What?'

'It is gone. The helmet's gone.'

'Shit. Okay. What's on the other side of the river?' Sullivan asked.

'Nothing. Just woods and fields. San Enrique is a bit further back. Do you think …?'

'The incident was phoned in by the anonymous caller. The MO used is pretty much the same as the Bernard killings – death by drowning. Am I right?'

'You're not a million miles away.'

'So, how do you get across there?'

'Quickest way is on the E-15 to San Enrique—' But before Consuela had finished her sentence, Sullivan was running for her bike.

Consuela called after her. 'What do you think you are doing?'

'Get a patrol car to follow me,' Sullivan shouted as she ran.

Consuela looked on helplessly. 'Come back here!'

But Sullivan was not stopping. Within seconds she and her Kawasaki were speeding through the streets of the old village, en route to the northern bank of the River Guadiaro.

Racing on from the San Enrique turn-off, Sullivan headed towards the small town, the sound of a police siren softly blaring in the distance behind her. A three-kilometre route to achieve the fifty-metre crossing of the river was clearly not a helpful equation, but still worth a try. Knowing that the river was on her left side, Sullivan looked for likely roads that would take her alongside the fields to the wooded riverside location opposite the crime scene. The chances of the watcher still being there were slight, but she had to give it a go. The thought that she was being fool-hardy had entered her mind a few minutes before. If it was the killer looking on from the opposite side of the river, it was likely that he was armed and most certainly dangerous. Sullivan was unarmed and vulnerable and had no jurisdiction as a police officer in Spain. Getting involved like this was pure insanity, and she knew what Gus Broderick would say if he ever found out. But she was a free citizen, and citizens could make arrests, couldn't they? How that procedure might take place was something she would consider when and if the opportunity presented itself.

The first viable left-hand turn was signposted ahead. Slowing down to approach the junction by the San Enrique

Public Medical Centre, Sullivan saw a motorcyclist pull out from the left, cross the main road and disappear into the streets opposite. There was no question in her mind as to who it was. The black helmet and leather top were the same. Taking a fast right and narrowly missing oncoming traffic, she gave chase. She was sure the rider had not seen her, so her plan was to keep on his tail and phone through to Consuela when a destination had been reached. That way the possibility of confrontation would be at least limited.

Weaving through the town in pursuit of the rider was not easy. It was clear that the motorcyclist ahead was far more proficient than she was. Taking a series of sharp lefts and rights, Sullivan began to wonder if keeping up was going to be possible. On leaving the narrow streets, the machines hit a clear stretch of road that followed the outer contours of the town. Increasing its speed, the motorbike in front pulled further away. Sullivan countered this as best she could, but it was clear that the motorcycle she was chasing was a good deal more powerful than her own Kawasaki. Sullivan had never ridden at the speed she was now travelling, and with her heart beating out of her chest and the noise of the engine loud in her ears, she hung on for dear life.

Several hundred metres on, a long bend in the road led to a T-junction. Hardly slowing at all, the rider in front swung right and continued to speed away from San Enrique and into the countryside to the north of the town. Unwilling to follow the same action, Sullivan slowed to a halt to check the road was clear. It was as well she chose the safe option: coming towards her from the right, a large lorry rattled through the junction in front of her. Had she blindly swung out into the road, the vehicle would have flattened her in an instant.

Finally clearing the junction, Sullivan could see that the watcher had put a lot of distance between them. Reality started to hit. If she stopped the chase now, nobody would blame her. She had done her best and the odds of her catching the other bike without being seen by its rider were not good. She should stop, call Consuela and report the watcher's present position and then return to the *finca* and feed the dog. That would be the sensible thing to do. So Sullivan opened the throttle of the Kawasaki and took up the chase once more. Sensible could wait for another day.

Half a kilometre ahead, the road reached another junction. Sullivan had lost sight of the watcher a few hundred metres back; now she was not sure if the motorcyclist had taken a left or a right. The road east was a continuation of the tarmac road she was currently on. The other road off the junction was an unmade farm road that offered a much rougher ride. Looking in that direction, she could just make out a cloud of pale dust rising in the distance. Certain it was the other bike, she once again took off, bracing herself for the tougher terrain.

Sure enough, the landscape either side of the road proved to be a combination of farmland and dry open countryside. Riding onwards, Sullivan passed nothing and no one. To her right, she caught a few glimpses of the E-15 a kilometre or so away. From this, Sullivan deduced that she was probably on the old route winding towards the Sierras and running parallel with the motorway as it cut through the land bypassing the coastal towns of the Costa. On the white dusty road before her, she could see fresh single tyre tracks. Although she could not see the watcher ahead, her choice to follow this road appeared to have been the right one.

Kilometre after kilometre flew by with the ride proving as uncomfortable as she had predicted. Her throat dry and her body dripping with sweat, Sullivan rode on as the heat of the late morning sun beat down on her with growing intensity. With no actual sight of the motorcycle she was chasing, doubt once again entered her thoughts. She had passed several tracks leading off the road, but had assumed they led to farmhouses or isolated villas. Could the watcher have taken one of them and given her the slip? Did they offer cut-throughs to other roads and different destinations? It was possible, but she was now committed to her route, and if she was wrong, she was wrong.

Pressing on, Sullivan steered her bike around a long bend in the road. Having taken the corner, she could see that the road straightened out and stretched far into the distance. She also saw the lone figure of the watcher standing beside his motorcycle in the middle of the road and looking straight at her. In the seconds it took Sullivan to take this in, she also saw that his arms were stretched out in front of him. The first shot from the watcher's gun cracked the air. The second did the same. Hurtling towards the helmeted figure, Sullivan could not believe she was actually looking down the barrel of a gun aimed straight at her. A third shot rang out and Sullivan was certain she felt the bullet narrowly pass by her head.

As she hit the brakes, the back wheel of her Kawasaki swung violently forward, sending the bike into a huge skid. Sullivan's body keeled over sideways with the bike, her right leg bouncing between the engine and the rough surface of the road. Her hands now flew from the controls as the motorcycle parted company with her, hurtling off the road and leaving Sullivan tumbling after it through a cloud of thick dust.

For a moment, Sullivan simply lay on the road. She was alive, but she was hurt. She could taste blood in her mouth and a fierce pain stretched from her right leg to her pelvis. Her breath was now forced and rasping as she lay waiting for a bullet to the head. It had come to this and it was her own stupid fault. She was helpless and soon she would die.

A few seconds passed and then footsteps approached on the harsh dried surface of the track. Her mind scrambled in an effort to do something. Should she scream and beg for mercy or just remain silent and hope his actions would be swift and painless? Opting for silence, she lay still and closed her eyes. The man reached her; she could hear his breathing close and hard. For several moments he hovered there. In her fevered mind, Sullivan started to pray. It was all she could think to do.

'Holy Mary, Mother of God.'

Nothing.

'Pray for us sinners.'

Still nothing.

'Now and at the hour of our death.'

And then he left, the sound of his footsteps replaced by an engine starting and the roar of his motorcycle speeding into the distance. Slowly, painfully, Sullivan turned her head towards the sound. The dust from the watcher's motorcycle hung in the air. The chase was over. Rolling onto her back and grimacing with the pain of her fall, she looked up into the clear blue sky and wondered at her own survival.

'Amen,' she whispered.

Chapter 18

'WE'VE CHECKED all missing persons notifications for the whole of 2005 and 2006 on both sides of the border,' Calbot said, addressing Broderick and the team from behind his desk in the Incident Room. 'Only three fitted Nefertiti's – sorry, *Eleanor*'s description. Two were found safe and sound and another was found dead in a canyon up in the hills near Casares. She'd been hiking and fell.'

'Extend the search then,' Broderick ordered. 'Keep looking till something comes up. Portillo says that death occurred most likely between 2005 and 2006. *But* "likely" doesn't mean absolutely. Trawl '07 and even '08 if you have to.'

'Doing it, Guv.'

'Checks on builders, warehouse employees, anyone with access to the warehouse over that period?'

Moreno looked down at a printout and put up his hand. 'Proving difficult to get a list of builders. The building contractors, Westport Building Ltd, went bust five years ago and they seem to have taken their employment records with them. We all know how some of these outfits work with cash in hand. I've talked to the old managing director and the warehouse architect, but the actual on-site builders are going to be harder to track.'

'And employees?'

'Better. Much. Line Wall Logistics have a full list. They maintained a basic crew on site week on week. Checking all the names that we've been given.'

'What about people with occasional access for deliveries, maintenance, et cetera?' Broderick asked.

'We have an agency that Line Wall used for general maintenance needs. Also a list as long as my arm of haulage companies that delivered over the years. Attempting to get the names of all drivers from them. It'll take time, Guv.'

'Something you have plenty of, Moreno.' Broderick turned to the rest of his team. 'Keep working the screens and the phones, everyone, and let's hope Forensics can help us focus in closer.'

'Might be able to help you with that, sir,' came a voice from behind Broderick. The latter looked over his shoulder to see Sergeant Aldarino. The tall, avuncular police officer stood in the doorway, a large envelope in his hand.

'Ah, Aldarino, welcome. Can we help you?'

The sergeant passed the envelope to Broderick. 'Professor Kemp just delivered this for you.'

'And scuttled off again, did he?'

'No, sir. He's with Chief Super Massetti at the moment.'

Broderick raised an eyebrow. 'Is he? I see.'

Ripping open the envelope, Broderick removed the papers within it. Skipping to the end of the many-paged document, he began reading through the report's conclusions.

'Right, here we go. Blah, blah, blah. "*One DNA profile found, belonging to the victim.*" Blah, blah. "*Profile not recorded on the National DNA Database. Checking Interpol and other International databases, but results from these sources may take several days to come through.*" Shit.'

Broderick read on in silence for a few moments before addressing the room.

'Okay. Not helpful.'

Moreno and Calbot nodded their agreement with this conclusion.

Broderick continued. 'Eleanor remains unidentified. Unless, that is …' He looked into the envelope once more. 'No Forensic report attached to the letter in here. Did Kemp say anything about that to you, Aldarino?'

'No, sir. Nothing.'

The phone on Broderick's desk rang. He reached for the receiver. 'Broderick. Uh, uh. Yes, ma'am. I'll come straight down.'

Throwing the envelope and report on his desk, Broderick left the room without a word. Whistling through his teeth, Calbot turned to his colleagues.

'Interesting.'

Chapter 19

'NOTHING IS BROKEN, by the looks of things.'

'Thank you, doctor,' Sullivan said, smiling weakly at the young woman and adjusting the light blue hospital gown she had been forced to put on.

'We will continue to dress the cuts and grazes on your arms and legs and give you some painkillers. You will probably experience some concussion and shock, so no driving, et cetera.'

'Do I have to stay here?'

'No, no. You can go home, rest and wait for the bruising to appear. There will be a lot of it, so I would get some arnica if I were you. It helps.'

'Isn't that a bit ... "alternative"?'

'Not these days. Whatever gets you through the night. That is what I say.'

As the doctor left the cubicle in the busy emergency department of Estepona Hospital, Consuela Danaher's face appeared between the curtains. Sullivan's heart sank.

'I know what you're going to say, so don't say it. Okay?' she said.

'You mean about you being a fool and putting your life at risk playing at being a police officer on foreign soil?'

'Yeah, that bit.'

'Okay. I will keep quiet about that,' Consuela said. 'What I will mention is that, if you ever do anything like that again, I will report you. Understood?'

'Yes, ma'am – *señorita* – *inspector* – whatever you call yourself,' Sullivan replied, not meaning a word of what she said. 'Don't you want to know exactly what happened?'

'I want to know that you are okay. I have been worried sick,' Consuela said, moving to Sullivan's side.

'I'm fine. Bruised in body and ego, but other than that, okay.'

'You chased a motorcyclist and the motorcyclist tried to kill you. Isn't that about right?'

'Spot on.' Sullivan winced as she shifted her position in the bed.

'The Guardia picked you up on the old hillside route from San Enrique to the coast road.'

'I'd no idea where the road was leading, but yes, they certainly found me.'

'Luckily your phone was intact.'

'Electronically, but the screen is badly cracked. I can't remember if I'm insured.'

Consuela rolled her eyes. 'First things first, Tamara. You told us the rider stopped in the road and fired at you, correct?'

'That's right.'

'And you are sure that it was a male?'

'Height and stance-wise, I'd say definitely.'

'After three shots, you fell from your bike and he rode off and left you.'

'Yes, thank God.'

'Agreed. Anything else?'

'If you ask my opinion, he was a professional. The way he handled the bike and his gun.'

'Then why not finish you off? I am sorry but I have to ask.'

'I don't know. Hopefully you'll get to ask him one day.'

'*Hopefully* you will be back on the Rock and minding your own business by then.'

Sullivan shrugged her shoulders. 'I guess. What about the body in the river?'

'I am not sure you should know anything more about that.'

'I'm not going to go charging off again. I promise. I'd just like to know. One professional to another.'

Consuela considered her answer for a moment. 'Okay. We know who he is. The killer left his wallet on him with everything in it. He's a local man. We are making enquiries.'

'What about the way he was tied up? Exactly the same as the Bernard killings?'

'It would seem so. Same plastic ties and tape for the mouth.'

'Uh huh. So this could be episode two of a possible series.'

'Who knows? But it is the same killer or killers, that much seems certain.' Consuela changed the subject. 'Look, Tamara. I'm afraid you are going to have to give a full statement about what happened to you. An officer is on his way.'

Sullivan nodded. The action brought a grimace to her face.

'Ouch. Sore neck.'

'I need to go,' Consuela said. 'When you are ready to go back to the *finca*, let me know and I will get you a lift up there. I am afraid neither you nor your motorcycle are going anywhere for a while.'

'Thanks, Consuela,' Sullivan said. 'You'll be back there yourself later?'

'Yes. Like you, I have nowhere else to go at the moment.'

'The odd couple, eh?' Sullivan said with a smile.

Consuela smiled back and left. In her place, a male nurse appeared, carrying dressings and medications. Sullivan leaned back on the bed and braced herself for the next round of pain.

Chapter 20

BRODERICK DESCENDED the stairs to the main reception of Police HQ. A few metres ahead of him, Richard Kemp was striding, on his way out of the building.

'Kemp?'

The Forensics professor turned to see the approaching chief inspector.

'Gus, I was just leaving.'

'Do you have the forensics on the letter?'

'They're with Massetti.'

'Why not bring them straight to me first? I'm the SIO on this.'

The normally fluent Kemp hesitated for a moment. 'Yes, sorry. I think she's waiting for you. Look, I'm afraid I have to dash. Sorry, Gus.'

As Kemp left the building, Broderick stood alone, wondering why he felt so unsettled by the encounter. Was it because Kemp had gone to Massetti first? Or was it the fact that the professor had called him 'Gus' for the first time ever? Deciding it was both, Broderick headed for the chief super's office.

———

'Take a seat, Gus,' Massetti said from behind her large antique mahogany desk.

Broderick remained standing. 'I believe you have the forensic report on the letter, ma'am.'

'I do,' Massetti said. 'Please sit down, Gus.'

Broderick was now doubly worried. Even Massetti was being pleasant to him. Considering it best not to disobey her a second time, he took one of the two seats opposite his boss.

'Richard's just delivered the report. He wanted me to take a look at it first. He considered the results to be somewhat delicate in content.'

'In what way?' Broderick asked, shifting in his chair.

'As you know, most of the lettering on the envelope and the letter itself was severely faded. However, scientific analysis has been able to reveal much of it.' Harriet Massetti paused for a moment, taking a sip of water from a glass on her desk. With a slight cough, she continued. 'It would seem, Gus – and I'm not sure how this can be – but it would seem that the letter on the dead woman's body was written by you.'

For a moment, Broderick thought he had misheard her. 'I beg your pardon?'

'And I'm afraid that's not all,' Massetti continued. 'The name on the envelope, the person to whom the letter is written, would appear to be ...' Massetti paused once again.

'Would appear to be who?' Broderick said, his frustration growing.

'Would appear to be Helen Broderick,' Massetti said at last. 'Your wife.'

The mention of Helen's name hit Broderick like a punch to the solar plexus. He felt as if all the oxygen had been forcibly extracted from his lungs.

'I know this must come as a huge shock to you, Gus.'

Broderick could not reply, his mind unable to process what had just been said. Massetti reached for the decanter on her desk and poured a glass of water. Rising from her chair, she moved across to her chief inspector and offered it to him. Without a word, Broderick took it and drank.

'Take your time. I appreciate that this is a lot to take in.'

'I don't … I just don't understand,' Broderick stammered.

'It's why Richard brought the results directly to me. He understood that this would prove difficult for you. I can see that this is obviously a terrible shock, but I know you'll understand that I have to ask some questions.'

Broderick was slowly emerging from the shock. 'Questions?'

'I'm afraid so. Although we haven't so far been able to formally identify the woman, we have to consider the possibility that …'

Massetti's words hung in the air as her obvious conclusion sank slowly into Broderick's befuddled mind.

'Are you trying to tell me that you think …?'

'It's all right, Gus. I really didn't mean to rush this.'

'Dear God, you think it might be her,' Broderick said, his eyes darting from side to side as he attempted to comprehend the horror of what was being suggested to him. 'That's right, isn't it? You think that body – those bones – that thing we saw out there – you think that's Helen.'

'I'm sorry, Gus, but we have to consider it a possibility.'

Broderick rose slowly to his feet, his large frame shaking with rage.

'You're upset, Gus. Obviously. We don't need to continue this now.'

Broderick's breath was now coming in gasps and his face had a pale and ghostly pallor. He tried to speak, to shout, to scream out, but nothing would come.

'Gus. Sit down, Gus,' Massetti pleaded.

But he swung around, lurched for the door and almost fell from the chief super's office into the corridor outside. Collecting himself as best he could, he walked quickly across the main reception area, Massetti rushing from her office behind him.

'Gus. Where are you going? Gus, please.'

Passing the main reception desk and pushing open the doors, the police officer stumbled out into the open court-yard. As the sun hit his face and dry air filled his nostrils, Gus Broderick vomited hard and fast over the ground at his feet.

Chapter 21

Sullivan sat in the hospital's emergency department reception. It was Saturday afternoon and mayhem prevailed in the busy corridors and examination areas that surrounded her. She was delighted to be escaping further incarceration and examination, and the thought of returning to Gaucín and Leggo especially pleased her. A police patrol car was supposedly on its way to pick her up. Consuela had said it would be with her in thirty minutes. That conversation had taken place over an hour ago. *Mañana, mañana,* Sullivan thought to herself.

She had been well looked after by the hospital staff and she was grateful for that. To her surprise, she did not hurt as much as she thought she would. Apart from some aches and tenderness, she had no complaints. The painkillers had clearly kicked in with great efficiency. She had a slight stiffness in her gait, but otherwise there were no other outward signs of her injuries. Her face was blessedly clear of cuts and bruises, and beneath her bedraggled clothing the dressings had been applied with care and dexterity. All in all, she had had a lucky escape. *Another one of my nine lives gone*, she thought.

Her mobile phone vibrated in her pocket. Taking it out, she was surprised to see the name 'Massetti' lit up on the badly cracked screen. Sullivan pressed the 'Accept' button.

'Ma'am. It's Sullivan.'

'Yes, obviously,' Massetti said. 'Look, I know you're clear this month, but something's occurred that you need to know about. More to the point, it's something I need your help with. In an unofficial way.'

'I see,' Sullivan said.

'You can't possibly see, Sullivan, because I haven't told you what it is yet. Can you make it in to see me tomorrow morning? I know it's Sunday, but I wouldn't ask if it wasn't important.'

Before she could tell Massetti about her present condition and the fact that she was not really supposed to drive anywhere, Sullivan heard herself say, 'Sure. What time tomorrow?'

'Make it eleven. I'll come straight from church,' Massetti said. 'And not a word to anyone about this, Sullivan. Nobody. Understood?'

'Yes, ma'am. Perfectly.'

When Massetti ended the call, Sullivan sat lost in thought. *What on earth was that all about? Massetti asking for help? 'Unofficial' help?* This was totally out of character for the chief superintendent. By the tone she had taken with her, nobody appreciated that more than Massetti herself. It had to be something important, but why would Massetti want to entrust it to the new girl on the block? Was it to do with the body at the warehouse? Something personal perhaps? With too many questions spinning through her mind, Sullivan almost missed the Guardia police officer looking in through the main reception doors. Spotting him, she raised her arm and caught his eye.

'Gaucín?' the officer called out to her over the heads of the passing infirm.

'*Sí. Muchos gracias,*' Sullivan called back, carefully rising to her feet. '*Muchos* very *gracias* indeed.'

———

The general demeanour of the two police officers tasked with driving Sullivan back to Gaucín hinted at their distaste at being reduced to taxi drivers. Their silence suited Sullivan well. She was in no mood to entertain small talk. Sitting in the back seat of the patrol car, she looked out at the sea and distant horizon as they made their way southwards along the old coast road towards the Casares turn-off.

The fact that she could easily have been killed earlier in the day had surprisingly taken second place in her thoughts. The call from Massetti was instead at the fore-front of her mind. The temptation to call Broderick, or even Calbot, was immense, but she had given her word not to and she was good for that. However, getting to Gibraltar the next morning did present a problem. Remembering that the old Mitsubishi was out of diesel Sullivan persuaded the police driver to stop at a petrol station and allow her to buy and fill a five-litre container with diesel. It would be enough to get her to the Rock the next day and discover what the mystery was all about.

Stepping out of the patrol car when they arrived at the old farmhouse, Sullivan instinctively knew something was wrong. Alerted by the fact that Leggo had not appeared to protest the approach of a strange vehicle, she asked the police officers to wait a few minutes while she checked the dog's whereabouts. Searching both buildings, she finally found the frightened dog locked in a small store-room in the main farmhouse. Crouching submissively in a dark corner and in some distress, Leggo was immediately relieved to see her. Fetching him water and bringing him slowly into the light of the kitchen, Sullivan waited for the old dog to show signs of recovery before alerting the officers outside to the situation.

'It looks like someone's been here and locked up the dog. The only other person living here at the moment is Inspector Danaher. She'd never do such a thing, so there must have been an uninvited visitor.'

Bemused by Sullivan's statement, the two officers nonetheless followed her as she looked for any signs of an intruder. She did not have to search long before realising that everything seemed to be in its place. Nothing appeared to be missing, but the feeling that someone had been there lingered in the atmosphere. She reached for her cracked phone and found Consuela's number.

'Hi,' Sullivan said, as she crossed the yard in front of the *finca*. 'I'm back at the farm and there's something not quite right up here. Leggo was locked up in the back room of the main building and seemed to be in distress. Nothing's been taken or moved that I can see, but I don't like the look of it, I'm afraid.'

'Are you okay?'

'I'm fine. Just a bit concerned.'

'Okay,' Consuela replied. 'Tell the officers to stay where they are. I'm on my way.'

'I'm on my way,' the policewoman said and the call ended.

Good, the man thought as he punched the red button on his mobile phone. *They're spooked.*

Bugging the woman inspector's phone had proven invaluable so far.

Monitoring Consuela Danaher's incoming and outgoing calls was hard work, but essential. As a constant update on the Cuerpo's investigation, it was delivering nearly all he had hoped. Not everything, of course, but tracking certainly helped him keep one step ahead. Or so he'd thought. His choice to watch the scene unfold on the riverbank that morning had been a blunder. That couldn't be allowed to happen again.

And who was the woman that had followed him?

After falling from her motorcycle, she had been taken to hospital and Inspector Danaher had gone to see her there. Once again, the bugged phone had come up trumps. There had been a window of opportunity. Leaving the woman on the road, he had ridden hard, before abandoning the motorbike and stealing an old Fiat parked in a narrow side road in San Luis de Sabinillas. This he had then driven to the last place anyone would have expected to find him – the hillside *finca* in the middle of nowhere. On arriving at the *finca*, the stupid dog had been a problem, but a sharp kick to its belly had made it considerably more pliable.

Entering the annexe first, he soon found what he needed: Sullivan's passport and RGP warrant card. He had learned from phone calls where she lived, but he had not known the full identity of the woman. The fact that she was a police detective made complete sense. Now he would dig deeper to find out more about Tamara Sullivan. Knowledge, after all, was power. Making sure to leave everything the way he'd found it, the man departed. Only the dog would be left locked up. That would spook them. He enjoyed the thought of that.

On his way to his next destination, the man realised that time was running out. Sighing as he put his foot down hard on the Fiat's accelerator, he saw the Rock of Gibraltar come into view in the distance. Rolling his neck to rid himself of his painful headache, he considered his next move. One thing was for sure. All work and no death was making him a very stressed boy.

Chapter 22

CONSUELA ARRIVED in a patrol car within forty minutes. This latest development had caught her off guard. The *finca* was her father's home. A line had been crossed.

Sullivan met her in the yard and took her indoors to see Leggo. The dog was ecstatic to see Consuela again and began licking her hand.

'Thank God he's okay,' Consuela said, hugging Leggo to her breast. 'Has he been beaten?'

'He's walking very awkwardly. I think he may have been kicked or something.'

'*Bastardo*,' Consuela said, holding him tighter. 'Who would do this? He's just a big softy. He would never hurt anyone.'

'I know,' Sullivan said, patting Leggo on the head. 'Nothing's been taken from the annexe. Not sure about over here though. Everything looks the same. Even so, he may have had a good look around.'

'*He?*'

'I think it may be the same man who shot at me earlier.'

'How?'

'I don't know exactly. We have to remember though that the anonymous caller will know who you are. He might also know where you live.'

'But I don't live here normally. I'm in Málaga.'

'You *were* in Málaga. Maybe he's been there too. Any news on how the flood started in your apartment?'

Consuela stood.

'Now that's not instinct. That's just a bizarre imagination, Tamara.'

'Maybe or maybe not. Here are some other questions. You believe there were two of them at the Bernard mansion. Why was only one of them observing the scene earlier and why risk being caught watching you?'

Consuela shrugged. 'Good questions, but I have no answers. I only saw one of them and that same person shot at you to stop being followed. If it is the same person, then perhaps he's interested in more than just me.'

Sullivan chose to ignore the last remark.

'One thing we can say for certain is that the killer or killers like to put on a bit of a show.'

'Maybe. But why come up here? That doesn't make sense.'

'I agree. It's more than a little disturbing.'

Both women stood in silence. It was very disturbing.

'Let's check the main house,' Sullivan said at last. 'I couldn't see anything different, but then I wouldn't know.'

Consuela did know straight away that all appeared to be intact.

'I'll still need to report this. I'll also get Forensics up here to look around. We'd better not touch anything else.'

'Well, I'm having a glass of something,' Sullivan said. 'I don't think whoever it was helped himself to wine. How about you?'

'No, I am still on the clock.'

'It's tough being a copper.' Sullivan smiled.

'At least I was not shot at.'

'Yes. There is that. Any other news?'

Consuela hesitated. 'Look, the newspapers are on to this now, Tamara, and I have just been told that an *inspector jefe* is being transferred from Cádiz to head up this case. I'm briefing him tomorrow and he takes over first thing on Monday. From then on, I cannot tell you anything. Do you understand?'

'Perfectly. But *until* then – any other news?'

Consuela smiled. 'The body appears to be that of Frankie DuPont. A resident of Sotogrande Marina. He had an apartment in the Plaza del Aqua. I was there earlier. That's where Forensics will be coming from now, if they can get away. DuPont lived there for about nine years or so. Ran a stall in the Soto market, selling hippy things. Was known as a bit of a psychic.'

'Clearly not psychic enough,' Sullivan said, pouring herself a glass of chilled rosé from a bottle in the fridge.

Consuela looked on with a touch of envy as she called in the incident to HQ and ordered the *forensic medico* up to the farmhouse.

An hour later, a team of two arrived, closely followed by De Galvez. After explaining the situation, Consuela left the team to their work and led De Galvez into the kitchen where Sullivan was finishing a second glass of wine.

'Anything new?' Consuela asked.

De Galvez flicked a look towards Sullivan, not sure if he should carry on in front of her.

'Tamara is fine. A fellow professional who, from now, will remain strictly outside of this investigation,' Consuela said.

Sullivan raised her arms in mock surrender. 'Absolutely. My work here is done.'

Neither Consuela or De Galvez believed that for a second, but the sergeant continued as directed.

'Frankie DuPont was last seen at a party for stallholders in Flaherty's Bar on Thursday night. Final night market of the summer; they were all celebrating in the marina. We have CCTV of him crossing the central plaza at 1.32 a.m. The surveillance camera in the Plaza del Aqua fails to pick him up returning to his apartment building. There is a blind spot that covers the connecting walkway between the two areas and a slipway to a small section of car park on the beach side of the marina.'

'So your thinking is that DuPont could have been abducted then and there,' Consuela said.

'Only place and time possible.'

'Have you checked the main security cameras on the gates out of the resort?'

'Yes. Fifteen cars left between 1.30 and 2.00 a.m. that night. All have been traced bar one. A silver Renault Megane leaving at 1.43 a.m. The car had false registration plates. We now know it had been stolen from Marbella two days before.'

'Any images of the passengers?' Sullivan asked.

'Tamara. Please,' Consuela said, her voice rising.

'Sorry, sorry.'

'Any images of its passengers?' Consuela asked De Galvez.

'Yes, but they're not good. A driver and front passenger, both wearing baseball caps. The pictures are being enlarged, but it looks as if they were camera aware. We are contacting the guards that were on that night to see what they recall.'

'False plates. Good,' Consuela said, starting to pace the length of the kitchen. 'A suspicious vehicle leaving Sotogrande at the time we believe DuPont went missing.'

'A good coincidence,' Sullivan said. 'I always like those.'

De Galvez's mobile buzzed. He answered. 'Hi. *Sí.* Okay, a *nuestra manera.*'

'What?' Consuela asked.

'A camera in San Enrique picked up the Renault driving north through the town at 1.51 a.m. on Friday morning. Diaz has just found the car hidden among trees near the river bridge alongside the Santa Maria Polo Club. Perfect place to throw a body into the water.'

'A body that was still alive, if the killers' modus operandi remains the same as in the Bernard murders,' Sullivan said. 'Not to mention that DuPont is French for 'bridge'. Do you think they may be trying to have a laugh?'

Consuela and De Galvez were out of the farmhouse door before Sullivan had even finished her sentence.

Chapter 23
CAPITOL HILL, WASHINGTON D.C.

An ocean away and in a time zone five hours behind, the congressman stood at his office window in Rayburn 2111 looking out at the view of the Capitol dome. It was a view he had enjoyed and prided himself on possessing for the last fifteen years. Not that it had been earned. The metal disk he had plucked from the office lottery bag in a downstairs committee room all those years ago had given him something his wealth and pedigree could not achieve. That he had won one of the best offices available to lawmakers on the Hill had been pure good fortune, nothing more. Many others of equal status and privilege had picked less successfully and been forced to accept far more humble workspaces in the nearby Cannon Building and elsewhere. Their rise up the office ladder would now have to rely on the death, resignation or loss of district of some other lawmaker, and a new chance to take part in the lottery all over again. Things had got so bad in one of the less prestigious buildings that one poor representative had been informed that he could no longer barbecue ribs on his office balcony. The news had caused quite a stir in certain Washington circles. Not that such a common leisure activity would ever have appealed to the occupant of the Rayburn suite presently enjoying his view of one of the greatest seats of power in the world.

The tastefully decorated blue and yellow walls of his office, with its mahogany panelling and personal trophies displayed with care and attention on surrounding furniture – a model of the Golden Gate Bridge from a leading world charity and many prized awards for good works within his district and in the national arena – were expected of the working environment of a politician of influence. Pictures of informal family gatherings, loved ones, world leaders and the obligatory handshake shot with the President – this last picture finding itself more concealed among others than one might have expected – adorned the walls and the surface of his majestic desk. It was the smiling, shoulder-slapping photograph of himself and the House Speaker that took pride of place in this politician's collection, and with good reason. Money and privilege certainly helped in life, but luck and who you knew were the magic ingredients that made the difference between achieving power and having none.

The thing most occupying the congressman's mind on this sunny Washington morning was just how to manipulate that luck, as always, to his further advantage.

Turning from the view, the congressman took a key from his jacket pocket and opened a bottom drawer in his large desk. The key turned with the heavy but smooth action of a lock installed for highly secure purposes. Upon opening the drawer, its metal lined interior confirmed its particular nature as a safe *within* a desk. In it the congressman kept certain papers and tapes of a very sensitive nature. He also kept three secured-line mobile phones, each dedicated to a specific and secret purpose. Taking one from the drawer and slipping it into his inside pocket, the congressman locked the drawer and left his office. The call he had to make could not be done with in the walls of the Rayburn Building.

Minutes later, the congressman left the polished-tiled, star spangled banner-adorned interior of the Rayburn. Crossing Independence Avenue and turning left, he walked towards Bartholdi Park, a few hundred metres along and opposite the US Botanic Garden Conservatory. The two-acre garden, with its stunning array of deciduous trees, plants, shrubs and flowers, offered an oasis of sanity to many stressed-out, nature-starved Washington citizens and visitors. At its centre stood the Bartholdi Fountain – also known as the *Fountain of Light and Water* – illuminated at night, but beautiful at all times. Finding a secluded bench under shade, the congressman sat, took out his mobile phone and awaited his call. It was not long coming.

'It's me,' he answered.

'Are you clear?' the voice on the other end asked.

'Clear.'

'DuPont has gone.'

'Fuck.'

Silence.

'Fuck!'

'That leaves just two, sir.'

'You know how urgent your mission has become. Finish this before it finishes us. Do you understand?'

'I understand.'

'Do you know where you're going?'

'I do.'

'Let me know when you've completed. I expect better news. Nothing less.'

The congressman terminated the call. Around him, people were taking in the beauty of the gardens as they enjoyed a late summer weekend in the capital. Couples strolled hand in hand. Tourists wandered in small packs, taking shots of all they saw. A nanny and her young wards walked by, the children ignoring her entreaties to stay off the flowerbeds.

If only they knew what really went on in the world, the congressman thought to himself. *They'd never feel carefree again. Ever.*

Chapter 24

THE MOTORCYCLES STOOD in the shadows of the small lock-up garage. Tucked away in a lower-ground-floor car park beneath the central buildings of Puerto de la Duquesa, the storage rental had proved invaluable to the couple since their arrival in Spain three weeks before. The bikes, helmets and gear would remain locked away, all now surplus to requirements. The two guns they would keep.

After securing an additional heavy-duty padlock to the garage door, the man took the woman's hand and both walked casually towards the ramp that led from the poorly lit subterranean chamber up to the service road. The noise from the busy coastal dual carriageway on the other side of a wire perimeter fence was loud and unpleasant. Taking a left, they followed a narrower road as it wound around the rear of the apartment blocks and back to their yacht mooring at the far, southern end of the marina. Passing a row of refuse bins, the man threw the keys to the lock-up into a half-open rubbish bag. Even though he'd paid a year's rent for the garage in advance, his instinct was not to make things easy for anybody at any time. Not that it really mattered: the forty-eight-year-old and his much younger red-haired companion would be long gone by then.

Things had not progressed entirely to plan since the murder of Frankie DuPont. The execution of his kidnap had gone like clockwork. Carrying the unconscious Frenchman to the stolen car and placing him in the boot of the silver Renault Megane had been simple. It merely looked like friends helping a drunk home. Not that anyone had been looking. They'd even had time to tape his mouth and secure his wrists and ankles with plastic grips. Driving off the Sotogrande estate had been easy; waiting for other cars to be on their way, they had followed them through the security point and then headed towards San Enrique. Minutes later they were through the town and on the empty road that led to the bridge by the polo club fields where they had earlier hidden their motorcycles.

Parking off-road in an area thick with greenery, they removed the gagged and bound DuPont from the car. Taking a moment to bring the Frenchman back to consciousness, they had then thrown him from the bridge and into the dark waters below. The look of pure animal fear in DuPont's eyes had delighted the man. It was the same sensation he'd felt with Ingrid Bernard just days before. At least there had been no collateral damage this time. The Bernard servants had had to die along with their mistress, loose ends that had needed to be tied up. A classic case of wrong place, wrong time.

The plan for DuPont had been simple. His body would float downriver overnight to the Estuario del Rio Guadiaro. A sandbank across the estuary mouth would force the outward-flowing waters of the river into a narrow channel before joining the sea. This natural phenomenon meant that there was a very good chance that DuPont's body would be washed up onto the sandbank, where it would remain stranded like a beached whale. As the good people of Sotogrande opened the windows of their villas or crossed the estuary bridge to the golf or beach clubs the following morning, the grotesque, bloated cadaver would be positioned centre stage for all to see. Like the bodies in the Bernard pool, the theatricality of it all pleased the man greatly.

However, the following morning had come and gone with no body found on the sandbank. Forced to scour the riverbanks for several hours, the couple found DuPont entangled in waterside branches. Abandoning the plan for a grand reveal, an anonymous call to the police directing them to the body had to suffice. A bit of an anti-climax, perhaps, but at least DuPont was dead. Now all their attention would be focused on their next victims.

An aroma of spices wafted to them on the warm evening air as they passed the open kitchen doors of the marina's Indian restaurant. For a moment, the man was taken back to happier times. Moments from his years on the Indian subcontinent came vividly to mind. Love, spiritual hope and communal comfort had been the sustaining forces of his life in those days. As they would be again once their work was done and justice had been achieved. With each death, hope had returned to his heart. Only she understood. The woman at his side was a true crusader.

Tightening his grip on her hand, he led her around a corner onto the main marina promenade. The night was still young and quiet. A few couples sat drinking in the cafés and bars that lined the marina. A similar number could be seen on their boats going about their nautical duties.

Anyone looking across to the tanned, grey-bearded man walking hand in hand with the much younger auburn-haired woman would have noted the gap in age between the two lovers but little else. To the naked eye, they looked like so many other couples sailing and staying along the Costas. Sun-kissed faces, salt air in their lungs and time on their hands. For them both it was the perfect illusion. Soon they would be aboard the yacht that had been their home for many months. It had served them well on the journey across the Mediterranean from Cyprus. In the morning, they would leave their mooring here in Spain and cast off for Gibraltar. Two more killings were needed before freedom was theirs. The man had mixed feelings about their visit to the Rock. His dread at returning to his past was only balanced by the excitement they both felt at the thought of completing their quest. Casting these thoughts aside, the couple put their arms around each other, as lovers do, and walked towards the setting sun.

Chapter 25
SUNDAY

THE SHOCK to Gus Broderick's system the day before had taken both himself and Massetti by surprise. For several minutes after falling ill in the Police HQ courtyard, he had been unable to move. A form of paralysis had seized him and it was some while before Sergeant Aldarino and Chief Superintendent Massetti had been able to bring him back into the building and call for a doctor. Broderick had protested all the way, but it was clear that his heart was not in it.

Fortunately, Hannah Portillo had been visiting HQ and was at Broderick's side in minutes. 'You've had a shock, Gus. You need to go home and rest,' she said, checking his pulse and the dilation of his pupils.

'I need to find out what this is all about. I'm going nowhere till then,' Broderick said, attempting to stand.

'I'm sorry, Gus,' Massetti said. 'There is nothing you can do here. We'll let you know everything we can as and when we find out ourselves. We'll get to the bottom of this. Trust us.'

'How can it be her?' Broderick said, the pain in his voice clear for all to hear. 'How can it be Helen?'

'We can't be sure it is, Gus. Let's just take this one step at a time.'

As the sun finally slipped from the western skies beyond the Strait and the distant shore of Morocco, Gus Broderick lay on his bed. As he stared at the last glimpses of red playing on the blinds of his bedroom window, his mind raced, his thoughts unable to build a logical pattern from the events of the day. Cath and the girls had been checking in on him regularly, all three deeply concerned and desperate to help. This was not like Gus. They had never seen him in such a state before.

For obvious reasons, it had been considered best not to tell Penny or Daisy the real reason for their father's sudden breakdown. Cath had informed them that it was just over-work that had brought their dad to his bed. 'A little rest and peace and quiet and your dad'll be as right as rain,' she had told them.

'Yes. Right as rain,' Daisy had replied with a smile and had gone to get her father a chocolate biscuit from the barrel in the pantry.

'He'll be all right, won't he?' Penny had asked in a concerned whisper.

'You bet,' Cath had said. 'He's your dad, isn't he?'

This put Penny's mind at rest. But as she watched her niece leave the room, Cath sat back in her chair and closed her eyes. Her own mind was very far from being at rest.

That night and early next morning, her brother lay still on his bed, two floors above. With eyes closed and arms outstretched, Broderick was lost in a maelstrom of distant memories. Helen's living, breathing body was beside him, his arms holding her in a passionate embrace; the softness of his wife's touch and her gentle breathing upon his neck. The warmth of love and desire possessed every cell of his body. These emotions, unfelt for so many years and banished to an unconscious world of dreams, were now strong and vivid visitors to his heart and mind. To his horror, Broderick felt the tears begin to fall down his cheeks. He had borne Helen's disappearance with as much strength as he could summon. It had overwhelmed him but he had survived. How could he bear her loss again?

━━━

Sullivan left the *finca* early on Sunday morning so as not to be late for her meeting with Massetti. At that time, the roads to Gibraltar were far from busy and the border crossing had taken mere minutes to achieve. The rough ride of the suspension-impaired Mitsubishi had increased the pains and aches she felt from her motorcycle fall the day before. Remembering the doctor's advice to get some Arnica for her bruising, Sullivan had stopped off at a duty chemist in La Linea on the way. Although sadly notorious for its gang and drug culture, she had always liked the Spanish town. Its colourful and energetic central food market was a joy to visit – the fresh fish and vegetables being of a particularly high standard – and the locals seemed always to be welcoming of visitors. With homeopathic remedy in hand and church bells ringing throughout the town, Sullivan had continued towards the Rock, her thoughts focused on the meeting ahead.

Arriving at her destination early, Sullivan got herself a coffee and sat in the central courtyard. It had been only a short time since she had last sat there – attempting a prawn salad lunch – but it might just as well have been weeks, so much had taken place. Sipping her strong black Americano, Sullivan enjoyed a few moments of peace, an oasis of calm soon shattered by the arrival of Harriet Massetti. Wearing her church-going clothes, Massetti paced quickly though the main gates and crossed the courtyard. Sullivan wasn't at all certain she'd been seen by the Chief Superintendent. It was only seconds before Massetti entered the building that the command came.

'My office, Sullivan. Five minutes, if you please.'

'Are you all right?' Massetti asked, as Sullivan entered. 'Hurt your leg or something?'

'Just a slight pulled muscle, ma'am,' Sullivan lied. 'On its way out.'

'Better sit down then,' the Chief Super said, pointing to a chair. 'I expect you'll be wondering why you're here.'

Sullivan sat in the chair and looked across to her boss. Massetti's small frame looked somewhat dwarfed behind her formidably large mahogany desk.

'You said it was something *unofficial*, ma'am.'

'In a way. We have a situation that's a little complicated, Sullivan.'

'Connected to the Eastern Beach discovery?'

'Very connected. Awkwardly so.'

Sullivan noted that *awkward* was precisely how she felt in the circumstances. Massetti continued. 'You are officially off duty at present. Between jobs, as it were.'

'It's certainly not proving to be much of a holiday, ma'am.'

'So what I'm about to say is off the record,' Massetti continued, ignoring Sullivan's remark. 'Let's just call this a casual conversation between work colleagues, Sullivan, and as such I trust you will be discreet about what I'm about to tell you and continue in that manner when considering the best actions to take in response.'

'I'm not sure I follow you, ma'am.'

'It's in regards to Gus Broderick. To be more precise, the possible relationship Broderick may have had with the dead woman found out near Eastern Beach.'

'Are you suggesting Broderick knew Eleanor?'

'*Eleanor*? Who the hell is that?'

'Working title, ma'am, until the body's identified. Has the body been identified?'

'Not quite. But a letter found on the woman was addressed to someone Broderick knew very well. His wife, Helen.'

Sullivan sat up in her seat, the shock of Massetti's statement scrambling her mind.

'Dear God. I mean, how is he? How's he taken this?'

'Not well, Sullivan. Not well at all.'

'I need to see him.'

'And you shall,' Massetti said, moving from behind her desk to give Sullivan a glass of water. 'But first you need to know some facts.'

Sullivan drank the water and composed herself a little.

'First, the letter. Broderick told me that he'd sent out upwards of twenty of the letters care of friends and acquaintances. It was just before he moved his family over here from the UK. His wife had been missing for some while and he suspected that friends of Helen had secret contact with her. The letters were sent in the hope that one might somehow reach her. At the very least it would inform Helen where he and the children were going.'

'I see. So Helen might have had it on her when she died. If the body is, in fact, hers.'

'Exactly. But we won't know if the body is hers until DNA tests have been fully run and matches found. This is the first area of awkwardness.'

'How?'

'Helen Broderick is not on the DNA register, so we have to take the DNA from the dead body and test it against a blood relation of hers.'

'I see.'

'I don't think you do. Helen Broderick has only two blood relations still living.'

It was a few seconds before the full implications of Massetti's words hit home.

'Oh no.'

'I'm afraid so,' Massetti said. 'Somehow we have to persuade Gus to let us take a DNA swab from one of his daughters.'

'And you want that someone to be me?'

Massetti placed her hand on Sullivan's shoulder.

'There is, of course, a second cause for awkwardness,' Massetti said. 'If the DNA proves the dead body to be that of Helen Broderick, our first person of interest, regarding her murder, would have to be …'

'Oh no, no, no,' Sullivan interrupted, shaking her head in disbelief.

'We would have no choice but to question Gus as a potential suspect. You understand that?'

'Yes.'

'Gus is no fool. He'll have figured this out for himself. I'm just concerned about his state of mind.'

Slowly, Sullivan raised her head to look Massetti directly in the eye.

'And you want me to talk to him.'

'Yes, Tamara, I do.'

———

Leaving the Police HQ, Sullivan passed the main reception desk. As it was a Sunday, Sergeant Aldarino was not at his usual station. The kindly Gibraltarian had been her friend from the very first day she had arrived on the job. His advice and practical help often guided her through the tough calls. Sullivan could not help but wish that her friend had been on duty today. *What would he say? How would he help me?*

Walking into the bright sunshine at the front of the police building, Sullivan looked out across the Bay of Gibraltar. Between the gigantic cruise liners and cargo ships going about their steady business, she marvelled at the teeming flotilla of sailing craft of many types and sizes. With full sails, their nimble passage over the white-topped waves and strong underwater currents created a wonderful pattern on the eye, zig-zagging across the Bay. *How nice it would be*, Sullivan thought, *to be out there at sea. Free of care and duty. With the sun on my face and the wind in my hair, dolphins leaping at the bow of my boat in play*. Forcing her eyes from the view and her mind from the fantasy, Sullivan moved to the jeep parked to her right. Now was not the time to dream. She had a job to do and the reality of that was hitting hard.

Chapter 26

Rounding Europa Point, the couple looked up from the deck of their fifty-foot yacht and took in the full majesty of the Rock of Gibraltar. The spectacle of the giant limestone miracle of nature had taken their breath away. The man had seen it many times before, but from a different vantage point – the mainland of Spain. For the woman, it was everything she had hoped it might be. The Rock was, without doubt, a worthy destination as their last port of call on the Mediterranean Sea.

They had started their murderous odyssey back in May. Arriving by air into Larnaca Airport, Cyprus, they had spent a week looking at yachts for sale at Limassol Marina. Comfort, sea-worthiness and a look that would not attract attention were the main requirements of the boat they were searching for. Eventually, a six-berth heavy cruiser sailing yacht caught their eye. Built in 1984, the newly refurbished yacht was perfect for their needs. It also had one other attractive buying point. It was named the *Adrestia*, after the Greek goddess of equilibrium, balance between good and evil and bringer of just retribution, a happy coincidence not wasted on either of them. Negotiating the yacht's price of £150,000 down to £125,000, the two had taken possession of their new home, stocked up with onboard provisions and prepared for their first killing.

Four months later, those early times seemed very far away. But the journey continued. Today, they had sailed from Puerto de la Duquesa at sunrise. As usual, the woman had taken charge of the boat. Born in Split, on the coast of Croatia, she had quite literally been delivered at sea. Her father had owned a boat-chartering business, and one summer's day, on a family boat trip along the coast, she had arrived prematurely. Growing up with boats and spending almost as much time on water as on dry land, she could handle all manner of yachts. It was a talent her partner was happy to exploit. Being in no hurry to get to their Gibraltar mooring at Marina Bay, she had charted a slow course that would take them out into deeper waters before turning westwards towards Gibraltar. This would give them time for a leisurely breakfast and allow her lover a few hours to indulge his passion for fishing.

Just before 9 a.m., he'd become inordinately excited by a pod of bluefin tuna passing beneath the boat. His furious attempts to catch one had ended in failure, sending him into a black mood, a dark cloud that did not leave him until the sight of the Rock lifted his spirits. A gentle command from the skipper had sent him below decks to collect the yellow courtesy flag. This would be raised and flown to announce the *Adrestia*'s desire to clear customs and immigration on its entry into Gibraltarian waters. Everything had been planned to the very last detail for their visit to the UK overseas territory. They worked well as a team, each knowing their particular jobs and acknowledging their separate areas of expertise. Together they could deliver death and mayhem to all who deserved it. Their talents, tested on several occasions, had not been found wanting.

'Looking good, Naida,' he called up to the woman at the helm.

'Me or the Rock?' she replied.

'From where I'm standing, *both*.'

'Thank you, Max. I'll take the compliment.'

'Please do.' Max said, his laidback accent as charming as the smile that accompanied it. Sitting back on deck, he started to go over the plans again for the coming days. The victim's address and workplace had been identified. Surveillance would allow them to decide on the exact location for the killing, somewhere that offered them the opportunity to execute the process of surprise, apprehension, containment and death by drowning. It was a specific modus operandi that offered both a completion to the act of murder and a rightful sentence for the victim.

One other thing had to be accomplished while on the Rock. Max possessed a key to a safety deposit box held in a Gibraltarian bank on Main Street. The key had been his mother's, but the contents of the box were unknown to him. She had died with so much left unsaid. Whatever had been precious enough for her to keep in such a place had to be of interest to her only son. Anything he discovered in the secret box could only bring him closer to his mother. It was all part of the journey, part of the odyssey. Despite this, a feeling of dread permeated his thoughts. It was a feeling he could not quite shake off.

Adjusting her course slightly, Naida brought the *Adrestia* into the Bay of Gibraltar. The sun was now high in a cloudless sky and the boat glided effortlessly across the waters, passing brightly coloured fishing vessels floating cheek by jowl alongside cargo ships, waiting like heaving metal giants to enter port for bunkering. Those gazing down from the Rock looked out on this marine amphitheatre with awe. The bustling industry of the waters and the diversity of its vessels were like players upon a stage.

Loisa Robba turned from her students and took in the narrow view of the Bay that was afforded to her through the church hall window, caught in the gap between the buildings opposite the church. In three hours' time she'd be out on the waters herself, enjoying the relaxation that would be a welcome contrast to her busy and energetic work as an art tutor. Not that she was complaining. For two hours, after morning service, she helped with these Sunday school sessions. These past several weeks, Loisa's particular talents as an art teacher had come heavily into play, as the children prepared an exhibition of paintings to be presented at John Mackintosh Hall. It would be entitled 'A Child's-Eye View of the Rock' and was part of a bigger event organised by all the denominations represented on Gibraltar to raise money and awareness of the refugee crisis in Europe.

Loisa loved her work both at the church on Sundays and during the week at her school. Teaching was the most rewarding thing she had ever done, and not a day went by without her giving thanks for the opportunities it had given her. The regular wage also allowed her to support her husband, Rahim, in his work as a sculptor. They had been a couple now for over eleven years and Rahim's wonderful talents had always been greater than his ability to make money from them. He worked in a coffee bar five mornings a week and spent the rest of the day in his makeshift studio in the small second bedroom of their apartment. It wasn't ideal, but it would suffice until his reputation had grown enough to guarantee regular commissions.

'Miss. Miss. What colours should I use?'

A voice from the far end of the hall drew Loisa's attention away from the view and her thoughts. The question came from Daisy Broderick – a member of the Sunday school and a pupil of Loisa's in the week. Daisy had made her artistic camp in one of the corners of the hall. Surrounded by her paints and paper, it was Daisy's special workplace and from it the fourteen-year-old was creating a very nice picture. As Loisa approached her enthusiastic student, she could see that Daisy was working on a beach scene.

'How can I help?' Loisa said.

'What colours do I need, please?'

'You'll need a turquoise for the sea, I think, Daisy. Try the blue and green together and then maybe add some yellow to make it pop.'

'Yes, pop,' Daisy said. 'Thank you, Mrs Robba.'

'No, thank you, Daisy. Your painting looks as if it's going to be super.'

Daisy stood and gave a little bow, her face beaming.

'It is. It's going to be big and super.'

Chapter 27

CONSUELA DANAHER'S first meeting with *Inspector Jefe* Manuel Pizarro could have gone a lot better. Her first mistake was to assume that the briefing would take place at the investigation's offices in Estepona. This assumption was entirely reasonable, but that was not always the way these things mapped out in a police officer's life.

Consuela had arrived at the Estepona Police HQ for the meeting at 1 p.m. Half an hour passed and Pizarro had failed to appear. Deciding to call him and check his whereabouts, she was surprised by a phone call from the disgruntled *inspector jefe* himself.

'Where are you, Danaher?' Pizarro said. 'I'm waiting for you and I haven't got all day.'

To Consuela's horror, the senior officer had been expecting her at Málaga Centro. After her apologies had been met with a curt cut-off, Consuela scrambled to her car and hit the *autopista*, driving fast to the capital town of Málaga Province.

The following two hours were spent going through the investigation's work to date. Nearly six days after the discovery of the first bodies, Pizarro needed to know precisely where the team's efforts had led them. The new senior officer's style was to ask question after question, but give little back in response. In his mid-fifties and eyeing retirement, Pizarro was not happy to have been called in from Cádiz Province. As a younger man he would have jumped at the opportunity to head up such an investigation, but now he wanted a quiet life. Nothing big and high-profile to put his respectable police career and reputation in peril.

The first murders had been reported during the week, but had not made the lead newspaper pages due to the bomb outrages in Granada and a huge drugs operation along the entire Costa del Sol. The DuPont murder had changed all that. Somehow the press had discovered that there was a possible link between the two murders. A headline in the main Saturday newspaper announcing, 'Costa del Serial Killer?' had proved a huge annoyance to the top brass, and questions were being asked about a possible internal leak. Up to now, the buck had stopped at Consuela; tomorrow it would be Pizarro's arse on the line. It was not a prospect he was entertaining with delight. As Consuela came to the end of her brief, Pizarro stood and started to pace the room.

'The killers have been busy. Two murder sites, four bodies, plus a possible break-in at your father's farmhouse. That last point is both baffling and, I'm sure, disturbing for you.'

'Very,' Consuela said. 'Sir.'

'Okay. Well, you seem to have done as well as can be expected under the circumstances.'

Considering I'm not an inspector jefe, *you mean?* Consuela did not voice this thought.

Pizarro continued. 'Forensics have delivered nothing useful as yet. Let's hope this changes in the near future. Other than that, all we seem to have is that it appears to be a professional hit job, plus the "*man in black*" description from your Gibraltarian friend.'

'From Detective Sergeant Tamara Sullivan, sir. And she's British born, as a matter of fact.'

'Same thing, isn't it?' Pizarro replied, looking at her with something approaching a sneer.

Consuela bit her tongue, considering it not the best time to talk politics and history with the new man. Although now a Spanish police officer, she remained half British by birth. From his last remark, she believed Pizarro knew this too.

'Clearly we need to discover if anything links the victims to each other,' Pizarro continued. 'Business, family, crime, love and relationships, et cetera. All boxes you are no doubt attempting to tick?'

'Yes, sir. We're still asking the questions.'

'I don't have to tell you there's a hell of a lot of pressure to deliver on this. Serial killers at large are great for the media, but don't play quite so well for the Costa's image.'

'Not too well for the friends and relatives of the victims either, sir.'

Pizarro turned a cold stare on Consuela.

'I took that as a given, Inspector. Now I suggest you get back to Estepona. I'll see you there in the morning.'

Pizarro walked from the room, leaving Consuela in no doubt that the next few weeks were about to get a whole lot tougher.

Chapter 28

THE NARROW THREE-STOREY townhouse in the upper part of Gibraltar Town had been the shared home of the Broderick family and Gus's widowed sister Cath for over ten years. Sullivan found a parking space on the next street down, and as she climbed up the steep incline of the cobbled passageway opposite, she could see Broderick's old Mercedes standing directly in front of his home. This signalled that he was most likely in and that she would have to somehow talk with him.

In the three months she had known Gus Broderick, both police officers had found – much to their joint surprise – an effective and respectful way of working with the other. It had proved a good match, and although their relationship was entirely professional and confined to working hours, Sullivan had developed a platonic affection for her older boss. She also suspected that Broderick felt the same, although he'd rather die than show it.

Sullivan rang the bell at the front door and it opened in

seconds. Cath stood in the doorway with a welcoming smile.

'Hello, Tamara. I've been expecting you.'

'You have?' Sullivan said, entering the hallway.

'Gus is out in the back. He said someone would probably be arriving from work. I assumed it would be you.'

'Is he okay?' Sullivan asked, moving through into the kitchen.

'To tell the truth, I've never seen him like this. Showing his emotions is not something he excels at. It's a shock, but it's the confusion that is getting to him, I think. Go and see him.' Cath pointed to the open door that led out to the courtyard. 'Would you like some coffee? Tea?'

'No thank you, Cath. I'm fine.'

As Sullivan stepped from the back door and into the paved and high-walled yard, she saw Broderick sitting out of the sun at a small table at the far end.

'Morning, boss.'

Broderick looked across to her. Sullivan noticed that his face was pale and his hair, although newly cut, was somehow more unkempt than usual. Broderick waved her over.

'I thought it would be you,' he said.

'Well, you knew considerably more than me then.'

'Nothing new about that, is there?' Broderick replied, the slight trace of a smile crossing his lips.

Sullivan was pleased to see that his sense of humour was at least still on automatic pilot.

'Ha, ha,' she said, taking the seat opposite him.

'What's with the limp?'

'It's hard work out there in the country. Nobody mentioned that to me.'

Broderick nodded his head. He didn't believe her, but he'd let it go for now.

'Look, I'm sorry about all this,' Sullivan said.

'Are you? I don't know why. We're not even sure what "*all this*" is about yet.'

'Yes, of course. I just meant—'

'I had a shock, Sullivan. That's all. I'll be fine.'

Sullivan attempted to order her thoughts. She truly didn't want to mess this meeting up.

'Massetti thought it was a good idea to come and see you,' she began. 'Not that I needed her to tell me that. I would have come anyway.'

'How's life on the farm?'

Sullivan hesitated for a moment, knowing full well that Broderick was trying to deflect the conversation away from himself.

'It's been quite, er, hectic, actually. Lovely views from up there, though.'

'Yes. There is that.'

'Look, I don't know how to say this really, but …'

Broderick interrupted sharply. 'Then don't say anything. Let me do the talking. I know the reason for your visit. I realise what must be going on.'

Sullivan began to speak again, but the look in Broderick's eyes silenced her. Broderick continued. 'Massetti needs to get a DNA test from either Penny or Daisy to confirm that the body is …'

Broderick stopped short of saying Helen's name out loud. Things were clearly too raw for that.

'… to confirm that the body is that of my *wife*,' he managed. 'But before that, I have to step down from the investigation and take leave from the force. If I don't,

Massetti will be forced to take those steps for me. Correct?'

Sullivan could only bring herself to nod her head.

'I understand also that if my daughter's DNA matches that of the body, I will, of course, be expected to help my colleagues with further enquiries.'

Once again Sullivan simply nodded, relieved that Broderick had taken responsibility for accepting the facts. This left one more question to be asked, but it was one that Sullivan knew she would never be able to ask directly. Once again, Broderick came to her rescue.

'I should point out that I didn't kill my wife, Sullivan. I never once, not ever, resorted to any kind of physical or mental abuse in our relationship. She left our family for her own reasons and perhaps we will now never know what they were. One thing I will make clear, is that I intend to find out who did murder that woman – be she Helen or some other poor soul – and I'll do it whether I am a serving police officer or not. Understood?'

'Perfectly, sir,' Sullivan replied. 'And you'll have my help every step of the way.'

Chapter 29
MONDAY

THE ADDRESS WAS a top-floor apartment above a restaurant in Tuckey's Lane between Main Street and Irish Town. Naida had arrived early to begin her surveillance, positioning herself in a doorway a few buildings down the lane. Knowing Loisa to be a teacher, she estimated that she would leave for work sometime between 7.30 and 8.00 a.m. She was not wrong.

At precisely 7.55 a.m., Loisa Robba exited the door of her apartment building and headed up the lane towards Main Street and her school, situated a ten-minute walk away off Town Range. By her side was her husband, Rahim. Naida recognised both from their Facebook pages. She had learned much from that particular social network platform – more than enough to build a picture of the couple's lives and daily routines on the Rock. Rahim Robba would start work in ten minutes at a café in a lane behind the Cathedral of St Mary the Crowned. Finishing at lunchtime, he would then return to the apartment and sculpt through the afternoon.

The couple's absence from their apartment in the mornings provided Naida with the perfect opportunity to gain entry and recce their home. If suitable, the apartment would provide by far the most convenient location for murder. Moving across the lane to the building's main door, Naida checked that no one was nearby, before picking the lock and gaining entry. That was the hard part of the job; the rest would now be easy.

As she climbed the stairs to the top floor of the building, Naida allowed herself to wonder how her partner was getting on with the task he'd set himself for the morning. One thing she knew was that it was a far easier job than the one she was now embarked upon. This pleased her. She could not bear the thought of him being pained by anything, by anything at all. She had dedicated her life to him completely. It was how it was meant to be and she would allow nobody and nothing to get in the way of that. He needed her protection. He was precious.

———

The bank on Main Street opened at 9 a.m. Max had not made a prior appointment. He possessed the safety deposit key and proof of identity and that was all that was needed for him to be taken down to the basement vault to be alone with the key and box left to him by his late mother.

After Naida had left the boat, Max had showered and dressed before strolling to Bianca's Café Bar on the marina front to enjoy a *café con leche*. Sitting at a table outside the friendly café, he pulled down the rim of his panama hat and took in his surroundings.

The *Adrestia*'s berth in the marina was just metres away

at the far end of one of the concrete pontoon walkways. The small marina was sandwiched between the majestic Sunborn floating hotel on one side and the runway of Gibraltar's International Airport on the other. It was undoubtedly very glamorous – in spite of the roar of the occasional passenger aeroplane taking to the skies – but hardly the most discreet of moorings. Not that it mattered, since nobody appeared to be on their trail. However, if the time came, he felt certain that both he and Naida would be easily remembered from their stay in such intimate surroundings. Gibraltar was impressive, but not big. All you could do was hide in plain sight, but this didn't bother him particularly. *If you've got it, flaunt it,* he thought, as he sipped his coffee. *Catch me if you can.*

Now that he was in the bank vault, with the larger than expected steel box before him, Max's relaxed mood was evaporating. He began to feel extremely anxious about its contents.

The journey to this point had been a long one. His mother had died over a decade ago, but it had taken until now for him to come to Gibraltar and use the key he held in his hand. It hadn't entirely been his fault. The drama and despair of his mother's passing had caused him to put off the task of sorting through her possessions for years. When finally he got around to the business, he'd paid little attention to the key and the bank information attached to it. The truth was that he'd had no interest in finding out about the box or its contents. Whatever it contained, he reasoned, would most likely cause him further pain, and only give him answers to questions he had never asked.

For many years he'd had no inclination to pursue the matter. His continued grief was punishing enough. His mother had died just miles from where he currently stood, and the idea of coming to this part of the world had filled him with a deep dread. After decades travelling and living in India, the Far East and Spain, he had returned home to California in 2006 in a perilous mental state and in need of profound medical and psychiatric treatment. After being involuntarily committed to psychiatric facilities on three separate occasions, his family had won the right to have him confined and hospitalised on a more permanent basis. The Goldenberg Neuropsychiatric Hospital in Oregon had become his home for nearly eight years. Now, just months after leaving the facility, he was about to complete the mission he had set himself during his long internment. That was why he was here in Gibraltar. That was why he would now have to finally turn the key.

Any expectations as to what he might find within the large box were quickly confounded upon lifting its metal lid. Max had supposed that its insides might reveal jewellery or small family heirlooms, or photographs, perhaps. None of these were present. Instead, filling the entire length and width of the box were neatly stacked piles of school exercise books. The different coloured covers produced a rainbow effect from right to left in the box, their chronological order also clearly defined – the older, more faded covers giving way to those in better condition as the line continued. He knew on sight what they were. His mother had written her diaries through the years and always kept them from him. Not that it mattered. They were her story and her son had no real interest in a chronicle of the past. His spiritual teaching had always concentrated on the present. To live in the here and now had been his constant mantra.

The only other item to be found in the box was a letter, folded neatly within a blue envelope. Upon it, written in pencil in his mother's unmistakeable hand, was his name. Removing the letter, he read its contents.

My dearest Max,

If you are reading this letter, I will no longer be with you on the physical plain. I understand the pain you will have been through to get to this point and how difficult it will be to read on, but I beg you to be brave and continue to do so. Although I have let you down so terribly badly, I hope you will forgive me. Thank you.

This collection of diaries is all I have to leave you in a physical sense. My money will join yours now and will manifest in your life in whatever manner you choose, although I know your spiritual path does not depend on it. As for the diaries, I do not expect you to read them,. Their pages are full of our life together and the journey we experienced. Happily, I know that part of the story is in your heart and needs no words to make it immortal.

Within them, however, will be found two things that you should know. Two things that I fear will cause you much pain. In life I did not possess the courage to share them with you. In death, I feel I have no choice.

Before we left the East, I told you my secret. That was a mistake. I have seen the changes in you that the revelation brought. But after so many years, I believed you had the right to know. There is now something else you should understand that I have not had the courage to tell you in person. It is detailed in my last entry. I cannot pretend that it will be anything but painful for you. But once again, it is your right to know. All is my fault.

The second thing you need to know is about my death, and that will be, in its own way, just as painful for you to discover. I found love and it destroyed me. All is my fault.

No mother wants to cause her child grief, so it is my great hope that you will simply take these journals, read them and destroy them. That you will then not think of the past but move strongly and happily into your future. That is my hope, but the choice must finally be yours. Forgive me.

My love for you has been the greatest part of my life. It has fed me and kept me. Our spiritual journey together is something I have cherished more than existence itself. Continue to bring love and peace to those you meet and to wherever you go. Be always yourself and let your light shine eternally.

Till we are together once more.

I love you.

Your mother.

Stepping back from the box, Max began to shake. As the letter fell from his hand, the violent tremble engulfing his body swept upwards from the solar plexus. Upon reaching his throat its force could be contained no longer. A wail of pure sorrow and loss erupted from him, filling the vault and rendering him hopeless in its wake. As his knees gave way and he fell to the ground, a darkness possessed the man, hugging him to its breast and rendering him helpless upon the floor.

———

The fourth-floor apartment was small. Fortunately, it had been easy to break into without leaving any traces. Starting at the far end and moving quickly from room to room,

Naida felt a growing sense of claustrophobia. The lounge doubled as a kitchen, its potential to fulfil either facility greatly challenged by its cramped space. Moving along the narrow hallway, she needed only seconds to take in the rest of the apartment. Rahim had taken the larger of the bedrooms as his studio, leaving himself and his wife to squeeze their three-quarter futon bed into the tiny box room, the couple's sleeping requirements clearly sacrificed to accommodate Rahim's artistic endeavours. The last room along the hallway was a shower room and toilet. Naida's heart sank. As a place to execute their murder, the Robbas' home was clearly not fit for purpose. It didn't even possess a bath.

Moving back to the kitchen area, she began to search for anything that might be of help to her. A large calendar pinned to the wall contained many scribbled notes alongside the month's dates. School commitments, doctors' appointments and dinner dates with friends were all prominently marked. So too were a series of other appointments that immediately took her eye.

Now that looks interesting, Naida thought to herself. *There's been no mention of that on their Facebook pages.*

Moving back to the larger bedroom, Naida entered and looked more carefully. Rahim's sculptures, both finished and as works in progress, filled most of the room, together with his art and research materials. To one side was a large wardrobe, which represented pretty much the only available storage in the apartment. Opening its doors, Naida found what she was searching for. The inside was crammed full of scuba diving equipment: two large cylinders, with '*nitrox*' stickers on their sides, plus wetsuits and two sets of masks.

'Da,' Naida said, punching the air. 'Da!'

Closing the wardrobe doors, she retraced her steps to the living room and looked once again at the calendar. For the next day an appointment had been marked in red pen – *6 P.M. SS ROSSLYN DIVE. SOUTH MOLE.* Naida smiled as a plan began to take shape in her mind.

Down the hallway a key turned in the lock.

'Jesus,' Naida gasped, turning in panic.

Rahim Robba entered the apartment and headed straight for his bedroom. He had forgotten his wallet and was now running late. Not finding it on the small chest of drawers at the end of the futon, he moved swiftly to the kitchen and living room. On entering the room he saw the object of his search on the sofa straight ahead of him. Rushing over to grab it, Rahim was unaware of the person squeezed tight against the wall behind the door, her breathing halted and eyes wide in alarm. Grabbing his wallet, Rahim ran from the room and back down the hall to leave the apartment. As the front door slammed behind him, Naida let go of her breath and stumbled forward from her hiding place.

Heading up Tuckey's Lane for the second time that morning, Rahim had no idea how close he had just come to death. Back in the apartment building, Naida slipped from the Robbas' home and moved down the communal stairs to the street level entrance.

That was close, she thought.

Being forced to kill Rahim Robba was the last thing she'd wanted. It was too early for that.

Chapter 30

HARRIET MASSETTI LEFT the Incident Room at HQ and walked with her customary hurried pace towards the main doors to the courtyard. The news that Gus Broderick was no longer leading the 'Eleanor' murder inquiry had already circulated amongst the force, although the true reason for him stepping down was known only to those working the case. Massetti had stepped in to take Broderick's place and had assured her officers back in the room that it was a temporary situation operational only until Broderick's return.

'Which will, I'm certain, be sooner rather than later,' she had added.

Passing Sergeant Aldarino on the reception desk, her mobile phone buzzed. As she exited the building into the courtyard, the Chief Superintendent took the call from Sullivan.

'Yes?'

'Just to confirm that Penny Broderick's DNA test will be carried out at HQ at 11.30 this morning,' Sullivan said. 'As you know, Penny is working part-time at our canteen, so she's taking half an hour off work. Kemp is coming over to carry out the test himself.'

'What's Penny been told? The truth?'

'No. Gus called me this morning. He says he and Cath have told her the test is just routine. That by adding her DNA to the database there might be a better chance of finding her mother.'

'So not a lie then.'

'Not the complete truth either, but Gus is insistent that he doesn't want his daughter upset by any of this.'

'Agreed, but let's hope the clock isn't ticking too fast on that one. Anything else?'

'Yes. He wants it all to appear routine. To that end he thinks that Cath and he should not be present. He's asked if I could be there for Penny. Be with her at the test and put her at ease if she gets worried.'

'I see,' Massetti said, aware that this was a little awkward. 'Well, you can be here as a friend, I suppose.'

'That's what I thought, ma'am.'

'Mind you, I've been considering the whole situation. Your absence is becoming quite inconvenient. With Gus off, we need all hands to the pump. Perhaps even yours.'

Sullivan couldn't quite believe Massetti's words.

'I'm sorry, ma'am, but are you suggesting—?'

'I'm not suggesting anything yet, Sullivan, but give me a little time and I'll see if something *suggests* itself.'

'Thank you,' Sullivan replied, failing to keep the excitement from her voice 'I'll be across in Gib by eleven.'

'Sooner, if possible, Sullivan.'

'I'm on it, ma'am.'

'Aunty Cath says that Dad just needs a rest. She's been telling him to take a holiday for ages.'

Penny Broderick was sitting in Massetti's office with Richard Kemp and Sullivan. The Chief Super had made it available to them and was discreetly going about her business elsewhere. At the desk, Kemp prepared for the DNA test, while Sullivan listened attentively to Gus's bright-eyed and animated eighteen-year-old daughter. If Penny was concerned about the test, she was showing no signs of it.

'Thing is, Dad still thinks a holiday means taking me with him.' Penny pulled a stricken face. 'I mean, that is so uncool. Can you imagine?'

Sullivan couldn't answer. The thought of Broderick on holiday was definitely something she had difficulty imagining.

Penny continued. 'I mean, okay for Daisy to go, but I'm eighteen, you know? My friends would just laugh. I mean, Dad's great, but he's so straight sometimes.'

'I'm sure you'd all have a good time.'

Penny pulled another pained expression.

'Last time we went on holiday he took us to York – the *old* York, not *New* York. All he wanted to do was look at museums and big churches.'

'Okay. Where would you like to go then?'

'Nowhere old, just somewhere fun.'

'Such as?'

'Ibiza. Ayia Napa. Cancun, maybe?'

Sullivan nodded her head.

'Yes, I can see you might have a problem with that.'

'Tell me about it. Thing is, if they did take off on a

holiday without me, I'd just sit here at home all week with FOMO. I can't win.'

'You mean you'd worry that they were having a good time by accident?'

'Exactly.'

Kemp turned from his preparations.

'And what, may I ask, is *FOMO?*'

'It stands for *Fear of Missing Out*,' Sullivan said.

'Goodness, Tamara, how very modern of you.'

'That's me, Richard. Always like to keep down with the kids.'

'Be that as it may,' Kemp continued, 'all is now ready for your little test, Penny. All I have to do is remove this cotton swab from its package and then gently place it inside your cheek and remove a little saliva. Does that sound *cool?*'

Penny smiled and shrugged her shoulders.

'Sick.'

⸺

Minutes later, Sullivan walked Penny back to the canteen and thanked her once again for helping out.

'No probs,' Penny said, heading towards the kitchen. 'If it helps find Mum.'

Turning to leave, Sullivan spied Calbot sitting alone at the far end of the canteen. Deciding to spoil his peace, she ordered an Americano and walked over to join him.

'No one cracking the whip now me and the Guv aren't around?' she said, sitting down in front of the young police officer.

'For someone who isn't around,' Calbot replied, 'you do a pretty good job of sticking around.'

'It seems I might be strangely indispensable,' Sullivan said, a smile curling the ends of her lips.

'Really? Who *knew*?'

'Not me, that's for sure,' Sullivan said, warming, as ever, to her colleague's cocky charm.

'How is the boss?' Calbot asked. 'He really is pretty indispensable around here.'

'Between you and me, he's not great. I'd say he was in shock. And who can blame him?'

'Yeah.' Calbot sighed. 'Shit happens, but if this goes the way it's looking—'

'This is going only one way,' Sullivan said. 'And that is we get Gus back here and working ASAP.'

'*We?*' Calbot asked, raising an eyebrow. 'Are you saying that *you're* back and working?'

'Not quite,' Sullivan replied, regretting her lack of candour. 'Let's just say I might be, but that's just between the two of us. Okay?'

'Lips sealed.'

'But it doesn't mean I can't start doing some prep. Any chance you could bring me up to speed on things?'

A look of slight alarm crossed Calbot's face.

'Are you serious?'

'Absolutely. And to show you just how serious I am, I'm prepared to buy you one of your favourite iced doughnuts.'

'Wow,' Calbot said. 'You really do mean business.'

'Don't I always? Stay there. I'll be back.'

As Sullivan stood and moved to the counter, Calbot watched her go.

What harm can it do? he thought. *And doughnuts aside, one good turn always deserves another.*

Chapter 31

THE BODY of Frankie DuPont lay naked on the autopsy slab. Late on Saturday afternoon it had been taken from the banks of the River Guadiaro directly to the Institute of Legal Medicine in Málaga. Forensic pathologist Dr Santiago Oriantes had carried out a lengthy autopsy on Sunday and was now ready to discuss his findings with police investigators. *Inspector Jefe* Pizarro had dispatched Consuela Danaher and De Galvez to Málaga, citing the extreme workload on his first day as an excuse for not attending himself.

For the second time in a week, the two police officers stood in the austere autopsy theatre awaiting Oriantes' verdict.

'If you imagined that Señor DuPont died from drowning, I'm afraid you're mistaken. In my opinion, death occurred when his head hit the surface of the water. Acute death from an upper spinal injury caused by hyperextension of the neck. Excoriation of the forehead and a subcutaneous haemorrhage in the dorsum of the nose are consistent with his head hitting the surface of the water after dropping from a height – in this case, I believe, from a bridge. The impact severed the intervertebral disc and the anterior longitudinal ligament between the fifth and sixth cervical vertebrae. I could go on, but all you really need to know is that he died from a broken neck.'

Consuela and De Galvez exchanged a glance. Oriantes continued.

'There was also an antemortem injury to the back of the skull. This may have been received at the time of Señor DuPont's abduction.'

'A wound that could have knocked him out?'

'Severe enough to achieve unconsciousness, I'd say.'

'And the exterior condition of the body, I take it, is simply consistent with his twenty-four hours in the water?' Consuela asked.

'Indeed. The skin macerations on the fingertips, toes and hands are in line with that, but he didn't drown. The fracture killed him.'

'I see,' Consuela said.

'I believe the body floated downriver,' Oriantes continued. 'That is odd. A human body weighs more than fresh water. Normally it would have sunk to the riverbed and only risen up after gases had built up due to gradual decomposition. That takes days, not hours.'

'It would appear that our killers had prepared for that possibility,' Consuela said. 'We found two inflatable armbands stuffed down the front of Señor DuPont's shirt. The combination of those and the strong river currents seems to have kept the body on the surface. This man's murderers wanted his body to be found quickly. As with the Bernard murders, they like to put on a show.'

'I see. You are obviously keen to establish a connection with the Bernard killings last week.'

'We have your autopsy report on those,' De Galvez said. 'Do you consider there may be similarities here?'

'Different causes of death, but the manner of approach and the confinement markings on the wrists and ankles are certainly similar. The tape covering the victims' mouths is also the same. It may well have been intended that Señor DuPont die from drowning. His death from a broken neck may have been chance and not factored into the killers' calculations. But this is conjecture. I cannot give a definitive answer to your question, I'm afraid.'

'Understood. Thank you, Dr Oriantes,' Consuela said.

'You are welcome. Good luck with your investigation.'

As the pathologist covered DuPont's body with a green sheet, Consuela and De Galvez headed for the door. Upon reaching the outside corridor, De Galvez turned to his colleague.

'The same perps on both cases, no doubt about it.'

'Agreed. Oriantes thinks so too.'

'We are still going to need all the *good luck* we can get.'

'Better not let Pizarro know that,' Consuela replied with a sigh. '*A mal tiempo, buena cara.*'

Chapter 32

THE BANK CLERK had been alarmed to discover the gentleman in a state of some distress in the vault viewing room. Immediately calling for help, he had been joined by two female colleagues from the main floor of the bank. Assisting their customer to a chair and giving him some water helped bring about the return of calm to the man's senses. Some minutes later, Max declared himself to be better and apologised for any distress he had caused.

'I need to leave now,' he said.

Finding something in which to carry the diaries away from the bank presented an immediate problem. The staff rallied round, locating some large plastic carrier bags to hold the books. Two of the bags advertised Morrison's supermarket, while the third had the emblem of the Gibraltar Football Association on its side. They were not ideal in a formal sense, but certainly adequate for the job in hand. Not long after, Max found himself being escorted by the bank staff to the door, where they bade him goodbye.

Back on Main Street once again, Max took his bearings

and began to retrace his steps to the marina. He was still in shock and the temptation to ditch the bags and their contents in a nearby refuse bin was strong. Balanced against this was a still-growing concern as to what the diaries' contents might reveal. For the first time in months Max found himself on the verge of a spiral back into mental chaos. He needed to restore control and quickly. Shaking his head and clenching the bags in his hands, he turned into a narrow passage leading down towards Irish Town and the marina. For now, he would lose himself amongst the locals and crowds of tourists thronging the centre of Gibraltar Town. The answer to his dilemma would have to come later.

By the time Naida returned to the *Adrestia*, she had planned how the Robbas would be murdered. It was now a question of making sure she had the correct equipment for the job and the ability to set the operation up properly. Naida had been a skilled diver since childhood, and her experience would now hold her in good stead. The couple's scuba diving equipment was stowed below deck in the second cabin. Ignoring the wetsuits and other diving essentials, Naida went straight to the cylinders. Two were nitrox cylinders – with a balanced blend of nitrogen and oxygen – while two others contained just pure oxygen. By the time she had brought the oxygen cylinders up on deck, Max had returned from his visit to town and was climbing aboard. The bags he was carrying looked heavy and the lack of any greeting put her on alert. All was not well.

'What's happened?' she asked.

'Nothing. Just not what I was expecting.'

'What's in the bags?'

'My mother's diaries. Nearly forty of them.'

'Jesus. They were in the safety deposit box?'

Max nodded his head.

'Anything else?'

'No,' he lied for a second time. 'How about you?'

Knowing that it would be pointless to ask more questions at this moment, Naida smiled, happy to tell him the story of her morning's exploits. Settling her lover on deck and making some fresh coffee, she set about sharing her plan.

'They both dive,' she said.

'Well, well. That suggests possibilities,' he said, stretching his legs and leaning back on the cushioned deck seat.

'It does. They have a dive tomorrow.'

Max sipped his coffee; its taste and the imminent hit of caffeine it would provide pleased him.

'And you intend to do what, exactly?'

'Exchange their nitrox cylinders with pure oxygen ones.'

'Sounds interesting.'

'Below ten metres the pure oxygen intake will lead them to experience convulsions and they will drown. Almost perfect, yes?'

'Almost, you say? Why not *absolutely*?'

'We have to exchange their nitrox cylinders with the two oxygen ones we have here on deck. Luckily they are identical to the ones they have in their apartment. We have to break in, change cylinders, attach the nitrox stickers to the oxygen ones and then get out. After that, they go diving and drown.'

'Won't they check?'

'Maybe, but it's hard to tell the difference straight away. With luck they'll simply dive and then die.'

Her words seemed to hit Max in a manner that could not be explained by the effect of the caffeine alone. Reaching for Naida's hand, the American pulled her down on top of him.

'I need you,' he said,

'I need you too, Max,' she breathed, 'I need you very much.'

Their lips met with force as the desire for each other consumed them. Sliding from the seat, the two lovers rolled onto the deck. Believing themselves to be out of sight from prying eyes, they made love, lust filling their bodies and minds with an unquenchable thirst.

From his top-floor balcony in the Neptune House Marina Bay apartment building, the man looked down on his prey. Adjusting his binoculars for a sharper focus, he looked at the couple making out on the deck of the *Adrestia* moored below. There was no voyeuristic pleasure to be enjoyed at this moment. Being a professional Peeping Tom was part of his job; he knew he had to remain immune to its strange and possibly shocking scenarios. But at the moment, there was no doubting that things had taking a turn for the best. After a disastrous start to the week and a frustrating end to it, all now appeared to be going smoothly. Travelling to Gib, he had left the Fiat in La Linea before crossing the border. He'd been lucky to get a holiday rental apartment at such short notice. Its marina-view frontage gave him exactly the proximity to his targets he had hoped for.

The last twenty-four hours had moved quickly. One extra piece of information from his contact in Washington had finally helped him to track the couple down and had precipitated his arrival in the British Overseas Territory several hours earlier.

He had been told that the couple may have been seen on a yacht called the *Adisto* in Palermo, Sicily. How this information had come to light he did not know. He hadn't asked. A six-hour internet search, plus several phone calls to harbour masters in Corfu, Sicily, Spain and finally Gibraltar, had achieved more than his previous weeks of searching had in total.

There was no yacht called the *Adisto*, but a yacht called the *Adrestia* had been purchased recently in Cyprus. That same yacht had left Spain and arrived in Gibraltar the day before. It was the breakthrough. Even his bugging of the Spanish policewoman's phone had proved ultimately useless. The man smiled in the knowledge that the police were nowhere near catching the two murderers he currently held in his sights. His search for the couple had been difficult. The only thing he had been given to work with until now was '*The List*', a crumpled piece of paper with names and one location scribbled upon it in pencil. It read:

Jackson
Kasoulidis
Taylor
Bernard (Marbella?)
DuPont

Robbas

His employer had told him that it had been found amongst Max's belongings and was the only pointer as to where he might possibly be found. As a piece of intelligence, it provided little to go on. But it had brought him to Puerto Banús and now it had delivered him his prey. Max and his companion were his now, but making them disappear was not going to be easy on the Rock.

Chapter 33
WASHINGTON D.C.

MARCEL'S at 2401 Pennsylvania Ave was one of the congressman's favourite restaurants; as he entered the heavily curtained entrance and vestibule of Chef Robert Weidmaier's famous French establishment, he felt quite at home. Greeted with an elegant respect by the *Maître d'* himself, the congressman was taken immediately to a table in the busy lounge bar. It was a few minutes after seven and as always, the place was buzzing with customers: members of the media and Washington elite, including several other high profile figures from Capitol Hill. Heads turned to see the congressman being led to his table at the far end of the room. A wave here, a smile there and a momentary stop to joke with a *Washington Post* political journalist made his progress a little slower than he might have wished, but this was Washington and Marcel's was the place to be seen, if being seen was what you wished to happen. Tonight it most definitely was.

Reaching his table, the congressman sat with his back to the wall. From this position he could see pretty much everything in the room. That was how he liked it. In truth, he had not visited the restaurant for several months. It had been refurbished in that time, its colours now soft and warm, the furniture in white leather and the new bar an impressive creation made from slabs of cool grey marble. The effect was subtle, modern and very French.

'I like the new look,' the congressman said. 'I see the piano has gone.'

'Thank you, sir,' the *Maître d'* replied. 'It was felt that the piano didn't quite fit.'

'Its absence also provides space for more seating, I see.'

'And very comfortable the seating is too, I trust.'

The congressman nodded. 'Yes. Very.'

'You are expecting someone to join you, I believe, sir.'

'Yes. James Leamore-Adair will be here shortly.'

'And you will be joined by further guests at eight in the Palladin Room.'

'Yes indeed.'

'May I offer you a drink, sir?'

'Just a sparkling mineral water, please. It's going to be a busy night.'

And it would be. In a few moments' time the congressman would be meeting with one of the top political fundraisers in the capital. James Leamore-Adair was respected as something of a kingmaker in American politics, and his abilities and talents for organising hugely effective Super-PACS was well known. Their meeting in such a public place would not go unnoticed by the press and the Washington gossip circus, and that, too, was just the way the congressman wanted it.

In an hour's time, the two men would join other heavyweight influencers for supper in the restaurant's private dining room. A positive response there would lead to the congressman deciding to run for president. It would be a popular decision with only a minority in the Grand Old Party and it would be a rough ride convincing the rest. To begin with, tradition had it that senators and governors were better qualified then members of congress to run for the highest executive office in the land. There were exceptions, but very few. The congressman knew it would be a tough fight against the other Republican candidates – except perhaps the buffoon TV showman who'd announced three months before – but it was one he was convinced he could win if the events unfolding in Europe could be dealt with and buried for good. Running for the top job was a now or never decision. The stakes were high, but so were his ambitions.

⊏⊐

As his water arrived, the congressman's thoughts were drawn to a Latin quotation that had played on a loop in his head for the last twenty-four hours.

Et stilla de fortuna valet dolca sedes sapentiae. The quote had stuck in his mind from the moment a relative had shared a story with him during the previous day.

⊏⊐

Since Max had gone missing, the congressman had desperately been trying to track him down. Managing to keep his nephew's escape below the radar had been easy at first, but it was now getting harder. Weeks and months had passed and no sign of his troubled relation had been found. No sightings, no paper trail, no nothing. And then the congressman had gone to a family wedding in Cheyenne, Wyoming. A passing conversation with a distant cousin – Abe Dillson – over an indifferent buffet and a bottle of warm beer, had revealed a possible location for Max.

'Six weeks back, me and Betty were just coming into Palermo Marina, out there in Sicily,' the cousin had told him. 'You ever been?'

The congressman had to admit that he hadn't.

'You gotta go. Just got to. Anyways, we were heading out of port, when I look over at this yacht coming in. We're no great distance from each other and I look across and I swear I see – no word of a lie – I swear I see that boy Max on deck. In his forties now, I guess, but it was him. Last I heard he weren't too healthy. Looked pretty fine to me though. What's the boy doing out there?'

'It can't possibly have been him, Abe,' the congressman lied.

'Sure looked like him. On a boat called the *Adisto* or some such. Betty caught the name – I sure didn't. We thought maybe to go back, but it was kinda too late for that.'

'You were right not to, Abe. Now, if you'll excuse me?'

Leaving his dull cousin in as much ignorance as possible, the congressman had exited the function room and made a call on a safe phone.

'It's me. I've new information. I know how they're travelling.'

A drop of luck is worth a cask of wisdom.

At the far end of the Marcel's lounge, the congressman spied James Leamore-Adair heading straight for him. Focusing his thoughts and slipping effortlessly into politician mode, he rose with a hand outstretched in greeting and a smile so broad it strained the muscles of his cheeks.

'Jim. Thanks for joining me.'

Chapter 34

SULLIVAN ARRIVED BACK at the *finca* later than she had
expected. The sun was about to fall out of the western
sky as she drove the Mitsubishi up the track to be met by
a barking and seemingly fully recovered Leggo. Early in
the day, she had spent over an hour talking to Calbot in
the police canteen. He had brought her up to date with
the 'Eleanor' investigation's progress. Calbot's general
conclusion was that they seemed to be getting nowhere
slowly.

'Hopefully, the DNA results will move things along a
bit,' he said. 'But as we know, that might prove to be a
double-edged sword.'

Sullivan had to agree. As they were about to conclude,
Massetti's number flashed up on her mobile. The Chief
Super was in brusque mode.

'Okay. You're back on the investigation starting tomorrow. I've pulled some strings upstairs and you're good to
go,' Massetti informed her. 'Only grit in the oyster is that
you'll not get paid till the end of next month, in line with

your pre-arranged contract of work. I'm sure you'll be able to cope till then. You can thank me in the morning.'

The line went dead. Sullivan looked to Calbot.

'I'm back tomorrow. Official.'

'It'll seem like you've never been away,' Calbot said, a sarcastic smile lifting his face.

'Tell you what. Give me some of your workload to get on with. I can get a head start this afternoon.'

Calbot stood to go.

'I'll bring something down. You don't want to be turning up in the Incident Room too early. Massetti said the morning and you know what she's like.'

'I do indeed, John. Thank you for your sweet concern.'

———

Sullivan spent the afternoon and early evening in the canteen working through lists of workers and visitors to the warehouse during the time of its construction and after. Calbot brought down some paperwork sent over from the maintenance company and emailed further information to her phone. Sullivan soon realised that she was in effect double-checking the work Calbot had already done: a standard procedure to catch anything that may have been missed on the first pass.

Nearly sixty people had been contacted during the previous week, and Sullivan now read through the paperwork with her usual intense concentration. It seemed that Calbot had been right. Nothing stood out as unusual. None of the building contractors, warehouse staff or delivery drivers who had been contacted or interviewed could offer anything to help them understand how the woman's body had come to rest beneath the floor of the Eastern Beach warehouse site.

At 6.30, and suddenly aware of how the hours had rushed by, Sullivan decided to call it a day. As she collected the mass of papers into a neat pile, she noticed several pages she had somehow missed. They were photocopied pages of a handwritten log made by the night watchman on the site covering the period of the second month after the warehouses had been opened.

Resolving to finish what she had started, Sullivan began to read. Each scrawled entry was written against a separate date of the week. For two pages she read the same thing: '*Night passed. No incidents,*' followed by the man's initials. On the third page her attention was drawn to a different entry: '*Bad smell in second warehouse. Reported to management.*' The next day the entries returned to their previous message and continued in that vein until the pages finished. In all she had read that afternoon, nobody else had mentioned there being a bad smell in the warehouse at any time. Yet the second warehouse was where the body in the air duct had been eventually found. Could there be a connection? It was probably nothing, she rationalised, but it was odd, and odd things sometimes led to interesting discoveries. Realising that it was a line of enquiry she would have to investigate in the morning, Sullivan packed up. Before leaving she put in a call to Cath to check on Broderick.

'How is he?'

'Not great, Tamara. Gus is tough, but this is really killing him.'

'Tell him I'm back on the case, will you? As of now.'

'He'll be pleased to hear that.'

'We'll sort this out, Cath. I promise you.'

'I know you will. Thank you, Tamara.'

The call ended, Sullivan finally left the Police HQ and headed for Gaucín. How she was going to deliver on her promise to Cath, she didn't quite know. But somehow she had to. *Whatever it takes, kid,* she thought to herself. *Whatever it takes.*

———

It was just after nine when Sullivan saw the lights of a car heading up the track towards the farmhouse. To her relief, it was Consuela. The fact that she was still jumpy from the previous few days' experiences took her a little by surprise. Leaving the annexe, she followed Leggo out to the yard to greet her new friend.

'You look tired,' she said, seeing Consuela's weary-looking face.

'Straight back at you,' Consuela said, kneeling to greet the excitable Leggo. 'But then nobody ever said our job was going to be easy.'

'Fancy a glass of something?'

'Oh yes. But come over to the main house and join me. Have you eaten yet?'

Sullivan had to admit that she hadn't.

'Good,' Consuela announced. 'I'm cooking and you're pouring the rioja. Deal?'

'You better believe it. But I'm supplying the wine.'

———

Consuela placed two bowls of delicious salmorejo soup – with bread, boiled eggs and Serrano ham – on the large farmhouse table when Sullivan arrived with the wine. The resting detectives devoured the exquisite Andalusian speciality within minutes. Now turning their attention to the red wine, they began to talk like friends who had known each other for years and not just days.

'It's good that you're back early with the RGP. It's what you wanted,' Consuela said. '*Sí?*'

'It is. The situation with Gus Broderick has been on my mind all the time. Now I might be able to help in a more practical way.'

'I hope so. He's a good man. I guess you'll be wanting to move back to the Rock early though.'

This thought had not occurred to Sullivan.

'I don't really think I can. Not for a few weeks. I've got a place in Catalan Bay lined up for a short period, but then I need to find somewhere more permanent. Is it all right if I stay here till your dad gets back?'

'Of course it is, Tamara. I'd love that. Besides, I think Leggo would be heartbroken if you left early.'

'Thank you. I think I'd miss him too.'

Leaving the table and moving to the sitting area, the women made themselves comfortable on the large sofas and poured more wine. As Consuela leaned back and placed her feet upon the large coffee table, Sullivan looked at the young, golden-haired woman before her and realised that she'd also miss her new friend. Her relationships with her own sex had always seemed difficult. She didn't know why, but somewhere in her mind she blamed her mother. Normally she would have been jealous of the twenty-seven-year-old, with her good looks and superior police rank. But she wasn't, and that came as an unexpected relief.

'How's the Bernard and DuPont investigation going?' Sullivan asked. 'Good day?'

Consuela shook her head vigorously.

'No, no, no. The opposite to good.'

'Oh?'

'No progress. Lots of questions being asked, but no useful answers coming back. The new *inspector jefe* is also – how would my father say it?'

'A real pain in the arse?'

'A bit stronger, actually, but something like that.'

Consuela smiled, but Sullivan sensed that something else was bothering her.

'Is that all?' she asked.

Consuela took a moment before answering.

'I think I screwed up today, Tamara.'

'How so?'

'Not me, in person. Another officer. But it amounts to the same thing. My responsibility, you understand?'

'Not yet I don't.'

Consuela took a large sip from her glass and then the words began to flow.

'It was Sergeant Cortez. It was his job, but he's lazy and I should have kept a closer eye on him. *Estupido*. This afternoon I phoned to check up on Izi Bernard and her father. He is out of hospital, but they are both in a bad way. I had to explain that we were having to delay the return of her mother's body at this stage. She got upset and started to cry. Understandably. I felt sorry for her and asked if her boyfriend Rudi had been able to comfort her at this terrible time. What she had to say surprised me.'

Consuela drank from her glass once more.

'In what way surprised?' Sullivan asked.

'She told me she hadn't seen him since the day after the murders had been discovered. They had talked on the phone just once after that, but then he had simply disappeared. She said she was upset, but understood how awful it must have been for him too.'

'How very understanding of her.'

'The point is, his running off worried me. I don't know why. Yes, it was too awful, but Izi needed him and I thought it very bad of him. Anyway, to tidy things up, I decided to check his paperwork. Cortez had checked him out and got confirmation of identity from the US sent over. Looking at the paperwork, I could see it all matched his statement. An investment banker based in California, visiting Spain briefly and then planning a holiday in Morocco. It all looked okay until I found a photograph attached at the back of the papers. His company had sent it over and Cortez had clearly missed it.'

Sullivan edged forward in her seat. Consuela's story was definitely getting interesting.

'The photo was not that of the Rudi Janson I'd met and interviewed at the murder scene. It was that of a bald man with a moustache.'

'A mistake?'

'We had a copy of Janson's passport. The passport photograph was that of the man I met at the Bernard mansion. It's a fake, of course.'

'Shit.'

'Pizarro hit the ceiling when I told him and I don't blame him.'

'But Cortez's fault.'

'And my *responsibility*.'

Sullivan stopped there. She knew only too well how the

system worked. She'd been on the wrong side of it herself enough times. Consuela continued.

'I had to ask if Izi had any photos of the man. She said no at first and then remembered she had taken a selfie in Banús with him in the background. I have it here.'

Consuela got the picture on her smart phone and showed her friend. The selfie had been taken in Izi's car. She sat in the driving seat and although behind her, the profile of the false Rudi Janson was very clear. A dark-haired, handsome man in his early thirties met Sullivan's eye.

'Well, Consuela, he has a lot of hair and no moustache, that's for sure.'

'I know. I know. But what does it mean? He couldn't have been involved in the murders. He was with Izi the whole time. But a person who pretends to be someone he is not is someone we as police officers need to know about. But he's just vanished and I'm the fool who must take the blame. *Soy estupido.*'

Sullivan reached over and filled her friend's glass.

'I'm sorry. It's not fair.'

'But, a little worrying, *sí?*'

'*Interesting*, certainly. I take it you're looking for him?'

'Of course, but he could be anywhere by now.'

'Of *course*, but in the meantime I suggest a toast.'

'To what?'

Sullivan raised her glass.

'To Sergeant Cortez getting screwed over too.'

Chapter 35

NAIDA STEPPED onto the deck of the *Adrestia* from the cabins below. The moon was high in the night sky and the lights from the surrounding apartment buildings, restaurants and casino prevented her eyes from seeing the full glory of the Milky Way above. On a clear night at sea, with no ambient light to interfere, the full canopy of stars above was a wonder to behold. She had studied them from an early age and knew many of the heavenly constellations by name.

The marina was still busy at this midnight hour, with people strolling along the promenades or drinking at the many bars that lined Marina Bay. Below her, Max lay asleep.

Earlier, they had made love and then prepared for the following day. They had gone into town and purchased two large suitcases suitable for carrying oxygen tanks. Transporting them to the Robbas' apartment would be easy. Getting them in and replacing them with the Robbas' own tanks would be a little more challenging, but absolutely possible. Naida enjoyed a little danger. It made her feel alive. The rest of the day had been spent on board the boat. They had cooked an early supper and Max had retired to bed. The experience at the bank that morning had affected him badly. Naida had not enquired as to the reasons why. She knew him well enough to know that he would tell her as and when he felt able to. That was his way. She remained deeply curious though.

Looking along the deck, she could see the carrier bags that Max had brought back from the bank lying neglected on the floor. Normally she would have simply put them away and let them be. Tonight she felt differently. For once she wasn't prepared to wait.

Picking the bags up, she moved along the deck. Settling further forward where the light from the pontoon walkway was bright enough for her to read by, Naida reached into the carrier and took out the first exercise book that came to hand. The date on its faded, orange-coloured front had been handwritten in ink and read, '*Diary. 1968–69.*' Flicking through its pages she could see that entries had been made sporadically over the months. Often several weeks were not accounted for, followed by a sudden flow of words and thoughts written over a number of days. Looking through the August entries, one particular passage caught Naida's eye and she began to read.

… Donna and me finally made it to the Whisky a Go Go. I mean she's been promising for how long? It's the most famous club in Holly-wood for god sake. Donna says it's the best in the world!! I had to dress up and put on heels to convince her that I looked old enough to get in. She's twenty-one and I'm nearly eighteen, but I'm so much taller than her and I looked just great. Her Dad's company does the

security at the Whisky and one of the guys on the door is hot for Donna, so she told me, 'Stay close, okay? I never have to show ID cos I'm the boss's daughter. If you're with me they'll let you through too. Just keep cool and look cool.' So I did. The guys on the door were real sweet. Smiled and asked Donna who her cute friend was. It felt great. Donna got pissed about it though. She gets that way with me when boys are around.

I was real nervous going in. I think I had the shakes, but it didn't last long. Inside was amazing. I mean THE most amazing place I've ever seen. As we entered the club the music was sooo loud – I got used to it though real quick – and the place was packed. I looked up and saw girls dancing above like they were hanging from the ceiling. They were wearing white boots and short skirts, but not a lot more. The lights were flashing everywhere, different colours and shapes, it was unreal.

Donna nudged my arm as a woman came past with two guys heading for the exit. She looked amazing. 'It's Faye Dunaway.' Donna said. All I could think to say was, 'Wow!' I did a lot of 'Wowing' as we moved around. I even saw two actors from General Hospital by the bar, but I just couldn't remember their names. It was like my mind had gone dumb.

We stood by the dance floor for a while. It was jammed. Donna reminded me about the 'Etiquette'. The 'Etiquette' is real important. If you want to dance, you have to wait for a space on the floor to open up. If you're an ordinary dancer you have to know this. 'You don't push in and you always, like ALWAYS, give way to VIPs wanting to get on the floor.' Donna said. 'It's the law.' Then she went to the powder room and left me on my own. I felt nervous again. Me and Donna were a long way from the two of us just talking about coming down here to The Strip. Sitting by the pool up at the beach club in Santa Barbara and planning our lives. Our freedom.

Then I heard this voice say, 'You don't need make-up.' I turned and looked down at this guy. How I'd heard him I don't know, it was so loud, but he hadn't shouted. Just spoke.

'You don't need make-up.' He said again. 'I can see your heart anyhow.'

I just stared at him. He was real short. Maybe five inches shorter than me. He had long hair down to his shoulder. Black hair, kind of untidy looking. And his eyes shone. I mean really stood out shining.

I didn't know what to do. I just started praying Donna would get back soon. Then he carried on and asked my name.

'I'm Yvonne Tremain.' I said, just straight out.

'Kinda formal. Your full name and all.' He said.

'Von. I'm Von. Donna my friend who's here and my other friends call me Von.' I said. I knew I was blushing and just blabbing. He just looked at me and smiled.

'I'm Charlie and you don't need make-up.'

Then he moved passed me and stepped onto the dance floor. I couldn't believe it, he just pushed his way through to the center. The other dancers seemed real unhappy about it and some looked as though they were telling him so. He just took no notice and started dancing.

I was just relieved that he'd gone and decided to move up to near the ladies room and wait for Donna. It was darker on the edges of the club and I could hide a bit and look down. When I turned back to see the dance floor again, I couldn't believe what I saw. Charlie was dancing flat out in the middle and people were just leaving the floor to give him space. He was dancing like I've never seen anyone dance before. I couldn't stop looking at him, it was kind of hypnotic, I guess. After a few minutes he was completely on his own out there and everyone in the whole place seemed to be watching him. They were actually loving it. His movements got bigger and bigger and his energy was just flying out of him. Maybe at times I don't know as much as I should, but I knew at that moment I was watching something extraordinary. Like magic.

Then he looked straight at me. The place was big and I was away in the shadows, but I swear on my life he looked right up at me and for a moment smiled. I was in shock, you know. That he'd done that. That he could do that. I mean, he was spinning and jumping and all sorts. He was manic, but he looked right up at me. It was like he knew exactly who I was and could see inside me. I don't under-stand how or why, but I knew right then that I needed to know him. That feeling is still in me, cos I still do.

Naida stopped reading for a moment and listened for any movement below. There was none. She was relieved that she could continue reading. Moving through the pages, she stopped at another entry.

September 21st, 1968

I found him! Last night Donna drove us down to LA and got me and her into the Whisky a Go Go again. It was even cooler than last time, with guys hitting on us as soon as we walked in. One even thought I was older than Donna. She got really pissed at him and walked off. I got her a drink and she came round. The only bad thing was this time Charlie wasn't there. I'd really hoped he would be. Like really hoped. This guy came over to us and started to hit on us both. Said he was an actor. I asked him straight out if he'd heard about Charlie and the dancing. He said, 'Who ain't?' Told us next that Charlie was a personal friend of one of the Beach Boys – I can't remember which one. Told us that Charlie and some friends had been living with this Beach Boy at his house just along Sunset Boulevard. He said that Charlie was wild and that the Beach Boy had had to close the house down and move to get rid of him. Word was that Charlie and friends had gone to live on the ranch where they'd made that cowboy series Bonanza. *My Gramma still watches that all the time!! Anyway, this actor just sat and talked about himself, so we went to the ladies room and never saw him again. On the way home, I begged Donna to drive me to the Bonanza ranch. She said that I didn't even know where it was. I told her I'd find out. So that's what I'm gonna do. Cool.*

September 23rd, 1968

Found it!! It's called Spahn Ranch and it's out near a place called Chatsworth. I got the address – 12000 Santa Susana Pass Road – my friend's brother Luke is a TV dork and knows everything. He says they even filmed The Lone Ranger out there and lots of other shows I'd never heard of. Donna's driving me down to the ranch this after-noon. Don't know why I'm doing this. I just can't help myself. If Mom, Dad or my brother found out they'd kill me to death. Who cares?

October 15th, 1968

The last few weeks have been shitty. Real bad. I'm going to try and think about it now. I guess it started on the day me and Donna took off to the Spahn Ranch. I had no idea it was in the middle of plain nowhere. It was just wild, with rocks and kind of hills and dust, just like the westerns on TV. Took us longer to get there than we'd guessed, but finally we pulled off the road late afternoon and there was an old sign almost hidden away. We drove down a track and suddenly there it was. Like a cowboy town, but not so big. There were old trailers, shacks and old cars. Lots of horses and stuff too. Then we saw them.

People just appeared from buildings and all around. They became like a crowd just walking towards us. Mostly girls like my age and

177

maybe Donna's. A few guys. Not many. None of them were wearing shoes and they looked dirty and we were both frightened. Donna wanted to turn right around and go, but then I saw Charlie. He came out of this trailer and just looked straight at me. I waved. He kept on looking at me real hard and just as I was going to say to Donna to go, he waved back and then slowly walked right over. All the others kind of just parted and let him through.

He came right up to the car and said, 'Hi, Von, I knew you'd turn up sometime. Who's your friend?' I just couldn't believe he'd remembered me. But he had. Then he called the others over and we got out of the car and Charlie introduced us. They were all smiling and kissing us on both cheeks. Charlie said visitors were always welcome and to come along and he'd show us around. Then he told the others to get back to work. Which they did.

I don't know where the hours went, but Charlie showed us around. The cowboy town was just the fronts of places like the saloon and store. Behind them were empty rooms or just big wooden frames to hold them up. We must have looked disappointed, but Charlie said that it was just like life. He said that people and things were never what they looked like up front and that we had to be aware of that. He said the other girls had come back from a food run and we should stay and eat with everyone and listen to him preach. Donna asked him what he meant and he said that he'd meant exactly what he had just said and gave her a cold look and left us for a bit. Donna whispered to me that we had to go as she didn't like the vibe. I told her I was staying and she could go if she wanted. We argued and she stormed away and drove off.

I told myself that I didn't care if she'd gone. Charlie was kind and interesting and what the hell? Charlie came back and just said, 'I knew she wouldn't stay.' He then told me to wash off my make-up and join the group. So I did.

Everyone was so kind and happy and I felt as if I'd known them always, you know. After supper Charlie took us out to a spot where there was a sort of cave, a large rock which everyone sat around and listened to Charlie talk. I sat with them and listened too. He got out a bible and said that everything in scripture was true. He said that he was Jesus returned to the earth and that he would protect only those who followed him. He said that we should all love each other and share that love with each other. That sex was good and should be shared as part of that love. He said we were all inhibited and that only drugs would release us to know our true consciousness. And then he came to us one by one and put a tablet in our mouths.

I didn't want to do it, but I couldn't stop. He said it was good and that no good would come from not trusting him and my new friends. All I remember after that was music. Lots and lots of music and faces. People saying that they loved me and that I was safe. I danced too, but I couldn't stand up straight after a while so had to lie down. And then it was morning.

I woke up and Charlie was lying next to me. We were in his trailer. He asked if I was happy. I said I was. He told me that's what he did – he made others happy. I said thank you. He told me it was love. If I hung around, he said, he'd fill my heart with all the love he had. He kissed my lips. I'd never really been kissed before. Not really kissed, but it felt so familiar. Then he pulled away, telling me to go outside and the others would show me what work I could do to show my gratitude for the welcome I'd received. I could have a little breakfast too as the days were long and nobody stopped for lunch. Outside the others were gathered around talking and drinking coffee. They welcomed me, and Ruth, one of the girls, said I could work with her in the stables. She was real pretty and nice and I felt happy.

As we walked over she asked if Charlie had taken care of me. I said that he'd been real kind. Ruth laughed out loud. 'Yeah, that's Charlie. He's real kind. To new ones, 'specially'.

We worked the stables through the morning and into afternoon.

Clearing out the stalls and polishing tack, then repairing wooden slats the horses had kicked out. It was hot and the only time we stopped was for water when our thirst grew strong. At last Ruth said we needed a break. 'You can never let Charlie catch you.' She said. 'He hates slackers. Goes crazy.' I said nothing, but Ruth read my face. 'If you don't believe me, you'll find out soon enough.'

We walked a little way from the back of the stables and out towards the shade of some small trees. The ground was dusty and covered in rocks, so we picked our way through. As we left the stables, we passed another girl carrying buckets of horse feed. I smiled and said hi to her. She didn't smile back. Just glared at me. It was a look that made me go cold. Ruth touched my arm and said, 'Don't you worry about Dianne. She's real close to Charlie. Real close. Gets upset when he shares.'

She must have seen that I still wasn't getting it.

'When Charlie's kind. To others. Like Charlie's bin' kind to you, sweet pea.'

Ruth walked on up to the shade, while I stopped, trying to figure what she'd meant. My mind was reeling, leaving me kind of dizzy. Moments later I started to follow her up the rocky slope to the trees. It was then the pain hit. I didn't hear the rattle, but I felt the bite. Looking down I saw the snake moving backwards towards the rocks. I must have brushed it as I walked, my mind so far away I hadn't noticed it. The rattler had struck my ankle. It was so quick and the shock so sudden, I couldn't even call out. I just stood shaking as I watched the rattler retreat, its body coiling as it moved, its mouth snapping and eyes looking straight at mine.

Next thing I knew, Ruth was by my side. She was calm and talking to me gently.

'It get you, sweat pea?' I nodded. 'Okay. Don't you worry' she said. 'It's going now, so you just breathe deep. You'll be okay.'

She took me by the arm again and slowly led me back towards the stables. Passing them we saw a group of the others across the way and Ruth called over to them. 'She's been bit.' Hearing this they ran over to us. That's when my mind went black and I must have fallen to the ground. Next thing I knew I was looking up and all I could see was faces. I caught some of what they were saying. Something about a tying my leg and getting me water. Then Charlie's face appeared, looking down at me. The others went quiet, waiting for him to speak. At last he said, 'You have all my love, Von.' He smiled sweetly and then nodded to one of the men and said, 'She can't die here, Tex. Get her to Chatsworth.'

I must have passed out again, because the next thing I knew I was being driven fast along a main road. We were in a dune buggy. I remember metal bars and what looked like fur hanging from a canopy or something. I was in the passenger seat and Tex was driving. Holding my shoulders from behind was a woman whose name I couldn't remember. My leg was hurting because of the strip of cloth tied tight above my knee. I tried to talk to them, but they weren't listening. I was panicking. I thought I was going to die. The woman gripped me hard from behind and I started to cry. Tex just drove on.

We hit the town and stopped at a small medical center. Tex got out then came around the buggy and picked me up out of the front seat. He carried me to the building and put me down against the wall near the main doors. The woman followed and told me to go in and see the doctor. I started to cry again. I asked if they were coming in too. Tex said that the center would look after me and walked back to the buggy. I grabbed hold of the woman's sleeve and begged her to stay and help me. She brushed me off. 'You're a big girl. Gotta look after yourself, see? And don't go telling them about Charlie, you hear? Just say you got bit out walking.' I asked her how I was going to get back. 'Just go home.' She said 'Charlie don't want you back. Get yourself home to Mommy and Daddy. Understand?' And she left.

As they drove off, a couple came out of the center and seeing me *crying, helped me inside. I told the lady at the desk just what I'd been told to, that I had been bitten by a rattler out walking. She got a nurse to get me in with a doctor straight away, but not before asking how old I was and then for my parents number. I didn't want to give her that, but she told me I had no choice. So, I did. The doctor told me I'd been lucky. The snake had only used a bit of its venom – I didn't know rattlers could do that. He said it had used enough poison to make me feel unwell for a bit, but the bite wasn't going to kill me. After treating the wound and giving me some drugs, the doctor left me alone. I started to cry again.*

I thought Charlie had wanted me to stay. That I was part of the family. That he loved me. I wanted to die and I still do.

Mom and Dad didn't kill me, but they shouted like they wanted to. Then Donna's Dad called to tell them where I'd been and to stay away from his daughter. That just made things a whole lot worse. It went on for days. Them telling me how disgusted they were with me. How I'd let them down. Let the family down. How I had nearly died because I was so stupid.

I've been grounded for weeks now and Donna doesn't want to have anything to do with me. I don't know what to do.

◆

November 1st, 1968

Have nearly gone out of my mind these last weeks. Finally got let out by Mom and Dad, but they treat me like a prisoner most days. Always asking questions as to where I'm going and who with. Donna still not talking to me, it's so unfair. Two nights ago, Mom and Dad had to go to a charity dinner down in Bel Air. They said they hoped they could trust me now that I'd learned what can happen when you go off the rails. I said I did, just to keep them from shouting at me.

After they had gone, my brother turned up with some of his friends and went down to the cabin in the garden. My bro didn't want me to go with them, but his friends insisted. I knew two of them. Dale Collins and Jake Brigston were neighborhood friends. The third was a guy from Santa Monica called Doug. They'd brought drink and were all smoking weed. I did too. My brother didn't care. I drank too much, I guess, cos I fell asleep and woke the next morning in my bedroom. I stayed in bed all day, telling Mom that I felt ill, which I did. Real ill. Still feel like I want to go and see Charlie, but know I can't. Still just want to die.

November 20th, 1968

I dream about Charlie. A lot. I know we have a bond that is special and that one day we will meet again. Mom said that I needed to build up mental strength to deal with the world outside and until that had happened I was in her and Dad's care. Anyways, I was still three and more years away from being twenty-one and the choice wasn't mine to make. They can't stop me though and they know it. Donna still not in touch. I wish I could see her. Why is life so hard? Think I've caught a bug: for the last three days I've felt sick to my stomach every morning. That's all.

Naida stopped reading. Her heart was racing as the enormity of what she had just read began to sink in. Turning the page to continue, her concentration was broken by the sound of Max calling her name from below. His voice was panicky and she knew at once that he'd just woken from one of his nightmares. She would have to go to him immediately. It was her job to calm and soothe him.

Placing the diary back in the plastic bag, she carried it across the deck to where it had been left and then descended into the quarters below.

From the balcony above the marina, Naida's every move was being watched. The man had spent the day working on a plan, and the following evening he would be ready to go. Breathing in the warm night air, he sipped a Spanish brandy and looked across to the waters of the marina glittering with the reflected lights of the shore.

The touch of his wife's breast gave him the comfort he desired. The softness of her skin and firmness of her purpose as she moved her body down upon him thrilled Rahim Robba as it always had done. His beautiful Loisa was everything he had ever wished for and needed. Her love, her patience and her passion had sustained them both for so long and had never wavered. Now, in the sanctuary of their marital bed, his eyes never left her face, as their breathing deepened in a rhythmical tantric pattern. Rahim now entered his love and they once again became one. Slowly and firmly thrusting forward, Rahim held Loisa tight as her back arched and her pleasure spread upward, bringing tears of joy to her eyes.

Throughout their years together they had always been able to seek refuge and peace in each other's bodies. Love was all Rahim had ever wanted and all he had ever wished for with Loisa.

Tonight they would sleep deeply and start a new day afresh. The joy of this was something Rahim would never take for granted.

Chapter 36
TUESDAY

RISING EARLY, Sullivan was at her desk in the RGP Incident Room by 7.30 a.m. It was good to be back and she could feel her adrenalin beginning to flow. For the next hour and a half she greeted her fellow colleagues as they arrived at HQ – Aldarino and Moreno showed particularly pleasure at seeing her back again – and reviewed the previous day's work. Reaching the same conclusions as the night before, she phoned the warehouse logistics company at 9 a.m. on the dot.

'It's Detective Sergeant Sullivan here. RGP. I'm going to have to call in and speak to you about something that we've found in your records.'

Thirty minutes later, she was sitting opposite the manager of Line Wall Logistics, Sandra Vinent. The sharply dressed and pleasantly mannered business woman seemed as keen to get on with things as Sullivan.

'I know you have been over much of this with my colleagues Calbot and Moreno,' Sullivan began, 'but I've spotted something that I hope you might be able to help me with.'

'I hope so too,' Vinent replied.

'You provided us with the records kept by your various night watchmen working at the warehouses from 2005 to 2008. They are sadly far from complete, but in the month of July 2005 there is an entry that stands out. I have it here.' Sullivan handed the relevant document to Vinent. 'You'll see all the entries against the dates are the same – "*no incidents*" et cetera – but on the night of July 11th, your night watchman wrote, "*Bad smell in second warehouse. Reported to management.*" However, after cross-checking all other documents around those dates, no response was received from you in management and no apparent action was taken to investigate and remedy the situation. Can you think of an explanation for that?'

Vinent looked at the page in her hand and shook her head. 'I'm afraid I have absolutely no answer for that. It is, after all, a long time ago and this "bad smell" may simply have blown away.'

'But wouldn't you have sent someone to at least check? A plumber or someone to see that the drains weren't blocked?'

Vinent shrugged. 'Normally, yes, perhaps.'

'You mean you might have done and not made a record of it?'

'If it was only a small problem. Maybe. The warehouses had just been put up. As you know we had contractors going on and off site completing and fixing anything that still needed to be finished.'

'This was six weeks after you'd opened. Are you saying that the building's contractors were still at work?'

'Not from Westport Building Ltd. They had completed their contract and were out of there, but there are always little things to be done on a site like that. You have the names of the people we have used on such occasions. Local electricians, plumbers and so on.'

'There is no record of any being on site that week.'

Vinent paused for a moment before replying. 'I'm afraid it doesn't mean they weren't there. Many such workers have several jobs on at any given time; they have been known to spread their work timetable over a longer period than the paperwork suggests.'

Sullivan reached into her bag and pulled out another file of papers. Looking through them, she came across an invoice dated the week before the report of the bad smell.

'This invoice, for example,' she said, handing it over to Vinent. 'That's from your regular plumbing engineer at the time, Jack Ocana. He worked at the warehouse from the 5th of July to the 7th fitting two extra wash-basins and extending pipework, et cetera. Do you mean he might have still been around to check things out a week later?'

'I've no idea. Someone may have asked him to check it out. It's possible. You'll have to talk to him.'

Sullivan stood and took back the paperwork.

'We've already talked to him. Only not about this particular query.'

Gus Broderick had taken himself for a walk. Cath had been encouraging him to get out of the house for days, but it was only now that he felt able to summon the purpose.

Even so, it might not have happened had Cath not mentioned the possibility at breakfast.

'Why don't you go and have a look at where they are building the Windsor Suspension Bridge this morning?' she'd said, as they sat in the courtyard drinking coffee and enjoying some tangy breakfast grapefruits. 'You've been wanting to go up there.'

'I'll see,' Broderick replied.

'Well, you won't see anything stuck out here with your crossword puzzles all day. How about this for an offer? I'll drive you up the Rock to the Nature Reserve, drop you off and you can walk back down. Do you good.'

To Broderick's surprise he had found himself nodding his head and saying, 'Okay. Sure.' It was a decision he immediately regretted, but looking at Cath's triumphant face across the table, he knew that there was no getting out of it now.

Not wishing to lose the initiative, Cath had hurried her brother out to her car and set off towards the steeply climbing roads that led to the Upper Rock Nature Reserve. Broderick was surprised at just how long it had been since he'd last taken the route. Rising steadily but sharply from the town below, the climb was as thrilling as it had always been. As they wove their way upwards, the sheer drop beside the road increased alarmingly with each bend they took. The view from such a height was spellbinding, and as they reached the off-road path where Cath could drop him, Broderick had thanked his sister for suggesting the outing.

'You're very welcome,' she said. 'Enjoy your walk. It might lift your spirits a little.'

'Quite a novel approach to dealing with my dark

moods,' Broderick replied. 'Dropping me all the way up here.'

'I have every faith you won't jump off, Gus,' Cath said. 'See down below.'

A hundred metre path led Broderick to the point where the bridge was being constructed. It would span the fifty-foot gorge on the western side of the Rock, connecting two World War Two gun battery sites, the first of which Broderick now stood beside. There was no question that the bridge would be an impressive piece of engineering and offer magnificent views. From his position beside the battery, Broderick looked out over the old Naval Docks and town below to the waters of the Bay. It was an uplifting experience. Cath had been right – this was taking him out of himself.

It was then a thought struck him. If mankind could use its intelligence and reason to create such a feat of engineering for the benefit of all, he too would find a way of getting through whatever the next few days might bring. Taking a deep breath of Upper Rock air, Broderick allowed himself to fully savour his moment of realisation.

Then his phone rang. It was Massetti.

'Gus? I've just had the DNA results back from Kemp. It's not Helen.'

For a moment Broderick felt as though his legs would give way. Reaching out for the side of the gun battery, he quickly steadied himself. To his surprise, another unexpected thing occurred. He began to laugh. It was not the laughter of mirth, but that of total and utter relief: a relief that the nightmare was over. The murdered woman was not Helen and hope that his wife might still be alive had been restored.

'Gus? We don't know who the woman is, but Kemp will keep checking. I don't need to tell you how delighted I am that you'll be back with us. We all knew that the chances of you being involved were slim. You understand that we had to check, though.'

'I do, Harriet. Thank you for telling me.'

'Don't rush back, though. Tomorrow at the earliest. Understood?'

'I promise.'

A large gull swept down and landed next to Broderick. Its loud squawk seemed to be like that of a triumphant herald. Massetti spoke again.

'Where are you, Gus?' she asked.

Taking a deep breath, Gus Broderick looked up at the clear blue sky above.

'I'm on the top of the world, ma'am. Top of the world.'

Sullivan had been back at her desk in the Incident Room for less than ten minutes when Massetti arrived to share the news about Broderick and the DNA test. A cheer went up from the gathered officers, none louder than Sullivan's own as she leaped from her chair and punched the air.

'All right, all right,' Massetti said, raising her arms to calm the room. 'It's good news for Gus and ourselves, but we still have a murder case to solve. The time for celebrations will be after we've caught whoever left that woman out near Eastern Beach. Keep your focus, okay?'

Sullivan had no need to take Massetti's advice. She was back working at her computer screen before the Chief Superintendent had ended her last sentence. She'd already left a message on Jack Ocana's mobile and was now checking reports she'd been unable to get round to the day before. At the same time she found Broderick's number and called him. Her call went straight to the answer machine. Sullivan left a message.

'Hi, Guv. It's me. Just heard the news and wanted to say how happy I am about it. I know you've been through hell the last few days, but it's over now. By the way, I'm back working the case – I'll tell you all about that when I see you – and I think I may be on to something. Look forward to seeing you. The whole team are.'

Sullivan ended the call and immediately worried that she'd sounded too sentimental. *Well, if I was, I was,* she concluded. *It's how I feel.*

Almost immediately her phone buzzed. It was Ocana. A minute later, Sullivan was out of the door and on her way to meet him.

        ⊏━━⊐

'It wasn't me.'

'I beg your pardon, Mr Ocana?' Sullivan said, looking the middle-aged Gibraltarian firmly in the eye.

'I'd got too many jobs on the go, so I subbed the work out.'

Jack Ocana was standing outside the gentlemen's lavatory at the rear of the Supreme Courthouse at the southern end of Main Street. Sullivan had been forced to find the plumber at his place of work for the day. Police business had brought her to the courthouse on several occasions before, but this was the first time she had accessed the private areas behind the courtrooms themselves. The building had been expanded in recent years and boasted four Supreme Courts, two Magistrates' Courts and one for the HM Coroner. The impressive mix of the traditional and the new co-existed well beneath the stately lion and unicorn sculptures on the royal coat of arms at the front of the building. For now, Sullivan and Ocana stood in the sombre, marble-floored corridor outside the gentlemen's toilets and spoke in needlessly hushed tones.

'You didn't mention any of this when Detective Calbot spoke to you,' Sullivan said. 'It might have helped if you had.'

Ocana looked down at his feet and muttered an apology. Sullivan carried on.

'So, who carried out the work over those days in July 2005?'

'My brother-in-law, Alberto.'

'Alberto, who?'

'Amigo. Alberto Amigo. He subbed for me, but the next week they called me to go and check out some smell in the second warehouse.'

'And?'

'It was coming from under the floor. The only access was a manhole cover, I remember, but it wouldn't budge.'

'You couldn't gain access to the underground passage?'

Ocana raised his shoulders. 'No. It wouldn't budge. Move, you know?'

'And then?'

'I told old Jerry – the night watchman – he's dead now, you know?'

Sullivan did know and nodded her head.

'There were no sanitation pipes running through that area, so I thought it must be a cat or family of rats, you know? Got in somehow and died. There were no flies around, so I had no real idea. I told Jerry to call me if it got any worse. Never heard another word.'

'Okay. Thank you,' Sullivan said. 'And where does Alberto live?'

'Who knows? He and my sister split, you know? Maybe six years back now. I heard he'd moved over to La Linea – his mother's Spanish – but could be anywhere now. I liked him, but, you know – shit happens.'

Chapter 37

THE VOICE on the phone recording was that of Consuela Danaher.

'The photograph of Rudi Janson sent from the States doesn't match the man we interviewed at the Bernard mansion.'

The man had been checking Consuela's bugged mobile for an update on things across the border. He was listening to a message she'd left a police colleague. confirming that his cover had been blown.

Shit. That was quicker than I'd expected.

The man would now have to move even more rapidly. His real name was Alex Weber, and although he was convinced that he'd disguised his tracks well, the margins for discovery had just collapsed dramatically. Bugging the Spanish detective's mobile had proved an increasingly useful source of information over the past week, but this news was an unwelcome game changer. When Consuela Danaher had given *'Rudi Janson'* her card and number up at the Bernard mansion, the detective had no idea that her phone would soon be working against her. She'd also had no idea that the real Rudi Janson was several thousand miles away in California and that the man she had found comforting the distressed Izi Bernard was an imposter. He was also a contract killer. Consuela knew nothing about this part of the story and Weber was determined that it remain that way.

Weber had been sitting on his shaded balcony overlooking the marina since just after first light. From there he could keep watch on the *Adrestia* and its occupants below and at the same time work on his laptop and make calls on his safe phone. There was much to organise. Making people disappear into thin air was not an easy procedure, and the challenges of his present mission were proving more substantial than he had estimated. The job had been difficult from the start. Given only a list of names and one geographical destination – *Marbella* – to work with, Weber had dived straight in, confident that his targets would somehow turn up. The couple he was chasing had been on the run for months; all he could think to do was arrive in Marbella and work through the list of residents with the surname Bernard who lived in that vicinity. Applied science it was not, but his strategy had eventually led him to his prey and today's business would now be about urgently finessing a plan to dispatch them. Somehow, he would have to get rid of the couple below before any contact with their next victim could be made. Killing them in the cabin of the *Adrestia* would be simple, but making both the couple and the boat disappear from the face of the planet was a more complicated logistic. With this in mind, Weber put in a call to a contact in Málaga. His Spanish fixer had proved invaluable so far, but the request that he was about to receive would challenge even him.

The first part of the plan was straightforward. Weber would board the *Adrestia* after dark and take the couple unawares at gunpoint. A bullet each to the head or heart would suffice. Weber would then take the *Adrestia* out of Gibraltar and head to sea. The next part of the plan was less in his control. At a planned co-ordinate he would meet with a Moroccan boat organised by his Spanish friend. With the dead couple below, Weber would then scuttle the *Adrestia*, leave the boat and head to Tangiers with his Moroccan colleagues. Behind him, the *Adrestia* would sink beneath the waves, taking its human cargo with it.

His call to Málaga was proving to be a positive one. The fixer told him that getting a boat for his transfer would not be a problem. A rigid inflatable boat would be perfect, but as the transport of choice for drug smugglers between Africa and Spain, this type of boat would attract too much attention. A more sedate motor cruiser would need to be sourced and crewed. It was short notice, but for the right amount of money, it could be done in time.

'Don't worry about the money. Just get me the boat where I need it and when,' Weber said.

'Consider it done, my friend.'

The line went dead. Weber took a sip from his third cup of coffee of the morning and checked his watch. It was 7.25 a.m. In the marina below, something caught his attention. On board the *Adrestia* there was movement. Putting his binoculars to his eyes, Weber could see that Max and the woman were about to leave the boat. Max wore his panama hat once more and both were carrying large black suitcases. Lifting them onto the marina walkway, they left their mooring and marched off towards the main promenade. Grabbing a small rucksack containing his passports, phones and other essentials, Weber rushed from his balcony and headed out of the apartment. All his careful planning would amount to nothing if he lost sight of Max and his accomplice. While the mechanics of their disappearance were being set up, Weber needed to stick to them like glue.

Taking the stairs to the ground floor, Weber ran out onto the marina front, arriving just in time to see the two turn right on Marina Bay Square and walk on past the Grille 53 steakhouse towards Gibraltar Town. Slowing to a fast walk, Weber concentrated on the twin jobs of following them closely and not alerting them to his presence. He was good at discreet surveillance, but this early in the morning, there were not as many people about as he would have liked. Blending in would not be easy. *Just don't look round, you bastards,* he thought to himself. *Just don't you look round.*

Fortunately for Weber, neither Max nor the woman turned to see their pursuer. Their journey into town took them through Ocean Village and up onto the roundabout at the junction of Waterport Road and Queensway. Café bars, shops and high-rise luxury apartments lined their route until this point. Crossing the roundabout, they moved on to Line Wall Road, skirting the edge of Grand Casemates Square. There were more people around in this part of town, early bird tourists and traders arriving at their shops and restaurants in preparation for the long day ahead.

Weber's watch now read 7.35 a.m. and he was pleased to have kept his prey in easy sight. Turning a corner into Irish Town the situation changed. Immediately ahead of him were several uniformed police officers standing outside a building on the left-hand side of the street. Two officers were putting crowd barriers in place, while a woman police officer talked to an elderly couple holding a map.

Weber saw Max and his accomplice walk on past the scene with an uninterrupted stride, rolling their cases behind them. His choice now was to get back onto Line Wall Road and run around to catch them further down the long central street, or simply drop his head and continue past the police officers. The first option brought with it the risk of losing the couple completely. Immediately dismissing it, Weber stuck to his course and walked on. He had no sooner passed the police officers when a voice called out.

'Rudi.'

At first the name did not register with him and he continued walking. The call came again.

'Hey, Rudi. It's us.'

To Weber's horror it was a voice he recognised. Pretending not to hear, he carried on. Again the voice came, but this time with footsteps hurrying behind him.

'Rudi. It's me, Eric.'

Before Weber could walk on further, a hand tapped his shoulder. There was no choice but to stop and engage.

'I'm sorry?' he said, turning to see the smiling elderly gentleman now at his side.

'Dah, dah!' the small bald and barrel-chested man said, triumphantly raising his arms like a showman. 'It's me. *Eric*. From the Madrid plane the other week. You haven't forgotten already, have you?'

'No, no, of course not. My apologies, I was miles away.'

'How's this for a coincidence, eh?' Eric said, his York-shire accent adding to the heartiness of his manner. 'Sheila and me were only talking about you yesterday. Saying what a very nice man you were. Come over, we're just getting directions from that very nice police lady.'

Before Weber could protest, the man had taken him by the arm and was propelling him towards his wife and the female police officer.

'It *is* him, Sheila,' Eric announced on reaching the pair. 'I told you it was.'

'Well, how's that for a coincidence, eh?' Sheila replied. 'Me and Eric were only talking about you yesterday.'

'He knows that, luv. I just told him.'

'We were saying what a very nice man you were.'

'I told him that too, luv.' Eric now turned to the police officer. 'You see, officer, we sat next to Rudi here on the flight from Madrid to Málaga. And now here we are in Gib. What are the chances of that, eh?'

'Quite a coincidence.'

'Yes, I just said that.'

'Well, you'll find Sacarello's Café just along the street there on the left,' the officer explained. 'Won't be open yet, but worth the wait if you want a good breakfast. Now if you'll excuse me, I must help my colleagues.'

As the officer moved towards the building, Eric called after her, 'Of course, off you go, luv. Thank you for your help.' He turned his full attention to Weber. 'She's got a busy morning ahead, by the sounds of it. That building there is the Greek Consulate and they're having a bit of a demonstration here or something. Forgot to ask what about.'

Weber smiled politely and began to back away.

'Well, it's been very … *nice* seeing you both again. Unfortunately, I have a meeting to get to, so I'm going to have to—'

'Busy, busy, busy. You young people, eh?' Eric replied. 'Mind you, look at Sheila and me. Up with the lark, that's us. Don't want to miss a thing on our Tour of Gib and España. Just Seville and Cordoba to go after this and then back to Ripon.'

'Yeah, well—'

'What are you doing afterwards, Rudi? We leave Gib tonight. Been staying on the Sunborn floating hotel, if you please.'

'Very posh,' Sheila added.

'Oh, yes. Nothing but the best for Mrs Bottomley, here. Five star all the way.'

'Why don't you join us for lunch, Rudi?' Sheila said. 'On board. The food's lovely. Very posh.'

'What a good idea, Sheila. How about it, Rudi? On us, of course. You can even go a la carte if you want to.'

'Yeah, that would be good,' Rudi said, backing further away from the couple. 'Let's do lunch.'

'That's the stuff. Shall we say twelve thirty? Sky Restaurant? The Sunborn.'

'You got it,' Weber called back. Turning from the couple he started to run up the street.

'Motherfuckers.' He spat out under his breath.

Watching the good-looking American running away from them along Irish Town, the Bottomleys raised their arms in a half wave.

'What a nice young man,' Sheila muttered.

'Yes,' Eric said. 'A very nice young man. A very nice young man, indeed.'

———

Reaching the crossing of Irish Town and Parliament Lane, Weber looked both left and right. There was no sign of his prey. Cursing once more, he continued along Irish Town, knowing that they might have entered any one of the buildings along the street and disappeared from sight. Losing them had been stupid, but unavoidable, considering the nearby police officers back at the Consulate. Weber just had to pray that Max and the woman were somewhere up ahead.

Reaching Sacarello's Café at the crossing of Irish Town and Tuckey's Lane, he once again checked to his left and right. There was still no sight of his prey along the lane. Nor was there any sign of them up ahead. Perhaps he'd missed them? Turning on his heels, Weber doubled back to check Parliament Lane once more.

———

A more thorough inspection of Tuckey's Lane would have proved beneficial to the American. In a disused doorway, several buildings up on the left-hand side of the lane, stood Max and Naida, their cases squeezed between them. From this position they could see the communal doorway to the Robbas' apartment building across the way. Here they would wait until the Robbas left for work. Once clear, they would enter the building, move up to the apartment and change the couple's nitrox mix diving cylinders for the lethal pure oxygen ones.

Naida checked her watch. If the Robbas left for work at the same time as the previous day – 7.55 a.m. – they had a ten-minute wait. The challenge now was to not draw attention to themselves. The lane was getting busier, with pedestrians and the occasional car or motorcycle passing by. Nobody seemed to be bothered by the presence of the couple waiting in the doorway. One passing old lady even wished them a good morning.

'And to you too,' Max replied. 'Have a nice day.'

The comment made Naida laugh.

'Must be the adrenalin rush,' she said, in reply to his look of surprise. 'We like this part, is that not true?'

Max had to admit that he'd come to like the set-up to their murders very much indeed, but before he could reply, Naida raised her hand to stop him. She'd seen something. Across the way, the Robbas both exited the building. They were early.

Loisa was first through the door. She stepped out onto the lane, her attention focused on stuffing some school papers into her handbag. Rahim followed her, his eyes fixed on the screen of his smart phone. Oblivious to their surroundings, they turned up the lane and headed towards Main Street.

Max and Naida watched them turn the corner, before leaving the doorway and crossing the lane. Reaching the main door to the Robbas' apartment building, they were surprised to see that it had not been properly shut – Rahim's concentration on his phone had worked in their favour. Pushing it open, Max and Naida picked up the cases and carried them inside, carefully closing the door behind them.

Back down the lane, as the internal lights of Sacarello's coffee shop came to life, Alex Weber turned the corner. Out of breath and severely out of patience, the realisation that Max and the woman had escaped him finally kicked in. His only choice was to now go back to the marina and await their return. The possibility that they might have left for good was something he was not prepared to countenance. His plan would shortly fall into place and this time he would not be distracted from seeing it through. Turning once more, Weber retraced his steps to Marina Bay, the colourful centre of Gibraltar Town coming ever more to life around him.

Chapter 38

GUS BRODERICK HAD PROMISED Massetti that he wouldn't return to work until the following day. But as the morning had gone on, his restlessness had increased. By the time he'd returned from his long walk on the Upper Rock, Broderick had convinced himself that popping into town via a quick visit to Police HQ would hardly do any harm. He'd even remember to smile a bit. Put everyone at their ease.

He wouldn't mention it to Cath. She'd gone to work, but had unexpectedly come back at lunchtime to pick up some files. Seeing her brother sitting out in the yard, she'd joined him for a moment.

'I haven't told the girls yet,' she said. 'It's Penny's day off and she's still in bed – of course. Let her know when she finally gets up. Daisy you can tell when she gets back from school. They don't understand what this has really been about, Gus, but they know that you've been unhappy. Just tell them that everything's okay.'

Cath reached over and kissed her brother on the top of his head. For once he didn't flinch with embarrassment.

'You've been through hell, Gus. But it's over now. Good news is good news and I think we should celebrate.'

Broderick gave his sister a look usually reserved for untrustworthy witnesses.

'Forget corned beef hash, I'll book a table at Roy's this evening,' Cath continued. 'Fish and chips in Casemates Square with the girls. I thought I'd invite Tamara too. What do you say?'

Gus couldn't think to say anything much. He simply raised his shoulders and grunted something Cath took to be an affirmative.

'Good,' she said, moving back to the house. 'Let the good times roll, eh?'

Two hours later, as Broderick walked through the gates of the RGP headquarters and into the inner courtyard, he finally allowed himself to feel free of the fears that had haunted him during the dark days of the previous week.

Before he could enter the building and head for the Incident Room, Broderick came face to face with Massetti heading in the other direction. She was clearly surprised to see him.

'Gus! What are you doing here?'

'Look, Harriet, I know I said that I'd wait—'

'We need to talk,' Massetti interrupted, looking behind her. 'But not here. Let's take a walk.'

Without waiting for him, she walked across the court-yard and out onto the street. Broderick followed.

'I just thought I'd pop in for a few minutes,' he said. 'Take a quick look at the state of play.'

'I'm afraid the state of play has changed, Gus. I've just had the second DNA results from Kemp.'

Crossing the road at the front of the police station, the

officers stopped by the low wall on the corner of Dockyard South Approach. A large ship was in for repair in the first of the three dry docks situated over the wall and below them. The noise of hammering and cutting loudly filled the air, but this did not seem to bother Massetti. It was clear that she had a preference to continue their conversation outside the precincts of the HQ. The fact that she was finding it difficult to look Broderick in the eye indicated a level of discomfort about the information she was about to share.

'This is difficult, Gus. As you know, the first DNA tests showed that the body was not that of your wife Helen.'

'Yes,' Broderick said, his answer sounding terser than he'd meant it to be.

'Does the name Gabrielle Johnson mean anything to you?'

The look on Broderick's face told Massetti that it did.

'Er … Yes … Gabby Johnson is the name of one of Helen's old friends.'

'I see,' Massetti said, Broderick's answer making the situation every bit as awkward as she'd imagined it might be. 'Kemp has somehow found a match with Johnson on the Austrian DNA database. She was apparently charged with an assault outside Vienna International Airport in March 2003 and had a sample taken. As such, there is no doubt that body found out near Eastern Beach is that of Gabrielle Johnson.'

Broderick's face froze in an expression of disbelief. Massetti continued.

'This clearly makes things rather more complicated. I'm afraid I have to ask if you knew her personally, Gus?'

Massetti's revelation appeared to have robbed Broderick of all breath. With shoulders sinking he fell back against the wall, seemingly unable to speak.

'I'm sorry. You understand that I have to ask.'

Broderick nodded his head and steadied himself.

'Gabby was an old school friend of Helen's. They'd grown up together.'

'What can you tell me about her?'

'Er … I don't know … Helen and Gabby were − very different people, I know that.'

'In what way?'

'Well, Gabby was a wildcard. A rebel. Always in trouble somewhere. Got chucked out of school early. Drugs were a problem for a while. She could never settle anywhere. Helen kept in touch with her over the years. Gave her money at times. Looked out for her. Felt sorry for her. Typical of Helen.'

'And you knew her?'

'Yes. She lived with us for a while. Just after Penny was born. She'd been homeless and drinking and we took her in for a few months.'

'And then?' Massetti prompted.

'Helen got her up and running, found her somewhere to live and she settled down a bit. About a year after she left us she called round to tell us that she was going travelling to India. Said she was going to find herself and finally deal with the shit that had hung about her over the years. That's what she said, anyway.'

'And did she? Find herself?

'I don't know. We gave her some money for the flight and never saw her again. Helen kept in contact. They wrote to each other, I remember.'

'The letter found on the body was one you had

addressed to Helen. Can you remember sending one of your letters to Gabrielle?'

Broderick tensed his eyes, trying to clear his confused mind.

'Yes. Yes, I did. Like all Helen's other friends, I would have written to Gabby enclosing a separate letter for Helen. I found an address for Gabby in India. Helen left behind her contacts book. Left behind everything, actually. It was Pondicherry, I seem to recall.'

'A letter sent care of Gabrielle that clearly never reached Helen,' Massetti said.

'Clearly.' Broderick stood up from the wall and took a deep breath. 'This doesn't look good, does it?'

'It complicates things, Gus. You know I'd be lying to pretend otherwise.'

'You're going to ask me next if I have any idea how Gabby ended up out there at the warehouse. The answer is simple, Harriet. I have absolutely no idea how or why she got there. The only thing I can tell you is that I had nothing to do with it. Nothing.'

Reaching out to touch her colleague's shoulder, Massetti could see the torment Broderick was suffering. She'd worked with him for over a decade and knew him to be, above all else, an honest man.

'I believe you, Gus. You know I do.'

'But that's not enough, is it, Harriet?'

'It certainly helps. And I won't be alone in my belief.'

'So what now?'

'You are going to have to go home and trust us to find out who did this.'

Broderick nodded his head in silence.

'We're going to sort this, Gus. Believe me.'

Turning from the wall, the two colleagues crossed the street. At the front of the police building they parted company. Massetti had an Incident Room full of murder detectives to brief; Broderick, a long walk home and a growing sense of dread in his gut.

Chapter 39

Finishing her interview at the courthouse with Jack Ocana, Sullivan headed out to the demolished warehouse site near Eastern Beach. A single officer stood guard at the gates and let her through to the dry and dusty site beyond. A crime scene tent remained over the trench where the body had been found, and beside it, spreading out for several metres around, lay the huge lumps of concrete and earth that had been displaced when the mechanical digger had fallen through the floor to reveal the grisly remains below.

Hidden amongst the disturbed ground works was the large cast iron manhole cover that Ocana had mentioned in his interview. It was still intact in a cement surround of broken flooring – even though it had been moved some distance from its original position in the warehouse floor. Bending down to inspect it at close range, Sullivan could see that the cover was heavy duty and would have needed some strength to have raised it – or get it to '*budge*', as Ocana had said. Sullivan paused for thought. Jack Ocana was a big man and should have been able to manage to lift the cover without much sweat. Reaching for her mobile, she called Calbot at HQ.

'Listen, I'm out at the warehouse site. I need you to get Forensics to pick up the under-floor access cover amongst the rubble out here.'

'Forensics must have checked it.'

'For prints and stuff, maybe. Jack Ocana told me earlier that he'd tried to lift it when he'd been called out to the warehouse back in 2005. He couldn't gain access to the area where the body would have been found.'

'He never mentioned that to me,' Calbot said.

'I know he didn't. Perhaps Forensics can tell us if the cover really was stuck or if Ocana is lying. You can also run a check on Alberto Amigo.'

'Who's he?'

'Another plumber. Last heard of in La Linea, but Gibraltarian. I'll fill you in when I get back.'

'On it,' Calbot said, ending the call.

For a moment Sullivan stopped and looked at the scene before her eyes. Above her, the east face of the Rock towered seemingly ever upwards, its majesty making everything seem insignificant by comparison. Except, perhaps, the view before her of the Mediterranean Sea, its waters spreading far into the distant horizon, its beauty a thing of wonder since the beginning of civilisation and beyond. And yet, surrounding her, in these few metres of dirt and rubble between rock and water, a woman had suffered a horrific fate. Murdered and forgotten, she had been left for dust. 'Eleanor' needed justice and Sullivan would move heaven and earth to get it for her. Whoever she was.

Sullivan's mobile buzzed. It was a text from Cath – *Hi*

Tamara. Fish and chips at Roy's at seven to cheer the innocent man up a little. Can you come?

Sullivan smiled. She was pleased to have been asked. Cath had a way of making her feel as though she was part of the family. It was a feeling she was unused to, but it made Sullivan feel good. Sending a text back in the affirmative, her mobile rang another tune. Massetti's name appeared on the screen. As Sullivan took the Chief Super's call, the smile left her face.

Chapter 40

ON HIS BALCONY overlooking the marina, Alex Weber paced back and forth. Max and the woman could be anywhere by now. The fact that they had been carrying suitcases only added to his agitation. It had occurred to him that they might be leaving the Rock, but he had dismissed the possibility, reasoning that they would hardly abandon the hugely expensive yacht moored below him. Besides which, he was certain that they had not yet accomplished what they had come to do. But as the minutes and hours of the morning ticked away, Weber had become less sure. He'd imagined that the couple were on their way to either prepare or carry out their next murder. Instead, they'd vanished and all he could do was await their return to the *Adrestia*.

Not for the first time, Weber noted that nothing about this job had gone quite to plan. He always seemed to be one step behind his prey, and as the events of the morning had proved, a step behind was one too many.

To his left, a British Airways Boeing hurtled down the

airport runway, before lifting into the cloudless azure skies above. If Max and his companion were on that flight, there was nothing he could do. The game was over. He would certainly have some explaining to do if he'd lost them after getting so close. The professional consequences would not be good. He relied on recommendations to earn a living, particularly as he was fairly new to the game. This last fact was something he had carefully disguised from his present employer, who believed him to be far more experienced than he was. A darker thought now presented itself. His failure might have consequences for his own safety. The historical whys and wherefores of the contract were something Weber knew nothing about, but protecting his own back was something he understood completely.

In spite of the sun on his face, the hitman felt a chill pass through him. Shuddering a little, he reached for his coffee on the balcony table. Such thoughts were unhelpful. Forcing himself to concentrate on a more positive outcome, he sipped the coffee. Patience would win the day. He would wait and they would surely return. From then on, he'd keep Max and the woman in his sights until the moment he killed them.

———

Exchanging the nitrox cylinders for the ones containing pure oxygen had been far easier than the couple had imagined. Max and Naida had already attached nitrox stickers to the replacement cylinders, and happily, both sets looked identical. After loading up the suitcases with the Robbas' set and placing the new cylinders in the bedroom cupboard, they had simply left the apartment and descended to the street. The next task was to dump the cases. Naida had found two large building skips the previous day that she thought appropriate. A large building was being renovated a few hundred yards away in College Lane. The skips were half full and positioned just off the lane. After checking that the coast was clear, they lifted their cases and hurled them into the containers, making a swift getaway up and onto Main Street.

The time was only 8.20 a.m. Loisa and Rahim Robba would not be diving until 6 p.m., so there was a lot of time for Max and Naida to kill before heading to the dive site at South Mole. As usual, Max intended to watch his plan come to completion. Afterwards, he and Naida would take the *Adrestia* back out to sea and sail for Morocco. But now they'd have breakfast at Jury's café near the courthouse, and then a spot of sightseeing beckoned. The cathedral-like subterranean wonders of St. Michael's cave would be fun, Max thought, followed by a trip out to Europa Point, perhaps. Then back to the yacht for a nice siesta, before setting out to visit the dive site at six. Max smiled as Naida placed her arm affectionately around his waist.

Chapter 41

THE NEWS that Broderick was now back in the cross hairs of the investigation completely poleaxed Sullivan. She could not comprehend this sudden reversal of fortune. Minutes before Massetti's call, the universe seemed to have been correcting itself. Broderick was in the clear and things were good with the world. Now, as the sun's afternoon light began to leave the eastern face of the Rock, Sullivan stood alone in the dry wasteland and stared out to sea. The woman who had been buried here was not Broderick's wife, but she was someone he knew. 'Eleanor' now had a name and an identity – Gabby Johnson. What's more, she'd once lived in the Broderick family home in London. Gabby was an old friend of Helen Broderick. A friend of Gus's too. How could that be?

For the first time, Sullivan allowed herself to imagine the impossible. Could Gus Broderick have had something to do with this after all? Might he even be the dead woman's killer? No sooner had these thoughts landed in her mind than Sullivan dismissed them. She would not believe it. That could not and would not be the outcome of the investigation. Pushing conjecture and doubt to one side, Sullivan knew it was now more urgent than ever to find the truth of the matter. Shaking her head clear, she allowed her lungs to fill with air. *Think rationally, not emotionally,* she told herself. *Just keep on keeping on.* Her immediate task was to track Alberto Amigo down and quickly. Calbot was on that job, but it might take time and the clock was running.

Scrolling through her mobile's contact list, she found Consuela Danaher's number.

'Hi, Tamara. How are things?' Consuela answered.

'Best of times and worst of times, I guess,' Sullivan said. 'Look, I need a favour. I know I shouldn't ask, but I need a fast track on an address for a Gibraltarian man supposedly resident in La Linea. Can you help me, Consuela?'

The line went silent for a moment.

'Consuela?'

'Yes, I will help, of course. I'm in enough shit with Pizarro. A little more won't make any difference. What do you need to know?'

'The name is Alberto Amigo.'

'Okay, Tamara. I'll check and see what we've got. I've just arrived in La Linea. A car we think was stolen by the fake Rudi Janson has been identified in the town. Shall we meet?'

'*Fake* Rudi Janson?'

'We seem to be in this together, Tamara, so I'm thinking you may as well know what's happening. Izi's boyfriend Rudi is not who he claimed to be.'

'Who is he then?'

That we don't know, but it's why I'm in La Linea looking at an old Fiat. You coming over?'

'Yes please, Consuela,' Sullivan said. 'I'll be straight over.'

━━━

Once again, Gus Broderick sat alone in the back yard of his home in the heights of the town. Rays of white sunlight shone through the large bougainvillea bush above his head, making a dancing pattern on the opposite wall that reminded him of fleeing fireflies at night. It was a welcome, but only momentary distraction from the painful thoughts that had once again possessed his mind.

To make matters worse, upon arriving back, he had seen the note Cath had left on the kitchen table reminding him of the fish and chip supper at Roy's in Casemates Square later. She'd already texted him an hour earlier about it and Broderick knew that a phone message was bound to follow if no reply from himself was forthcoming. Cath had long ago learned that steady persistence was the only method she could use to stop her brother wriggling out of social commitments. But how was he to tell her and the girls that things had gone back to where they had been before? And not just that. Things were now somehow much worse.

Reaching for a glass on the French dresser, Broderick poured himself a generous shot of his favourite Lagavulin, Isle of Islay sixteen-year-old single malt. The deep amber liquid slipped down his throat all too easily. It was always the first thing Broderick turned to in either triumph or despair. Now in the yard, sitting alone with his thoughts, his second glass of scotch sat on the table before him.

———

By mid-afternoon, Alex Weber's patience had reached its limits. For hours he had waited in vain for Max and his companion to return to the *Adrestia*, and his mind had exhausted every potential scenario regarding their possible whereabouts and the future moves he'd be forced to employ to track them down once again. The sense of help-lessness he felt was driving him insane. How had he let things get so sloppy? His job was to control events and carry out his contract. Why did everything seem to work against him? His only comfort had been the boat itself. Wherever they were and whatever they might be doing, the *Adrestia* remained moored in the marina and Weber's instinct stubbornly told him they would surely return to the vessel.

At 2.45 p.m. precisely, his faith was finally rewarded as he spied the couple strolling into the marina. They were holding hands as they headed for their yacht. The next thing he noticed was that neither had the suitcases they'd carried with them that morning. But what had been in them and where they might have gone, were things he couldn't worry about now. Although his relief at seeing the couple was immense, there was still far to go before his plan could be brought to completion. Putting his binocu-lars to his eyes, he watched as Max and the woman boarded the yacht and immediately went below deck, closing the doors behind them. Having witnessed a similar action the previous afternoon, Weber surmised that the couple would most likely be taking a siesta. At least they hadn't returned to continue their preparations to sail. Not yet, anyway.

Timing was all from here on in. If there was any sign of them leaving harbour, he would move immediately to stop them. He would have to synchronise things so as to meet up with the Moroccan boat in the Straits after dark, but that would still be achievable. It was a plan more complicated and open to chance than he would have wished, but circumstances permitted no other permutation. The couple had to disappear. That could not be executed on the Rock, so off the Rock they would all have to go.

Happy now that his prey were within striking distance, Weber settled down to focus on both the *Adrestia* and his watch.

Chapter 42

ALTHOUGH NOT YET RUSH HOUR, the long line of vehicles at the border crossing to Spain meant that Sullivan was forced to use her police status to jump the queues. The Spanish border officers knew her on sight, and a cursory glance at Sullivan's RGB badge allowed her to drive the old jeep over the crossing and onto Avenida Principe de Asturias and into La Linea. Crossing the duel carriageway, Sullivan headed north along Calle de Gibraltar, passing the fast food restaurants Burger King and McDonald's on her left and the unexpected greenery of the Parque Princesa Sofia on her right. Taking a left turn at the next junction, she saw – some fifty metres ahead – a Spanish police patrol car parked across the front of the sloping entrance to an underground car park.

Minutes later, Sullivan stood beside Consuela Danaher in the darkened subterranean car park looking at a battered green Fiat Panda. Forensics were already at work on the exterior.

'What's this about?' Sullivan asked.

'We think this may have been used by the motorcyclist who shot at you,' Consuela said.

Sullivan raised an eyebrow.

'But I thought he had a motorcycle.'

'He did. But he abandoned it in San Luis de Sabinillas after the shooting.'

'Really?'

'We got a break from CCTV footage taken near the Medical Centre in San Enrique. It caught his bike. Managed to pull a close up of the number plate. The bike turned up in a back street in San Luis. Officers discovered it when they went to investigate the theft of this Fiat from the same street on the same day.'

'Coincidence?' Sullivan asked.

'I don't think so. Do you?'

'No, not really. Let's just put it down to police work at its finest.'

'Thank you, Tamara.'

'But how did you track it to down here?'

'A bit of luck involved in that one,' Consuela admitted. 'The night security guard at this car park is married to a Guardia call controller. She'd mentioned the appeal for the car to him yesterday and last night he found it parked down here.'

'Now that is a coincidence.'

'Where would we be without them?'

'Gus Broderick would say, "*up shit creek without a paddle*." My default position.'

Consuela laughed. 'Now we both know that's not true.'

Sullivan shrugged her shoulders. 'Sure feels that way some days. But this is good news.'

'And I have better.' Consuela nodded to the entrance. 'Let's get out of here.'

The two officers headed for the ramp and towards the sunlight that flooded through the entrance above.

'We've just received some intelligence from Interpol,' Consuela continued. 'They've been cross referencing details from the Bernard and DuPont murders to see if any similarities arose from other cases Europe-wide.'

'Of course.' Sullivan nodded, knowing the procedures. 'And?'

'They think they've found one.'

'Great.'

'In fact, they think they may have two matches.'

'No kidding?'

'Not at all. I'm quite a serious person, as you know,' Consuela said, a slight twinkle in her eye.

'If you say so. So where and who?'

'A woman's body found weighted down in a harbour in Limassol, Cyprus, and another one found in the same condition at the bottom of her pool near Sidari in Corfu.'

'Wow.'

'And both within the last three months. If further details match, I think we have a serial killer operating across the breadth of the Mediterranean.'

Sullivan nodded her head as she and Consuela reached the top of the ramp and the sunlight hit their faces. 'That's a hell of a break.'

'I hope so.'

Sullivan now got to the question she'd been waiting to ask since she'd arrived. 'I know this is all hectic, but did you manage to—?'

'Get Amigo's address?'

Sullivan nodded once more.

'Of course. He lives further into town, in the Plaza de Toros.'

'Thank you, Consuela.'

'If you want to go now, I'll come with you.'

'Really?'

'I think it best, Tamara. I don't need to tell you that you have no jurisdiction over here.'

'I know, but I thought—'

'I know,' Consuela interrupted. 'But it might be best if I came along. I don't want either of us getting into trouble.'

'But what about here?' Sullivan said, looking down into the gloom of the car park.

Consuela smiled. 'They'll be a while yet. A loader is on its way to take the car to Málaga. Anyway, I won't be far away, will I?'

'Okay. Thank you.'

'Just follow me,' Consuela said, already moving past the patrol car to her own vehicle parked across the street.

'Sure,' Sullivan answered, following behind. 'How's your hand, by the way?'

'Better, thanks. How are your aches and pains?'

'Can't feel a thing,' Sullivan said, hoping that her slight limp had not been noticed. 'Top of the world, really.'

———

It was a five-minute drive north to the Plaza de Toros and the La Linea de la Concepcion bullring. The whitewashed and circular arena stood at the centre of the plaza, its high walls almost castle-like in their defiance of those who believed that its bloodthirsty entertainments were a thing best consigned to history.

Sullivan and Consuela drove their cars into the plaza, circling the stadium before turning onto Calle Alemania and coming to a halt opposite the northern door of the bullring. The door was painted dark red, but someone had sprayed graffiti across its centre. The single word in black paint stood out in silent protest –*ABOLICION*.

The address Consuela possessed for Amigo had no number, just the name of the house – La Parador. Leaving their cars, the detectives hit the pavement, following the line of neglected one-storey homes – some derelict and with their windows bricked up – until they reached a small mauve-coloured end terrace building with a hand-painted sign next to the door announcing the name they were looking for.

'Doesn't look much like a *parador*,' Sullivan said, knocking on the door with a sharp rat-a-tat.

'I think they may mean it with some irony, no?'

'Who knows? The inside might be a palace.'

'I think you are a little over-optimistic, my friend,' Consuela said, grinning.

After a few moments with no response, Sullivan knocked once more.

'I'm afraid I may have to leave you here to wait,' Consuela said.

Stepping back from the door, Sullivan looked further along the street. A few metres away, an elderly man carrying two heavily laden carrier bags turned the corner. Seeing the two women ahead of him, the man froze momentarily before turning on his heels and heading back around the corner.

'Did you see that?' Sullivan asked.

'Yes, I did,' Consuela replied, following Sullivan along the sidewalk in the direction the man had gone. Turning the corner, they witnessed him trying to run. Hampered by his bags and in no fit condition for speed, he was making heavy going of his effort.

'Alberto Amigo? Police.'

Sullivan had only guessed that it might be her man, but as he continued to attempt an escape, she knew her instinct had been correct.

To get away, Amigo released his grip on his carrier bags, allowing them to fall to the ground. There was no real chance of escape, but he desperately needed to try. He'd been dreading this for years: the nightmare that haunted both his sleeping and waking hours. Judgement had come, and it was every bit as terrifying as he had feared.

Glancing round, Amigo saw the two women giving chase. What he could not see was the can of cheap kidney beans that had rolled from one of his bags onto the pavement ahead of him. As Amigo's foot came down upon the small item of grocery, his ankle twisted and his knee buckled, causing him to lose all balance and tumble to the ground.

Sullivan and Consuela were with him in moments. Checking that he was fully conscious and not in any pain, the policewomen helped him slowly to his feet.

'Are you certain you are in no pain? You may need a doctor,' Sullivan said.

'No, no, no. *Warraso*. I fell, but I'm good. No fuss. I need to go home. Please.'

'You are Alberto Amigo, *sí?*' Consuela asked the man.

'Yes,' Amigo said, his eyes looking off into the distance.

'I am Inspector Danaher of the Cuerpo Nacional.'

'And I'm Detective Sergeant Sullivan of the Royal Gibraltar Police. I need to ask you some questions.'

'Yes,' the man said.

'It's in connection with a body discovered in Gibraltar.'

'I know,' Amigo said. 'The English woman?'

Avoiding an answer, Sullivan looked Amigo in the eye.

'It's been a long time,' he said. 'I'd hoped you'd never come.'

Alberto Amigo sat in the front passenger seat of the ancient Mitsubishi Shogun as Tamara Sullivan drove across the Gibraltar International Airport runway on her way to Police HQ. In Amigo's hands was clasped the passport he had nervously shown the officers as they'd passed through the customs checks at the border.

Before this, in La Linea, Sullivan and Consuela had accompanied the man back to his small rented home next to the bullring. The inside of the dwelling was a mess. Shabby furniture and a worn Moroccan-style rug covered in cigarette butts were crammed into the tiny front sitting room. A smell of damp and old frying fat emanated from the kitchen next to it.

'How long have you lived here?' Sullivan asked.

'Six years. Since my wife chucked me out,' Amigo replied, with little self-pity in his tone.

'I'll need you to come over to Gib,' Sullivan said. 'Are you willing to accompany me?'

Amigo nodded his head.

'Inspector Danaher here is witness to your allowing me to escort you over the border to answer questions. Is that understood?'

Once again, Amigo nodded. Minutes later, the officers led him to the Shogun and sat him in the front seat. Closing the passenger door, Sullivan turned to Consuela.

'Thank you for this. I owe you.'

'It's not by the book and you might have difficulty if Amigo's lawyer gets picky about how you got him over to the Rock, but I'll back you up.'

'Nothing ventured, nothing gained.'

'Sometimes we venture a lot and still get nothing. Apart from being yelled at from above. Which reminds me, I need to get back before Pizarro kicks off.'

'A regular occurrence, is it?'

'Very much a part of his management style,' Consuela said with a shrug. 'Good luck, Tamara. Hope Amigo helps.'

As Consuela moved towards her parked car, Sullivan considered how fortunate she and Consuela's instant friendship was proving. *Sometimes it takes an amiga to find an Amigo,* she thought, choosing not to dwell on the poor quality of her joke. That Amigo had freely agreed to come with her was a good sign. As she jumped into the driver's seat, Sullivan hoped that this positive spell would continue.

Chapter 43

INTERVIEW ROOM 2 on the ground floor of the RGP HQ was typical of police interview rooms anywhere in the world. A single table occupied its centre with chairs either side of it. The room's bare walls and concrete floors were unadorned. A tape recorder on the table and a camera set high on the wall were the only other objects in the room upon which a person might rest an eye.

Sullivan's arrival with Alberto Amigo had caused quite a stir at New Mole Parade. Sergeant Aldarino had immediately got hold of Massetti, who promptly asked Sullivan to explain exactly what she was doing.

'Amigo's agreed to answer questions about Gabby Johnson's death.'

'Did he actually use her name?' Massetti asked.

'No. He called her the English woman.'

'Where did you find him, Sullivan?'

'Living in La Linea.'

'And he's here willingly?'

Sullivan nodded her head.

'Doesn't even want a lawyer present. Says he just wants to talk.'

'I see.' Massetti said. 'Get on with it then. I'll listen in.'

———

'She told me her name was Gabby.'

Sullivan and Calbot looked across the interview table at Amigo. No question had been asked, but Amigo had launched straight in anyway. The man continued, apparently wishing to unburden himself of his story without interruption from the detectives who had summoned him.

'I was driving back to Gib from Cádiz – I'd gone to fix something for my wife's aunt who lived there. She'd been going on about it for days. My wife. On and on. So, I took an afternoon off from the warehouse site I was working on and drove over.'

'Which warehouse site?'

'The one near Eastern Beach.'

'Run by Line Wall Logistics?' Sullivan asked.

'Yes. Those.'

'Do you remember the date?'

'Yes. It was July 8th.'

'2005?'

'Yes. Anyway, I was driving back from Cádiz. I'd reached the main beach road at Tarifa when I saw her. A blonde woman hitching a lift. She was not a whore. I could see straight away. I was going to drive on, but I stopped. I don't know why. I wish I never had, but it's what happened.'

Sullivan kept her eyes focused on Amigo, hoping her silence would add more pressure for him to talk. Not that he was having any trouble recalling the events of that distant summer. Stopping only to roll his neck and shoulders to relieve the stress-induced pain he was feeling, Amigo continued.

'She said she needed to get to Gibraltar. I said it was where I was going, so she got into my van. She seemed nervous because she could not stop talking. She told me her name. Said she was running away from someone. She told me that the person would kill her if he found her. She was scared and needed to get to Gib. Told me she had a friend there who would help her.'

Amigo stopped for a moment. Sullivan and Calbot remained silent. When she had first seen Amigo, Sullivan had thought him to be an elderly man. His teeth were rotten, his skin heavily lined and his hair bedraggled and unkempt. The man was in his fifties, but something had led to his premature ageing, and Sullivan was certain she was about to discover what that something was. Amigo continued.

'I told her I would take her to the Rock. She was so grateful. She thanked me again and again, with tears rolling down her face. She was in a terrible way. I felt sorry for her. Anyone would have done as I did. No?'

Neither detective responded.

'And so I drove on. After the tears she became very happy. Talking all the way. She was English, she told me, and had been travelling for years. India, Thailand, Australia, everywhere. She told me she was part of a group of people who lived together. A spiritual group, she said, but it had all gone wrong and she had to get away. I told her I understood, but I don't think I did.'

Sullivan noticed that Amigo had begun to wring his

hands in a constant nervous motion. His mind, however, was focused elsewhere.

'As I drove into La Linea I told her we would need our passports at the border. That's when things went wrong. She told me she had no passport. Been forced to leave it behind. And then, *se armo un zapatiesto*, all hell broke loose. She was hysterical. Crying, punching my arm. I pulled over at the side of the road to try to calm her. I didn't know what to do, but I promised I would help. She was in real pain.'

'So, what did you do?' Sullivan asked.

'I told her to get into the back of my van. I could cover her in worksheets and then I would drive her through the border crossing. I told her that the guards on both sides all knew me and never stopped my van. Which was true. One or two were old school friends.'

'And did she do as you suggested?' Calbot asked.

'Yes. She calmed down, and I drove to a quiet street and she got in the back of the van and I covered her with sheets and told her to keep silent. Once we reached a safe place on the Rock, I said I'd get her out and she could then find her friend.'

'What happened next, Alberto?' Sullivan asked gently.

'We crossed the border. I was waved through like always. No problem. But then as I drove on towards town, there *was* a problem. I saw that a police car was behind me. I panicked. I knew I couldn't just stop and drop Gabby in the street. I had to think quickly. That's when I went to the warehouses at Eastern Beach.'

'And that's what you did?' Sullivan said, sensing that the end of Amigo's story was approaching.

'It was dark now. I got to the warehouse and old Jerry

opened the gates. I'd had to call him. He was a little deaf and pretty blind, you know, and he was watching a football match on his TV in his shed. I'd had to shout and rattle the gates to get him to come out. I told Jerry I was picking up equipment I'd left that morning. He opened the gates and I drove through and over to the second warehouse on the far side of the site. My plan was to let Gabby out over there. She could then sit up front in the van with me and duck down as I drove back out. I would then drop her at a good place in town. It was simple.'

'What happened, Alberto?'

'I opened the doors of the van and she got out. It was dark out there and even though I told her it was fine, she panicked. She was hysterical again. I tried to calm her, but she wouldn't listen. Then she started to shout out.'

Amigo stopped. Remembering was proving too much for the man. His mouth opened and closed several times, but words would not come out.

'Tell us, Alberto. What did you do next?' Sullivan asked.

'I didn't kill her,' Amigo said, his voice pitching higher and his breathing becoming more intense. 'I know you think I did, but please believe me. I didn't kill that woman.'

'What did happen then?'

Alberto Amigo's answer was not the one Sullivan had expected.

Chapter 44

ON HIS BALCONY overlooking the marina, Alex Weber checked his watch. It read 17.05. Over two hours had passed since Max and the woman had disappeared below deck on the *Adrestia* below. Despite the shade provided by the balcony's parasol, Weber had struggled with the afternoon heat. A couple of times he had accidently nodded off. It had only been for a few seconds on both occasions, but the panic he'd experienced at the thought of missing the couple leaving the yacht had made him focus with an even grimmer determination on the job in hand.

As his watch showed 17.09, the sight of Max and his accomplice rewarded Weber's patience as they both stepped up onto the deck of the yacht. They immediately left the *Adrestia* and started to move along the pontoon walkway in the direction of Ocean Village. By the time they had passed the Sunborn floating hotel and turned right onto the main promenade, Weber was only metres behind them.

During the long afternoon wait, he had found time to

consider another plan to catch the couple unawares. Stopping at the end of the pontoon walkway, Weber watched as they walked on ahead and into the crowds promenading through the marina village. Once Max and the woman were out of sight, Weber turned right and followed the walkway to where the *Adrestia* was moored. His plan now to board the yacht, gain entry to the cabins below and then await the couple's return. Once they were on board he would surprise the two of them and set sail for the Straits. As with his first plan, lying in wait for his targets had its own risks, but the task of completing his contract on the couple was now severely limited by lack of time and opportunity.

As he approached the mooring, Weber checked the boats that surrounded the *Adrestia*. Most were uninhabited, but one or two of them had people on board, going about their sailors' business or sitting and enjoying the late afternoon sun. None of them appeared interested in the tall, dark-haired man who boarded the neighbouring yacht and disappeared out of sight below its deck.

Happily for Weber, the cabin door was unlocked, and after descending into the darkened interior, he quickly sized up the location. He decided on a precise plan of action and then placed his Ruger automatic pistol on the table beside him. The gun's integrated suppressor would be a vital element in containing sound levels if things got a little out of hand.

It was now just a waiting game. A deadly one.

It had taken Max and Naida the best part of half an hour to reach their destination at the Queensway Quay Marina. It took a further ten minutes for them to take possession of the RIB they had hired and take to the waters of the harbour. This course of action would give them the best view of the dive that was about to take place on the other side of the harbour on the South Mole – the imposing breakwater that separated the calm waters of Gibraltar Harbour from the stronger currents of the Bay.

The couple's timing was precise. As they sat in the small motorboat, they could see that several divers were on the South Mole and boarding a boat that would take them the short distance out to the waters above the wreck of the SS *Rosslyn*. The 3,600-ton steamer had sunk off the South Mole in 1916 and had lain on the sandy bottom of the bay beneath twenty-three metres of water ever since.

From his viewpoint, Max could just about make out the figures of Loisa and Rahim Robba as they took their places amongst their fellow divers. Only he and Naida knew that the tanks attached to the Robbas' backs were filled with pure oxygen, not the nitrox mix displayed on the equipment's false labels.

Max, as always, was eager to see his work in action. Although he would not be able to see the distress below the waters, he needed to be nearby to be sure they had achieved the couple's murder. Being afloat nearby offered the best chance for him to witness the Robbas' last ever dive together. Any chance of the couple surviving the dive was comfortingly slim. Once Max knew they were dead, he and Naida would return to the *Adrestia* and prepare the yacht for a dawn sailing on the following morning.

———

Across the harbour, Loisa and Rahim were the last to board the waiting boat, which was carrying seven fellow divers and two crew. The last hour had been a mad rush for them both. Loisa had run late at the school, and the knock-on effect had caused them to miss a lift down to the harbour. The tension had led to an uncharacteristic squabble between the pair as they gathered their equipment and rushed from the apartment in search of a taxi to make the journey to the South Mole. Once there, they had been forced to change quickly and board the boat, which was already full of their diving companions.

Minutes later, the boat pulled away from the South Mole and headed towards the harbour entrance. From here the ride became bumpier as the party left the calm waters of Gibraltar Harbour and hit the incoming force of the sea. Taking an immediate left, the boat steered a course along the outer walls of the Mole towards the wreck site a few minutes away to the south.

———

Max and Naida followed the diving expedition at a respectable speed. As Max opened the throttle on the RIB's outboard motor, Naida noticed a look on his face she had seen several times over the previous months. It was an expression even more familiar to her from her childhood. Often her father would strap his hunting rifle to his shoulder and take his young daughter hunting with him. Where they lived, it would mainly be for mouflon and red deer, but several times he had taken her further into the

Croatian countryside in search of wild boar and European brown bear. Even at that early age, she had noticed the change in her father's manner and expression as a kill approached. It was the look her lover now possessed. The look of the hunter.

The divers were to go down to the SS *Rosslyn* in pairs. This was usual with the group – each separate couple comprising one diver with more experience than the other. Loisa and Rahim had both been diving for eleven months, but the fact that her diving partner, Mateus, was someone she could rely on in the event of any problem arising, comforted Loisa. Rahim was impatient to get on, so after a hurried routine pre-dive check, he and his partner, Ali, began their dive ahead of Loisa.

Rahim had dived the wreck twice before and was hoping to enjoy once again the haunting site of the sunken vessel and its myriad inhabitants of octopi, moray eel and sunfish. The waters offered a good ten metres plus of visibility on this summer's evening, and as he and his diving partner moved down towards the twisted, dark remains of the *Rosslyn*, Rahim marvelled at the sheer beauty of his surroundings. Despite an eagerness to get to the wreck as quickly as possible, both divers moved steadily downwards in an unhurried manner.

It was on reaching a depth of twenty metres that things started to go wrong for Rahim. He began to have problems with his vision. There was a blurring, which he put down to trouble with his face-mask. This was swiftly followed by an uncontrollable twitching of the muscles of his face.

Turning to Ali, he signalled that something was not right. Swimming closer to him, Ali could see that Rahim's breathing was becoming laboured. What she couldn't make out was that Rahim was now feeling nauseous and had been overtaken by a sudden sense of light-headedness. Taking her diving companion by the arm, she pulled him upwards towards the surface. Knowing she could not handle her increasingly agitated partner alone, Ali did her best to signal to the divers above her for help. Within a minute they were with her and together the three divers slowly and with great difficulty brought the fast-deteriorating Rahim to the water's surface.

On the boat, Loisa and Mateus were about to start their dive when the waters beside them broke in a frenzy of activity and the emergency became clear. Loisa could not make out what was happening. Only the call from the crewman gave her the information she needed.

'Diver in difficulties. Make room to bring him on board,' the crewman yelled, reaching over the boat to help.

Even then, it didn't register to Loisa that it was her husband in distress in the water. At the moment the truth finally became clear, Loisa froze in panic. She could feel the blood draining from her face, and an attempted cry stuck in her throat as the shock of what was happening momentarily paralysed her with fear.

'We still have divers below. We can't leave them,' the second crewman yelled. 'I've called for help. Rescue services are launching.'

A hundred metres away on their RIB, Max and Naida looked across at the evolving crisis. Rahim had fallen victim to the oxygen toxicity as planned and the likelihood of saving him was remote. But something had gone wrong. Rahim had been brought to the surface before his wife had entered the water to begin her own fatal dive. Naida could see that the expression on Max's face had now changed to one of fury.

'Shit!' he screamed. 'Shit, shit, shit!'

Naida knew better than to speak to Max. He had no mechanism available to him to deal with defeat. With negativity of any kind, in fact. He was like a child. His mental illness severely exacerbated his responses, but Naida had long realised that his reactions came from somewhere buried much deeper in his past. Somehow, she would talk him down; she always did. But for now, it was safer to remain silent and let him rage alone.

Chapter 45

'I KNOW you think I did, but please believe me. I didn't kill that woman.'

'Then who did, Alberto?' Sullivan asked.

The man couldn't speak, his eyes flickering from side to side as he tried to process the horrific memories from so long ago. Taking a deep breath, he continued.

'She fell. Backwards. She thought I was going to touch her.'

'And were you?' Calbot asked.

'Yes, but just to stop her from shouting. Not to hurt her. I never meant to hurt her.'

'Then how did she die, Alberto?' Sullivan pressed.

'Her head. She moved backwards. Quickly. She lost her balance and fell back onto the ground. Her head hit a rock, and she stopped. No sound. No breathing. Just blood. In her hair. Her neck. It happened so quickly.'

'And what did you do, Alberto?'

'I panicked. I didn't know what to do. I was in shock, you know?'

'What did you do?'

'Her eyes were open. Just staring. I knew she was dead for sure. I knew I should take her to the hospital at least, but then what would I say? No one would believe me. I had picked her up and smuggled her over the border and then she died. Who would believe it was all an accident? I meant her no harm. I only tried to help her. Please say you believe me.'

Sullivan's expression did not convey her thoughts. With Massetti watching everything via the camera set high on the interview room wall, she knew there could be no margin for error. Her guide, as ever, was the voice of Broderick in her mind.

'Just ask the questions and listen to the answers. Follow where the answers take you, but give nothing away. Nothing.'

'What did you do, Alberto?'

'I hid her. There was a ventilation duct running below the floor of the warehouse. There'd been plans to use it to run cables and pipes for services, but the builders had found better ways to do that. So it was just there, you know. It was all I could think of. I pulled up the cover and put her down there. It was terrible. I cried, you know, but there was nothing else I could do.'

'Just take your time,' Calbot told the man.

'I can't. I need to tell you,' Amigo said, his hands gripping the side of the table as he rocked gently back and forth. 'There was just enough space for her down there. In the duct. And I left her. It was horrible. No one should end in such a way.'

'And then?'

'I had to replace the cover, but I knew somebody could lift it and find her, so I got the soldering equipment I had at the warehouse and bonded the top of the cover to the entrance. It would seal the top and make it impossible to open. That is what I thought.'

'And you were nearly right,' Sullivan said.

'Then I left the site and never went back. What happened that night, what I did … it has haunted me every day. My life has been worthless since that time. I should not have done what I did, but I did not kill her. Please. I did not.'

Sullivan and Calbot looked on as Amigo's shoulders heaved and tears poured down his cheeks. His pain was horribly real and raw, but then so had been the death and burial of Gabby Johnson. There was a price to pay for what had happened on that night, and both detectives knew that, despite his grief, Amigo's account had yet to be fully paid.

'So, what do you think?'

Massetti stood beside the large screen in the monitoring room, addressing her question to both Sullivan and Calbot. The detectives had wound up the interview with Amigo minutes before, and Sullivan was keen to get the go ahead to tell Broderick that he was off the hook.

'My instinct says he's telling the truth, ma'am. A good turn that went tragically wrong,' Sullivan said. 'His description of Gabby Johnson cracking her head on a rock will have to be examined by Portillo, but in the light of what we already know, it sounds like a convincing explanation of her death.'

'I'd concur with that, ma'am,' Calbot added.

'Well, we'll see,' Massetti said, moving to the door. 'One thing seems clear: Amigo was solely involved in Johnson's death, which happily leads me to conclude that Chief Inspector Gus Broderick had nothing to do with it. Our colleague, as we all knew, is entirely innocent of any suspicion.'

'Brilliant,' Calbot said.

'I think it appropriate that you break the news to him, Tamara,' Massetti said. 'You did the spade work.'

'I'm supposed to be having a fish and chip supper with him and his family in half an hour,' Sullivan said, checking her watch. 'I thought they'd cancel, but I've had no word. I'd like to tell him in person, ma'am. We still have to remember that he knew Gabby Johnson as a friend.'

'Sensitive to the end, Sullivan. Well done,' Massetti responded as she left the room. 'Enjoy your cod and chips.'

'Thank you, ma'am.'

'And have a pickled onion on me, Sarg,' Calbot said, following his superior. 'I'll square it cash-wise with you in the morning.'

'And pigs will fly, John Calbot,' Sullivan called after her colleague with a laugh.

Turning to the monitor, she saw the black and white images of Alberto Amigo being escorted from the interview room to the cells. The forlorn and dishevelled man cut a pathetic figure as he shuffled from the room, his head bowed and his wrists handcuffed. *Sometimes everyone loses*, Sullivan thought as she switched the screen to black.

Chapter 46

MAX AND NAIDA arrived back at the *Adrestia* aboard their hired RIB. They'd arranged to leave it at the mooring after they'd sailed that night, with the hire company picking the boat up the following day.

The sound of the couple's arrival and subsequent boarding of the yacht had surprised the waiting Weber below deck. Expecting them to return on foot, Weber had to adapt quickly to their sudden appearance by water.

Checking his gun, he moved to a position at the side of the steps that led down from the deck above. He did not have long to wait for his first victim to descend. Above Weber, the doors opened and light flooded into the large saloon and galley area. Seconds later the woman climbed below. From his hiding place behind her, Weber sprang forward, holding her tightly around the neck, covering her mouth with his hand and ramming the end of his Ruger pistol forcefully into her back.

'Fight me and you're dead. Do you understand?' Weber hissed in her ear. To his surprise, the woman did not try to struggle or cry out. All he had to do now was to wait for Max to descend and he would have them both. A bullet through the woman's head and two or three aimed at Max would complete the first part of the plan. Weber would then sail to meet his Moroccan associates, scuttle the *Adrestia* and head for Tangier, contract completed.

'Naida? I need a drink,' Max's voice came from the deck, his tone urgent and irritable. '*Naida?*'

Looking up, Weber now saw Max's foot take the first step down. Seeing it too, Naida dropped her centre of gravity and pushed back with all her strength. The move caught Weber by surprise, propelling him back onto the saloon floor and sending his gun flying from his hand across the cabin. Springing forward to the bottom of the steps, Naida screamed up to Max.

'Run. Go. Go!'

Without a moment's hesitation, Max disappeared from sight. Taking her chance, Naida started up the steps towards the deck. Behind her, Weber had rolled across the floor and retrieved his Ruger. As Naida reached the top of the steps, the suppressed crack of his gun sent a bullet upwards, piercing into the woman's upper body and sending her flying forward with an agonised scream onto the deck of the *Adrestia* above.

Charging up the steps, with his gun in hand, Weber saw the splayed body of the woman on the deck, blood pooling around her. Looking to the marina walkway, he could also see Max running flat out with a fifty-metre advantage on him. To his horror, Weber then saw something else.

The commotion had drawn the attention of those on other boats in the marina. Across the connecting water, a couple stood on a yacht, staring in disbelief at the sight they were witnessing. Weber could not think about that now. He had to focus on Max. Replacing his gun in his jacket, Weber leaped from the *Adrestia* and hit the pontoon walkway at speed. He had nearly two decades on the man he was chasing, but he'd need every bit of that younger strength to stop Max making good his escape.

Across town at the Royal Gibraltar Police HQ calls began to come in. Something terrifying was taking place in Ocean Village and help was urgently needed.

Sullivan was late for supper in Casemates Square by ten minutes. She'd left Police HQ just before 19.00 and parked the Mitsubishi off Line Wall Road five minutes later.

The early evening sun was still hot as she entered the crowded square and made her way past the many restaurants, bars and kiosks that surrounded the grand gateway to Main Street and Gibraltar's town centre. The bustle of tourists flocking beneath the multi-coloured table canopies, was only slightly at odds with the imposing arches and converted Victorian barracks that surrounded them. Her objective was in clear sight – Roy's Fish and Chip Restaurant, the favoured eating place for the Broderick family and, since her arrival on the Rock, for Sullivan as well.

Cath, Gus and his daughters were sitting at their usual outside table. The girls were laughing, and the sight of this made Sullivan suspect that perhaps Broderick had not passed on the ominous news he had received earlier. Although she herself brought good news, Sullivan decided not to make a big announcement straight away.

Daisy Broderick was the first to see her approaching,

and leaped from her seat to greet her. 'Tamara!' she yelled, hugging Sullivan and pulling her towards the restaurant at the same time.

Arriving at the table to kisses from Cath and Penny and a firm handshake from Broderick, Sullivan sat and joined the party. After a few minutes it became clear that her instinct had been correct. As his family relaxed and joked, Broderick seemed tense and unable to join in. Sullivan had to admit that her boss was not the most relaxed of people anyway, but she knew him well enough to spot a deeper unease.

'Sorry to be a party pooper,' she finally said, 'but I'm afraid I will have to take my Guv'nor here to one side. Two minutes' work talk and we'll be back for the fun, okay?'

'Of course,' Cath said. 'But two minutes only. This is a celebration.'

As Sullivan and Broderick stepped away from the table, it was clear that Broderick was far from happy at the interruption. She could also smell whisky on his breath, which she guessed had not been drunk in a celebratory mood.

'Look, I haven't told them, Sullivan, and I don't want you to. They deserve one night of happiness before all hell breaks loose. Do you understand?'

'I understand one thing, sir, and that's that you don't have to worry about it any more. We've discovered how Gabby died, and as we all knew, you had nothing to do with it.'

Broderick stood open-mouthed for a moment, struggling to take in Sullivan's words.

'You're in the clear, Guv,' Sullivan continued. 'It was an accident by the look of things. An accident with complications, but I'll tell you more about that after the celebrations.'

Back at the table, Cath looked across to where the two police officers were standing. To her great surprise, she saw her brother reach over and give Sullivan a huge bear hug. For a moment it looked as though he was squeezing the very life out of her, but thankfully Sullivan was laughing and seemed delighted by the gesture. *Well, well, well,* Cath thought to herself, a smile playing on her lips. *That doesn't look like police business to me.*

Returning to the table, Sullivan and Broderick were greeted with applause by the girls and menus by Cath. As Broderick reached for his beer, Sullivan noticed how the years seemed to have suddenly dropped from his face. She wasn't used to seeing Gus Broderick smile, but at this moment he seemed to be able to do nothing else. For a few seconds, Sullivan allowed herself to feel at one with the world. Life could be sweet, and here at this table was the proof.

The moment was soon broken by the sudden wail of police and ambulance sirens. They were coming from the west of the square and sounded as if they were heading for the marina. All conversations stopped.

'That sounds like a comprehensive response to something,' Broderick said, taking out his mobile phone to check for messages.

'I hope it won't spoil the fun,' Cath said, years of experience telling her it probably would.

Then another noise joined the cacophony. People were shouting in the square. Standing to see what the commotion could be, Sullivan saw a tall, bearded man running through the centre of Casemates. He was pushing people out of his way, looking back over his shoulder, and appeared to be running from something. Looking in the same direction as the man had glanced, Sullivan saw his pursuer. Running from the arches of the Grand Casemates Gates was a man Sullivan instantly recognised from Izi Bernard's selfie photograph. Weaving his way across the square at speed, his eyes firmly fixed on the bearded man, was Rudi Janson. But Sullivan knew he wasn't the real Janson, but an imposter. Before Cath or Broderick could utter another word, Sullivan ran from the table.

———

A large party of South Korean tourists had entered Casemates Square from the southerly direction of Main Street. Max had run from the square just seconds before they arrived, but for Weber, the mass of over fifty holidaymakers presented a wall of bodies to weave through. This slowed him down, and he got through to the main thoroughfare to find no Max. He'd lost sight of him for a matter of seconds, but it was enough to leave Weber stranded at the junction of several streets and passages and desperately searching for the fleeing man. A decision had to be made.

To his left, the narrow passageway of Lynch's Lane would have been Weber's choice of escape if he'd been in Max's shoes, so he sprinted towards that. However, once he had run halfway up the steps of the lane, Weber realised that he was approaching a dead end and there was no sign of Max. Turning back towards Casemates and cursing his bad luck, Weber now saw a familiar face appear through crowds on Main Street. Tamara Sullivan saw him too, and they locked eyes. Sullivan called to him.

'Police!'

For a moment, Weber's mind turned to a frenzied mush. *What the fuck am I going to do now?*

Moving towards the panic-stricken man, Sullivan saw him dive into Turnbull's Lane to his left and disappear from view. Sullivan was running now; the hip pain she was experiencing was agony, but her infirmity was not affecting her speed. She knew the lane ran for only a short distance before rounding a corner to turn onto Main Street. As she raced into Turnbull's she could see that the man was halfway along the lane and running for dear life. Continuing the chase, it surprised Sullivan to see him suddenly stop and turn towards her.

Taking out a gun, he raised his arm and took aim. The image was one Sullivan instantly remembered. The tall figure who now meant to kill her was definitely the same man who'd shot at her on the dirt road out at San Enrique. As he squeezed the trigger of his gun, Sullivan dived to the side of the lane, falling into a doorway.

The two .22 low velocity rounds ricocheted off the stone archway as Sullivan pressed herself back against the door, hoping to limit his target. Further down the lane, Weber backed away, his gun still aimed towards the hidden police woman. Nearing the turn in the lane, he swivelled on his heels and ran around the corner, hoping to make good his escape. The punch that now connected with his jaw seemed to come out of nowhere. The ferocity of its force sent Weber reeling backwards, his gun flying from his hands for the second time that day and landing metres away against the high flagstone curb of the lane.

Back along Turnbull's, Sullivan had dared to look out from the doorway. Shocked to see the man now sprawled and unmoving on the ground at the end of the lane, she moved quickly from her protected spot and ran to the corner. The nearer she got, the more it became clear that the man was unconscious. As she reached the corner and looked around it, Sullivan was doubly shocked to find Gus Broderick leaning against a wall, sweat dripping from his face and his breathing heavily laboured. He'd seen Sullivan give chase back at Lynch's Lane and decided to carry on along Main Street, hoping to cut the man off. He'd succeeded, but it had come at a cost. Neither his pace nor his knees were what they once had been. Reaching for her mobile to call for back-up, all Sullivan could think to say to her boss was, 'Thanks for that.'

'You're welcome,' Broderick said, finally regaining breath. 'And before I go into a full cardiac arrest, perhaps you'd have the grace to tell me what the fuck's going on here?'

Chapter 47

SOMEHOW, Max had found his way back to the Ocean Marina Village. After running from Casemates Square, he'd ducked into the crowded Irish pub, The Venture Inn. Hiding among the pint-drinking customers, thronging the pub to watch an early evening football match on the bar's TV screens, Max waited until he judged the coast outside to be clear. Moving swiftly across Main Street, he'd headed down Cooperage Lane and passed the large Debenham's store on his way to the marina. The shock of finding himself the target of a killer was sinking in. He could feel his heart pumping through his chest and his hands were shaking. He'd had no idea where the man had come from or who had sent him, but one possibility was forming in his mind.

Fortunately, Max had both his wallet and his two fake passports with him – all, he hoped, he'd need to effect an escape from the Rock – but first he had to check on the *Adrestia*. Although certain that Naida must have been killed by the man who had been chasing him, he needed to know if the police and ambulance sirens he'd heard earlier had been sounding because of the discovery of her body. Retrieving his laptop from the boat would also prove immensely useful. It would be dangerous, but there was a gun on the yacht, and if his pursuer returned while he was there, he'd be ready for him.

As for Naida? He'd have to deal with the possibility of her loss later. For now, his own survival was paramount.

Keeping a low profile among the crowds walking through the village centre, Max headed for Leisure Island. From there he could look across to the *Adrestia*'s mooring in comparative safety. Within seconds of reaching the island and the Sunborn floating hotel, he was grateful that he had approached the area with caution. Opposite – on the main promenade adjoining the marina – were parked two police vehicles and an ambulance. Looking over to the mooring, Max could see that the deck of the *Adrestia* was full of paramedics and police officers. The medics appeared to be at work near the main doors, and Max presumed that the focus of their attention would be Naida.

The hard fact was that, whether Naida was alive or dying, there was no going back to either her or the yacht. Max now had to concentrate solely on his own escape.

His first step would be to get clear of the Rock and back to Spain. From there he'd find a way of leaving Europe entirely.

Turning his back on the *Adrestia*, Max walked to the front of the Sunborn floating hotel. Parked directly beside the covered walkway that rose to the hotel's main reception was a large coach. Its driver was at the side of the vehicle, loading luggage into the hold. Next to him was a woman with a clipboard, talking to a couple who were clearly about to board the coach.

Looking up to the driver's front window he saw a plastic sign with the name 'Seville' followed by that of a holiday company. From where Max was standing he could see that the coach was fairly full, although some seats appeared to be empty towards the back. Checking that both driver and holiday rep were looking in the other direction, Max boarded the coach at the front. Climbing the steps, he caught the eye of a man sitting on the front seat.

'When are we supposed to be leaving?' Max asked.

'Ten minutes ago, by my watch,' the elderly man replied. 'Won't be getting into Seville till nearly ten now. That's if the driver takes the A-381 and the AP-4. If he takes another route, then God help us.'

'But they've promised a nice finger buffet upon arrival, Eric,' the woman sitting next to him interrupted.

'Very nice, I'm sure. You staying at the Gran Melia?' Eric asked.

'Yes, I am,' Max lied.

'Sheila and me have never stayed in a Melia before.'

'Very posh, I believe,' Sheila added.

'I'm sure it is,' Max said, edging his way past them.

'Five star all the way for Mrs Bottomley, here. Nothing but the best.'

'Have a good journey,' Max said as he left the smiling couple and headed to the back of the coach.

Taking a seat two down from the back row, he lowered himself from view and closed his eyes. At the border an officer would no doubt jump on board and give a cursory check of the passengers' passports. After that, they'd cross into Spain and head for Seville. With the police checking the *Adrestia* and a killer looking for him, Max knew the time had come for him to disappear once more.

As the coach moved out of the marina village, Max caught a fleeting glimpse of a trolley being loaded onto the back of the waiting ambulance. There was a wrapped body on it, although it was not clear if it was dead or alive. *If that's Naida,* Max thought to himself, *I hope she's dead. Things will be simpler that way.*

Chapter 48

WHEN DR ALMA FELICE had started her 6 p.m. shift at St Bernard's Hospital, the A&E department had been relatively quiet.

'Not a lot going on today. Typical Tuesday,' her colleague Dr Budrani had told her as he'd left the department for home.

'That suits me,' Felice had replied, heading to the locker room to change. 'I'm all for a quiet life.'

Thirty minutes later, the work tempo in the department had changed dramatically. A diver suffering from convulsions had been rushed from the South Mole by boat and unloaded directly to the hospital at Harbour Views Road. Felice could see that the patient, Rahim Robba, was exhibiting classic signs of oxygen toxicity syndrome. It was presenting as a series of grand-mal seizures brought about by an excessive amount of oxygen in his system. Although Felice and her team went to work immediately, it soon became clear that the patient was not responding to the emergency treatments. A steady deterioration over fifty minutes finally led to the man going into cardiac arrest. Neither adrenalin nor persistent attempts at defibrillation could save him, and at 19.23, Rahim Robba was pronounced dead.

In the corridor outside the emergency theatre, Loisa Robba sat in silence. At her side, Rahim's diving colleague, Ali, offered support. It would be another thirty minutes before the tragic news of Rahim's death would be given to them, a period that saw the work of the surrounding A&E department escalate dramatically.

At 19.35, an ambulance delivered the young woman to St Bernard's. She had taken a shot to the upper right-hand side of her body, was still unconscious and had lost a lot of blood.

Fifteen minutes later, another ambulance brought with it the wheelchair-confined and deeply concussed Alex Weber. Suffering a suspected fractured jaw, he was wheeled into a cubicle for examination by an on-duty intern and nurse. The two armed police officers who had escorted him from Turnbull's Lane also stood in attendance, the patient being deemed to be of a dangerous nature.

Sullivan and Broderick had followed the ambulance in a patrol car and were now in a quiet corner of the hospital reception area talking to Chief Super Massetti on speaker phone.

'Witnesses in Marina Bay say a tall, dark-haired man with a gun jumped from the boat soon after some shouting and a scream were heard,' Massetti said. 'Two of the witnesses say they saw a woman fall to the deck of the yacht and another says she saw a dark-haired man chasing an older man with a beard into the centre of the village.'

'I saw the two men running through Casemates Square,

ma'am,' Sullivan answered. 'I gave chase and confronted the dark-haired man in Turnbull's Lane. He took out a gun and fired at me. Fortunately, Chief Inspector Broderick intervened and took him down. Forensics have his gun, a wallet and a mobile phone for examination. We're with him now in St Bernard's.'

'Is this a domestic that's got out of hand?' Massetti asked.

'No, ma'am. I believe the man may be implicated in murders being investigated by Spanish police. In particular, a triple murder just outside Banús. He's been travelling under a false American passport in the name of Rudi Janson. However, we've just found two other passports on him bearing different names. Also, his gun is a Ruger. A professional's weapon of choice, I'd say. With your permission I'd like to contact the Cuerpo and inform them of developments here.'

'Of course. Calbot and CSIs are on the boat – it's called the *Adrestia*. Aldarino's running checks on it now. Witnesses say the bearded man and the woman had been on the boat since it arrived yesterday morning, so I presume it to be theirs. Where the man has got to is anybody's guess.'

'If I was being chased by a gunman, I'd lie low, ma'am,' Broderick said.

'Indeed. Well, let's identify him and flush him out, shall we? Any luck with the other one?

'He's got a fractured jaw by the sounds of it,' Sullivan said. 'Might be a while before he can fully communicate.'

'Okay. Keep me up to date.'

Massetti hung up.

'I take it your knowledge about all this comes from a

certain Spanish police officer by the name of Consuela Danaher?' Broderick said.

'It does. I've also seen our friend with the busted jaw before.'

'Oh, yes?'

'He shot at me while I was chasing him near San Enrique.'

'Please tell me you're kidding, Sullivan?' Broderick said, his eyebrows raised to their full extent.

'He could have killed me too. But he let me go. Something he may regret right now.'

Before Broderick could respond, Sullivan moved off quickly towards the A&E department, scrolling her mobile for Consuela's number as she went.

Chapter 49

CONSUELA DANAHER HAD BEEN WORKING LATE in Estepona and she was looking forward to getting back to Gaucín. The Fiat car discovered in La Linea had been delivered to Málaga and she'd been awaiting an update on the forensic report. Her mother had also called to make sure she'd be going for dinner on Sunday. Seeing her mother would be good, but the dinner was also being attended by several rather tiresome cousins and their children. It would not be fun.

The good news was that Pizarro had flown to Cyprus that afternoon to meet with police on the island. Hopes were high that they could make a connection between the Limassol murder and those in Banús and Sotogrande. It had been good to see Pizarro go off on his glory hunt. As much as Consuela would have enjoyed the change of scene herself, she was glad to get her boss momentarily off her back. As she considered calling it a day, her mobile buzzed and Sullivan's name lit up the screen.

'And how are you, my friend?' Consuela asked.

'I'm up to my eyes in a huge amount of very interesting shit,' Sullivan replied. 'In fact, I think you'd benefit from getting over here right away to wade through some yourself. We've found the owner of your abandoned Fiat. There are also some other things I think might interest you. I know it's late, but what do you say?'

'I say yes, Tamara. On my way.'

———

An hour and a half later, both police officers were sitting in the RGP HQ canteen, eating sandwiches and comparing notes. The news from the hospital was that the woman from the yacht was still undergoing surgery. It was going well, but she remained in a critical condition.

'The man we know as Janson is also in hospital under armed guard. Doctors say he won't be able to speak till tomorrow and even then, not too well,' Sullivan said, chewing on her tuna sandwich. 'We know he's not who he says he is, and that he was present at the discovery of the Bernard murders with Izi Bernard. We also know he flew from the States via Madrid two days before that. There's one other thing I believe I know about him. I'm certain he was the man I chased after the discovery of DuPont's body in the River Guadiaro.'

'I see. And so now he comes over here and tries to murder the couple on the *Adrestia*? Yes?'

'It looks that way. We still don't know the identity of the man Janson was chasing. But Calbot found several passports on the boat with the woman's picture in them. All different names, although the most authentic looking of them is an American passport with name Naida Horvat and a birthplace in Croatia. My colleagues have also recovered a laptop, a gun and some bags containing a set of what appear to be handwritten diaries. There was also a letter attached. It's written by a mother to a son called Max. Reads like a suicide note to me. Forensics have it all, but I've requested the return of the diaries ASAP.'

'And if the fake "Janson" is the man who shot at you, he also abandoned his motorcycle before stealing the Fiat discovered in La Linea today,' Consuela continued.

'Parked there before crossing over to the Rock. The question is, is he the same person who committed the murders at the Bernard villa and then went onto kill DuPont?'

'And if so, might he also have carried out the murders in Cyprus and Corfu?'

'And why? What's the connection between them all?'

The detectives continued eating in silence for a moment, their thoughts finally broken by the entrance into the canteen of Broderick.

'Hi Consuela,' he said. 'Good to see you, *Inspector* Danaher. Sorry to interrupt your dining, but I think you both need to come upstairs. Aldarino's got something on the *Adrestia* and the CCTV footage is with us from Ocean Village and Casemates.'

———

Although it was late, Broderick, Aldarino and several other officers had been setting up an Incident Room for the new investigation on the first floor. It had not yet been officially sanctioned, but Broderick had taken the role of SIO with immediate effect. How Massetti would view that was anyone's guess. She was in a meeting with the Commissioner of Police, so it wouldn't be long before they would find out.

Entering the large room, the three detectives went straight to Sergeant Aldarino, who was sitting at a desktop terminal. In his hands were several email print-outs.

'I sent out a general enquiry about the *Adrestia* to Mediterranean harbour masters about twenty minutes ago. I've got four confirmations of the yacht's recent whereabouts already. Puerto de la Duquesa, Palermo in Sicily, Corfu Town and Limassol in Cyprus have all had the *Adrestia* moored in their marinas. Two of the dates directly correspond to the murders in Spain and Greece.'

'I'll contact Pizarro in Cyprus and tell him. See if he's turned up anything there,' Consuela said.

Broderick nodded. 'Either way, that puts the two on the *Adrestia* pretty much in the frame.'

'We're also checking available CCTV footage,' Aldarino said, handing several copies of the image to his colleagues. 'We've already got this enhanced image of the bearded man.'

'Good work,' Sullivan said, immediately recognising the man in the image as the one she had seen in Casemates Square.

'Wait, a minute,' Consuela said, gazing closely at the remarkably clear picture in front of her. 'I've seen this man before.'

Without further explanation, the others watched as she punched in the number for the Cuerpo Incident Room in Estepona.

'Hello, Diaz. It's Danaher. The interior shots of DuPont's apartment – we have a close-up image of the large framed photograph on his sitting room wall. Send it, will you?'

Minutes later, all had gathered around the image pinged over from Spain. It showed a large colour photograph of a group of people partying on a beach. A wooden sign in the sand announced the location to be 'Phra Nang Beach'.

'Looks like Thailand,' Sullivan said.

'It is,' Consuela replied. 'Now look at the tall man in the middle of the group of women on the right of the sign. Tell me if I'm wrong, but I think that's the same man we have in the CCTV picture from Casemates.'

There was no mistaking the similarity of features. Although the man was younger by some years and sported a less fulsome beard, there was no doubt in anyone's mind he and the man in the CCTV shot were the same person.

'Well done, Consuela,' Sullivan breathed. 'This is major.'

'Wait, a minute,' Broderick interrupted, having spotted something else in the picture. 'I think I recognise her.'

He was pointing to one of the young women sitting on the sand at the man's feet. Like the others, she was gazing up at him in clear adoration.

'Who?' Consuela asked.

'I'm certain that's Daisy's teacher. Here in Gib. Miss Robba. Teaches art.'

'I think you're right,' Sullivan said, examining the woman's image closely. 'I met her at the school's summer concert. Looks just like her. But how the hell could it be?'

Broderick could not answer. He wasn't even looking at the girl now. Instead, his eyes were on the other side of the picture and the shock he felt at what he saw had momentarily robbed him of speech.

'Sir?' Sullivan said. 'Are you all right?'

Slowly Broderick raised his arm and pointed to other group of people in the picture. They were all dancing and one of the men was playing a guitar and laughing.

'What is it, sir?' Sullivan asked, concerned at the look of shock on Gus Broderick's face.

'It's her.' Broderick said at last. 'Can't you see?'

He was now pointing directly at a blonde woman dancing at the centre of the group. Her arms were raised, and her expression was full of exhilaration and joy. 'It's Helen,' he gasped. 'That's my wife.'

The plain walled chapel of Our Lady of Lourdes, on the ground floor of St Bernard's Hospital, is more a place for grieving and fervent prayer than regular worship. Directly next to the hospital's A and E unit, the chapel has often provided the first place of refuge for those experiencing the sudden loss of a loved one.

It had been nearly three hours since Rahim Robba had died from the effects of acute oxygen toxicity, and his wife now sat in the hospital chapel with the duty priest, Father Hernandez, by her side. The shock of Rahim's sudden passing had not manifested in tears or hysteria. Instead, a silent state of grief had overcome her, and the priest's arrival had only confirmed this path as the best way to survive the tragedy that had taken place. If Loisa had realised that one of the architects of her husband's demise was undergoing major surgery in the same hospital, her response may not have remained so balanced. Not that the sudden arrival of two female detectives wasn't proving enough to keep her fully occupied.

—

Sullivan and Consuela arrived at the chapel to find its door guarded by Rahim's diving companion, Ali.

'I'm sorry, but Father Hernandez is comforting a bereaved woman in the chapel at this moment.'

'I'm sorry too,' Sullivan said, flashing her warrant card. 'But we have some urgent police questions to ask Mrs Robba.'

With that, the woman stood aside.

The multiple revelations that the DuPont photograph had brought forth at Police HQ had increased with the mention of the name Robba. Sergeant Aldarino had earlier been informed of an emergency services launch to a diving accident off the South Mole. The condition and name of the injured diver – Rahim Robba – had also been reported to the station. The distressed diver had been taken, at speed, to St Bernard's Hospital for emergency treatment. Since then, Aldarino had been distracted by the rest of the evening's events.

A quick check confirmed that Rahim was Loisa Robba's husband, and a phone call to the hospital pinpointed her location to the chapel. Although reeling from the photographic image of his long-lost wife, Broderick had the clarity of mind to dispatch Sullivan to St Bernard's, considering it best to remain in charge of the new Incident Room himself. As Sullivan left Police HQ with Consuela at her side, she couldn't help but note how cross-border police procedures were taking second place to the furious pace of the investigation.

Inside the chapel, Father Hernandez protested that Loisa needed to be left in peace.

'She is in a fragile state. She has no relatives here and her in-laws are away on a holiday. Can you not wait to interview her later?'

'I'm sorry, but we have no choice, Father,' Sullivan told him, moving to the front of the chapel to where Loisa sat. The woman was in a contained state; her hands lay open on her lap and her eyes, although not tearful, had a distant look of sadness.

'Loisa? I'm DS Sullivan,' Sullivan whispered. 'We met briefly at your school's concert this year. My colleague here is Inspector Danaher of the Spanish Cuerpo. I know this is the worst time for you and we're sorry for your loss, but we have questions we urgently need to ask.'

Without looking up, Loisa simply nodded her head.

'We have a photograph we'd like you to look at,' Sullivan said, nodding to Consuela to place the large copy in front of the grieving woman. 'Do you recognise this picture, and if so can you tell us what you know of it?'

Glancing down at the photograph, Loisa's eyes widened. The effect of seeing the image was immediate and dramatic. Her head shot upwards and her hands clenched. It was as if an electric current had suddenly coursed through the poor woman's body.

'You've seen this before, Loisa?' Consuela asked, edging the photograph a little closer to her face. Summoning strength, Loisa nodded her head once more.

'Is that you in the foreground?' Sullivan asked.

'Yes,' Loisa said at last.

'And someone took it in Thailand, yes?'

'Yes.'

'When?'

'2004. 2005, maybe.'

'Who took this picture, Loisa?'

'A friend. Frankie DuPont, I think. He took pictures everywhere.'

'Have you seen him lately?'

'No. He lives in Spain, but we never meet. Why?'

Sullivan and Consuela glanced at each other. They'd touch on DuPont later.

'Were you both on holiday?'

'No. We lived there. For nearly two years.'

'With your husband?'

'No. I didn't meet Rahim till the commune moved to Spain. But Frankie was there.'

'A commune?' Consuela said.

'Yes,' Loisa said, her tone making it clear she was finding the interview exhausting.

'And the man you seem to be smiling at in the picture. With the beard. Who is he?'

Once again, Loisa tensed.

'He was one of this commune, yes?' Consuela asked.

Loisa nodded once more.

'What is his name?'

'Max. That's Max,' Loisa said, almost swallowing her words.

'And his surname?'

'No one knew. It was just Max. The commune was his. And his mother's. We just knew him as Max.'

'And his mother?'

'She was Von.'

'And this woman here?' Sullivan pointed to Helen Broderick on the other side of the picture. Loisa looked at the image carefully.

'I can't remember her name. She was English, I think. Didn't stay for long. A month, maybe. She was a friend of Gabby.'

Sullivan could feel her heart rate rising dramatically.

'Gabby? Gabby who?'

'Gabby Johnson,' Loisa replied. 'Please, I need this to stop now.'

Chapter 50
WEDNESDAY MORNING

SULLIVAN AND CONSUELA returned to Police HQ just minutes after the clock on the Incident Room wall passed midnight. To neither's surprise, Broderick and Aldarino were still busy at their desks. The officers had now been joined by John Calbot and Harriet Massetti. Consuela Danaher's presence drew a sharp remark from the Chief Super, but Sullivan's explanation of her importance to the rapidly unfolding investigation proved sufficient to halt further objections.

'We've been trying to track the bearded man,' Broderick launched in. 'He was last seen back in the marina, but CCTV is down for repair near the casino and main thoroughfare, so God knows where he's got to.'

'His name is Max,' Sullivan announced. 'Don't have a surname yet, but we've got considerably more.'

'Go on?' Broderick said, a definite note of impatience in his tone.

'A lot more,' Sullivan said. 'The DuPont photograph has opened the full Pandora's Box on this one.'

Although Loisa Robba had reached her limits during the interview at the hospital, Sullivan had pressed her further. Much further. Eventually, Father Hernandez had persuaded them to stop. This was a huge frustration to Sullivan, who had many more questions to ask. She had, however, got the names of those associated with the Thai commune, with Loisa giving up as many as she could remember. Moving swiftly to the central white board, Sullivan took a black marker and wrote the names for all to see.

Frankie DuPont
Ingrid Bernard
Gabby Johnson

'These three people are dead. Gabby Johnson we believe was killed here in Gib, either by Alberto Amigo or by accident. Bernard and DuPont were both murdered in Spain. All three victims were members of a small commune based near Phra Nang Beach in Thailand. Loisa Robba, or Kennard, as she was then, was also a member of the Thai commune. She told me tonight that the commune was disbanded by Thai authorities in 2004 and it subsequently moved, with only ten members, to an old *finca* north of Tarifa on the Costa de la Luz in Spain.'

'Was Helen among them?' Broderick asked, unable to hide the need to know.

'No, sir. According to Loisa, your wife visited the Thai commune for about a month. To see Gabby, I imagine. She then left. Loisa Robba has no idea where she went after that. I'm sorry.'

Broderick could only nod his head, his disappointment clear.

'Continue, please,' Massetti ordered.

'One new member joined the Spanish commune from Gibraltar; his name was Rahim Robba. Today he was declared dead after a diving accident in the Bay.'

Aldarino raised his arm to interrupt.

'We have an update on that. The diving group have reported that both the diving tanks used by the Robbas were full of pure oxygen only, although labelled as a nitrox mix. Pure oxygen is lethal if breathed at certain depths and almost certainly led to the death of Rahim Robba. They've no idea how such a thing could have happened, but reported it to us for investigation.'

'So, we now have four members of this commune dead and the possible attempted murder of Loisa Robba,' Massetti observed.

'Bloody hell,' Calbot said, his shock shared by the entire room. Sullivan continued.

'Loisa also gave the names of the last three members of the Spanish commune.' Reaching to the whiteboard, Sullivan wrote them up.

Jana Kasoulidis
Domonique Taylor
Savannah Jackson

'Consuela has checked the named victims of the murders in Cyprus and Corfu.' Sullivan nodded to Consuela to take over.

'Jana Kasoulidis was discovered drowned, now presumed

murdered, in Limassol marina in July. Domonique Taylor was found dead in her villa swimming pool on the island of Corfu, two weeks later. We know the *Adrestia* also stopped in Sicily, so perhaps there's another murder there we don't know about.'

'Dear God in heaven,' Massetti said, leaning back on the side of a desk.

'Of the ten members of the commune over in Costa de la Luz, six are now dead, believed murdered,' Sullivan continued. 'We know nothing about Savannah Jackson or Von, the mother of Max – she was the commune leader. But we know that Max was in Cyprus, Corfu and Spain at the times of the murders there. He was also in Gibraltar today when Rahim Robba had his accident.'

'We know also that the man I stopped in Turnbull's Lane tonight was chasing Max after shooting Naida Horvat on the *Adrestia*,' Broderick said, his head beginning to throb with pain.

'It's a lot to take in,' Sullivan said.

'Well, there's an understatement,' Calbot muttered, avoiding Sullivan's glare.

'Well, whatever it is, we need to nail all this,' Broderick continued. 'I know it's impossibly late, but where are we going from here?'

'We've sent the images of Max and his pursuer to Interpol and the FBI for identification,' Aldarino offered, turning to Consuela. 'I'll be sending them to your colleagues in Málaga too.'

'In Estepona, actually. Thank you.'

'We're also checking the false Janson's phones and his gun. Forensics will be back ASAP.' Calbot said.

'And we'll be interviewing him at the hospital first thing in the morning,' Sullivan added.

For a moment there was an exhausted pause, broken by Massetti standing from the desk.

'It's a maze. I'll give you that,' she said. 'But I don't have to tell you how important it is that we get this right. Whatever you need, I'll do my best to get it for you. You have to do the rest.'

'There is one thing, ma'am,' Sullivan said. 'The diaries found on the yacht. I'd like to see them as quickly as possible.'

'That's an easy one,' Broderick interrupted. 'They're on my desk. Done and dusted from Kemp. All yours.'

Sullivan turned to Consuela.

'I feel an all-nighter coming on. Care to join me?'

'*Hasta la estrella de la manana, mi amiga,*' Consuela replied. 'Let's do it.'

Chapter 51

After an intense six-hour operation, Naida Horvat had been taken down to the James Giraldi Intensive Care Suite on the second level of St Bernard's. Meanwhile, in a private room under police guard, Alex Weber lay in a state of heavy sedation. An update from the hospital had been sent to Police HQ at 2 a.m.

Since their return to the Incident Room, both Consuela and Sullivan had been feverishly working through the diaries. Having sorted the bags full of handwritten school exercise books into a proper order, Sullivan made an executive decision that they should first read only the diaries covering the time the commune was in Spain. It was agreed that Consuela should start at the commune's arrival in the Costa de la Luz, while Sullivan herself would read Von's last entry and work backwards. Sullivan's thinking was that the end might give more useful information pertaining to the murders in question. It soon became clear that her instinct had been correct. The last entry read:

· · ·

September 5th/6th, 2005

Everything has changed. Irreparably. I haven't kept this diary for nearly two weeks now. Not since the hell began. I couldn't think, let alone write. It started the night that Max discovered Gabby and me kissing down by the river. He'd followed us from the farmhouse, so he must have suspected something. Later he said he'd suspected us for some time but had prayed that it wouldn't be so. He screamed at Gabby. Calling her a whore. Calling her unfaithful to him – although they'd never coupled together. Not once. Loisa has always been his favoured one. I tried to intervene, but he pushed me away. Actually, pushed me to the ground. I knew then that something had snapped. Had broken. That this wasn't just an ordinary blackness. He'd never done such a thing before. Not even in the East when I told him the secret.

Last evening, we discovered Gabby had gone. She was not at supper and nobody had seen her since the afternoon. Max told me he'd said he'd kill her if he found her with me again. I knew then she would never come back. In that moment, I think my heart broke in two. Max says she'll come back because he has her passport, but I know she won't. Gabby is gone. I cannot write it without tears.

But the pain has come from yet another place. I am writing this in Gibraltar. Sitting in the Botanic Gardens looking upwards to the Rock. It's all exquisite and strange. So different to anything I've known for the last twenty-five years.

Today I had a doctor's appointment here, Max not wanting the local doctors in Spain to know anything about us at the commune. It seems that I may have cancer. The doctor thinks I have a good chance of survival, but that I will need treatment. The extraordinary thing is, as he spoke I realised that I no longer cared. For myself? Not at all. Because something worse than Gabby leaving and cancer coming has happened. Something that has made my whole life seem nothing but a desperate sham. A total façade.

Before this visit to the doctor, I collected my monthly post from the Main St post office. There was yet another letter I'd sent to my brother that had been returned unopened, a spiritual magazine I subscribe to and a letter from a genetic testing company in Berkeley.

For years I have been trying, in vain, to persuade the authorities to allow a blood test to prove that Max is Charlie's son. They refused every request. I had always thought, from his birth, that Max possessed the shining side of Charlie's spirit. Where Charlie had lost his way, Max had found the path. That is what I thought although it was difficult for Max to sometimes reconcile himself with that. He has been brave and strong always. It is me who has been weak.

The letter I received had the results of a DNA test. I had sent them samples of Max's DNA. The laboratory told me that they would be able, to within a close margin, match them to Max's birth father or a next of kin. This they did.

The fear I now have in my heart is stronger than anything I have ever felt and that is why I will never be able to tell my son to his face. The letter told me that the name of Max's father is not Manson. It is Brigston. The Brigston family traced to Santa Barbara. That name and the place were enough for me to know. Instantly. Jake Brigston was a friend of my brother's and I believe, although I cannot fully remember, that he and his friends raped me in my brother's cabin at the family home in the November of 1968 My brother was there. Of that I'm certain.

I had always believed Max was Charlie's. That he was special like Charlie. That he would use his power to make things better. And he did. But then I foolishly told him and things were never really the same again. And now this. Our whole life a lie.

I'm leaving these diaries in a safe deposit box in the bank here in Gibraltar. I don't know if Max will ever find them, let alone read them. If he does, I pray that he'll find it in his heart to forgive me, for I will not have forgiven myself.

. . .

Two words had sprung from the pages to shock Sullivan's mind. The first was *Charlie* and the second, *Manson.* Filtering through the other major information in the two diary pages – Von's love for Gabby; the power and fear of Max; the news of Von's cancer; her rape and the mis-iden-tification of Max's birth father – the name of Charles Manson stood out as both the cause and effect of all the other elements within Von's tragic story. Could it be possi-ble? Could Von have believed her son's father to be one of the most infamous personifications of evil in the world? How would it be possible to forget and bury the facts of a brutal rape?

Looking to Consuela, Sullivan realised they would have to read from the first diary entries in the hope of finding some corroborative connections. If they were not there, it would be clear that the diaries were nothing more than the ramblings of a madwoman.

Within a short time, the detectives had found more than enough information from Von's first entries to back up the horrors the diary would later reveal. From Von's first meeting with Manson in a Hollywood nightclub, to her subsequent obsession with seeing him again, the entries rolled out the reasons for the unstable and dangerous foun-dations of her later life with Max.

Last night Donna drove us down to LA and got me and her into the Whisky a Go Go again … The only bad thing was this time Charlie wasn't there … Word was that Charlie and friends had gone to live on the ranch where they'd made that cowboy series …

.   .   .

Von's story now consumed Sullivan and Consuela. Although both realised the diaries could easily be a work of utter fantasy, the growing feeling was that they seemed to have an undeniable feel of authenticity.

Found it! ... me and Donna took off to the Spahn Ranch ... it was just wild, with rocks and kind of hills and dust ...Then we saw them. People just appeared ... Mostly girls like my age ... but then I saw Charlie ... All the others just kind of parted and let him through. He came right up to the car and said, 'Hi, Von, I knew you'd turn up sometime.' ... Donna whispered to me that we had to go as she didn't like the vibe ... we argued and she stormed away and drove off.

With the clock displaying 3 a.m. neither woman showed any signs of tiredness as they continued to read. What all this meant for the investigation would have to be worked out later, but for now, both were driven by the need to find out more about Von and Max and how their story might have led to the murder of so many people over the past weeks.

After supper Charlie took us out to a spot where there was a sort of cave ... He said that we should all love each other and share that love with each other ... That sex was good and should be shared as part of that love ... And then he came to us one by one and put a tablet in our mouths ... All I remember after that was music ... People saying that they loved me and that I was safe ... And then it was morning

… I woke up and Charlie was lying next to me…Then it all went wrong. I went and got bitten and they drove me away. Left me… I thought Charlie had wanted me to stay. That I was part of the family. That he loved me… He kissed my lips. I'd never really been kissed before. Not really kissed, but it felt so familiar.

'Dear God,' Sullivan muttered under her breath. 'She thought her child was conceived during her night on the ranch.'

'And with him,' Consuela said, her eyes still concentrated on the pages before her.

Reading on, they came to another passage with equally disturbing content.

Two nights ago, Mom and Dad had to go to a charity dinner down in Bel Air… my brother turned up with some of his friends and went down to the cabin in the garden … My bro didn't want me to go with them, but his friends insisted. I knew two of them. Dale Collins and Jake Brigston were neighborhood friends.

'Brigston,' Sullivan said. 'It's all here. Everything.' The diary continued.

They'd brought drink and were all smoking weed. I did too … I drank too much, I guess, cos I fell asleep and woke the next morning in my bedroom … I felt ill … Real ill … Still feel like I want to go and see Charlie, but know I can't … Still just want to die.

. . .

Then a later entry.

I dream about Charlie ... I know we have a bond ... I turn eighteen next week so I guess I can make up my own mind about what I do ... Think I've caught a bug: for the last three days I've felt sick to my stomach every morning. That's all.

Consuela and Sullivan stopped reading for a moment.

'These last entries are from 1968,' Sullivan said. 'If you match her story to the things Von says in her last entry in 2005, it's not difficult to see where all this went.'

'Two nights. Two probable rapes.'

'Only she acknowledged only one of them and even then, not as a rape.'

And then *this*, Sullivan said, pointing to a diary entry from 1969.

Today my baby was born. I've named him Maddox. He's a beautiful soul and I love him more than anything ... Mom and Dad are telling me that Charlie's done terrible things ... that he is a monster ... that he's killed people ... Dad says Maddox will have to be adopted now ... Mom says that he is the child of the Devil ... They both say the Tremain family name will be ruined ... I won't listen to them ... I hate them ... I will take Maddox and run away if I have to ... I will protect him...he's an angel ... he is love.

Finally, exhausted by what they had discovered, Sullivan and Consuela sat in silence, the only noise in the room coming from the hum of computer terminals and the ticking wall clock. It was 4 a.m. As both struggled to assimilate all they had learned, Sullivan found herself focusing on one word. Finally, it fell from her lips.

'*Tremain.*'

Chapter 52

THE SIGHT of Calbot's face staring through the driver's side window was not the best way for Sullivan to wake from a deep sleep. His smug smile only added to her irritation.

'This is your early morning call, Sarge,' Calbot's raised voice announced.

A middle finger was all Sullivan could think to offer in response. It had been a long night and the clock on the Mitsubishi dashboard showed 7.10 a.m. When no place to sleep within the HQ had presented itself, Sullivan and Consuela had retired to the comparative comfort of the SUV parked outside. With the time at 4.37 a.m., both detectives had automatically reclined the vehicle's large leather front seats and fallen into an exhausted slumber.

'*Buenos dias*, Tamara,' Consuela said, with an attempt at brightness.

'I hope so,' Sullivan replied, opening the car door and heading to work.

Before calling it a night, Sullivan had emailed to the States requesting urgent information regarding the

Tremain family of Montecito, California. Sullivan hoped something useful would be sent back, to go alongside the details already gleaned from the diaries.

As she and Consuela entered the busy Incident Room, Broderick was already waiting with a reply from Washington.

'And this email would be about what exactly?' he asked, taking in the somewhat dishevelled state of the two women detectives.

'We took Von's diaries apart as much as we could last night,' Sullivan replied, scanning the email. 'The whole thing's extraordinary, but for now we're concentrating on finding Max. We discovered his family name is Tremain. This email is, by the looks of it, confirming that.'

Moving to the whiteboard, Sullivan took the black marker and wrote up the latest information.

'Maddox Tremain, AKA Max, born to Yvonne, AKA Von Tremain, in Santa Barbara on July 23, 1969. Von's father, Gerard, was a banker from a successful banking family. Mother, Jannette, a non-professional from an equally respected Californian family. One brother, Richard, who is now ... shit ...'

Sullivan stopped, taken aback by what she was about to read.

'Is what?' Broderick questioned, appearing to be irritated at feeling so out of the loop.

'Who is now,' Sullivan continued, 'a leading Republican congressman and a possible future presidential candidate.'

'Wow,' was all Consuela could add.

'Still not understanding,' Broderick replied, as Sullivan continued to read the FBI email.

'Yvonne and Maddox Tremain left the US for Goa, India in 1979. There is no subsequent knowledge of their time in that country. In 2004, *Max* Tremain – as he had become known – and his mother turned up in Thailand seeking help from the US Consulate in Bangkok. Max had been charged with the sexual assault of a woman in a commune in Krabi Province in the south of the country. After diplomatic intervention, the charges were dropped on condition that Tremain leave Thailand. In September 2005, both he and his mother reappeared on the Costa de la Luz, in Spain. Yvonne Tremain was subsequently found dead in the swimming pool of the farmhouse the Tremains were leasing, in the countryside near the Rio de los Molinos. Her death was considered accidental, although suicide was not completely ruled out due to an excess of sleeping tablets in her system mixed with alcohol.'

'That's where Gabby Johnson was escaping from when she was picked up in Tarifa,' Broderick said, doing his best to join the dots.

'Looks like it,' Sullivan said, continuing to read. 'Max Tremain returned to the USA in October 2005. He lived in Santa Barbara at his uncle Richard's home in Montecito for six months before being confined to a high security mental facility in Oregon State. Records show him as having experienced a complete mental and physical break-down after the death of his mother. The condition presented with extreme rages of violence and prolonged periods of psychotic disturbance.'

'We're definitely getting warmer.' Calbot smiled, giving Sullivan a double thumbs-up.

'Max escaped from the facility in April of this year. He

is believed to be in the company of a former day-visitor to the institution by the name of Naida Horvat.'

Calbot punched the air. 'Nailed.'

A cold stare from Broderick quickly took the wind out of the young detective's sails.

'It is believed that Tremain is travelling abroad. He is known to possess considerable private funds available to him from off-shore accounts. No information exists regarding the identity or whereabouts of these accounts.'

'Or as to the bastard's exact current whereabouts,' Broderick added.

'No, sir,' Sullivan said, a little disappointed by her boss's response.

'But, er … well done, Tamara,' Broderick added, just in time.

'Inspector Danaher, too, Guv. She set this whole ball rolling.'

'And you too, Consuela. If only all our dealings with the Cuerpo were this easy.'

'Thank you,' Consuela said. 'Happy to be the bringer of détente.'

Aldarino raised his arm for attention.

'Just in. We think Max Tremain may have left Gib last night on a coach bound for Seville. We've notified the Cuerpo in the city as well as your colleagues in Estepona, Inspector Danaher.'

'Thank you, Sergeant. I'm going back there now.'

Broderick stepped up to the whiteboard.

'So, we suspect Max Tremain and Naida Horvat of being the main killers; now we need to find out their reasons for murdering.'

'I've a theory it could be about what happened after the

death of Max's mother and the end of the commune. I assume it broke up and everyone went their own way. Maybe it wasn't amicable. Maybe Max held a grudge about that.'

'Conjecture, but a good conjecture. We also need to discover why our fake Janson was trying to kill both Max and Naida,' Broderick added. 'Kill you too, Tamara.'

'I have a theory about that too,' Sullivan said. 'May I suggest we get across to St Bernard's to interview him?'

'Suggest away, Detective Sergeant,' Broderick said, a glint in his eye. 'We are all mere mortals in your presence.'

'I wish.' Sullivan said, marching to the door. 'Oh, how I dearly wish.'

Chapter 53

THE COMBINATION of rush hour and roadworks along Queensway meant that Sullivan and Broderick's drive to the hospital took longer than expected. Phoning ahead, they'd been told that 'Janson' was awake but struggling to speak. The hospital also informed them that an interview with Naida Horvat would not be possible until her condition improved. She remained in Critical Care.

Sitting in the passenger seat, Sullivan looked to her boss.

'I'm sorry we found nothing on your wife's where-abouts, Guv.'

'Thank you,' Broderick said and continued driving in silence.

As they entered the St Bernard's reception area, Broderick's mobile buzzed. It was Kemp phoning to tell him that Janson's phones had already delivered intelligence. The burner phone had called and received from a number in the Washington D.C. area. The smart phone was also found to be running a sophisticated mobile phone bugging device linked to the Spanish police number of Inspector Consuela Danaher.

'So that's how he got his information,' Sullivan said. 'He'd have listened in to what Consuela knew about the investigations. I spoke with her on that number too. He'd have known what we were thinking, where we were going. Those bugs are highly effective.'

'It's all Sanskrit to me,' Broderick answered. 'Last time I used a satnav, I nearly drove off Europa Point.'

Two armed RGP officers guarded the private room on the second level of the hospital, one stationed outside and the other within. A nurse escorted Sullivan and Broderick to the patient's bedside.

'Mr Janson has been operated on for a broken jaw. He also nearly severed the end of his tongue, so communication may prove difficult,' the nurse told them before leaving. As Broderick nodded to the armed officer to also leave the room, Sullivan looked across to the man on the bed.

'Well, one thing we know for sure is that you're not "Rudi Janson",' Sullivan said, moving closer to him. 'The real Janson is in San Francisco. The passports we found on you are clearly false, so they don't help. And I'm guessing you're not going to be much help to us either.'

Alex Weber lay in silence, his heavily bandaged head propped up a little and his wrist handcuffed to the bed. In spite of the heavy doses of medication he was receiving, the pain in his head and mouth remained hugely uncomfortable. Answering questions was not something he was planning on doing any time soon.

'I thought you wouldn't,' Sullivan continued. 'In case you don't already know our names, although I'm sure you do, I'm DS Sullivan and this is Chief Inspector Broderick of the RGP. You met Chief Inspector Broderick briefly last evening. In fact, he's the reason you're the one in hospital right now and not me with a bullet in my chest.'

With still no response, Sullivan looked to Broderick.

'Okay if I continue, Guv?'

'Fill your boots, Detective Sergeant.'

'Good,' Sullivan said, returning her attention to the patient. 'So, if you're not going to tell us anything about yourself, why don't I let you know the things we've learnt about you?'

Sullivan moved yet closer to Weber's side.

'You arrived in Spain from San Francisco via Madrid eleven days ago. You met Izi Bernard in Banús and were with her when she discovered her mother, housekeeper and gardener murdered in the pool of the Bernard family villa. There you gave the Spanish police your name as Rudi Janson. That name was false. As was your story about stopping in Spain for a little business before heading over to Morocco. I believe your real intention for being here was to track down the two people we believe carried out the Bernard murders, together with several others. Your getting caught up with the police in Marbella was the first of several rather poor decisions I believe you've made over the past week. Wouldn't you agree?'

Weber did not reply. His eyes fixed on a spot high on the ceiling. Across the room, Broderick had sat down on the one comfortable chair available, happy to let Sullivan take the lead.

'You next popped up in San Enrique. I saw you spying on the recovery of Frankie DuPont's body from the Rio Guadiaro. In fact, I chased you and we met on that dirt road heading out of San Enrique. That was the first time you tried to kill me. As it is, I hurt myself falling from my motorcycle. For some reason you decided to show me some mercy. A decision I suspect you regret right now.'

Sullivan noticed a slight twitch in the man's left eye. She was getting to him.

'With DuPont, you were one step behind again. But you thought you were being clever. Somehow, you'd got a bugging device on Inspector Danaher's mobile phone. Well done for that. Brilliant. Probably how you discovered who *I* was. Definitely why you broke into the Danaher *finca* up in Gaucín and had a root around. But once again, you made a bad mistake. You hurt the dog. Why? Did it make you feel better? Leggo wouldn't hurt you. He's hardly got any teeth. Anyway, that was a very bad mistake and, in my book, unforgivable.'

Weber moved slightly on his bed. The chain of his handcuffs rattled against the metal bar at his side.

'But then you must have received intelligence about the whereabouts of Max Tremain and Naida Horvat, because you crossed the border and tracked them down to Marina Bay. Where or who you got your information from is something we are particularly interested to know. I believe that holds the key to all this. So, this is my question: who sent you here?'

At last Weber spoke. Just one word.

'Lawyer.'

'You want a *solicitor* present, do you? We haven't charged you with anything yet Mr ... Mr? You see, there we go again. We don't know your name. But if you're considering talking to us, we will of course get you a legal representative. Are you willing to talk to us?'

Weber once again lay in silence. Sullivan went on.

'Okay. The thing is, I don't think you'd be able to answer my question even if you wanted too. You see, I believe you're a hired killer. A *contract* killer if you will. A pretty poor one, it has to be said, but certainly good enough to be charged with three attempted murders. Two attempts on my life and one nearly successful attempt on the life of Naida Horvat. In fact, you're not really a *"hitman"*, more a *"hit or miss man"*. However, such is the nature of your business, I believe protocol often insists that the person or persons buying your services remain anonymous. Which is probably just as well. They can't be too thrilled with the way things have worked out up to now can they? In fact, if I was them, I'd consider you to be something of a liability. Might I be correct in that assumption?'

Sweat was now forming on Weber's forehead, his eyes flicking from side to side. In the corner of the room Broderick was looking on in complete amazement. *Where the hell is Sullivan going with all this?*

'The thing is, if you were willing to tell us the things you *do* know, it could be very useful for you later in court. We have your mobile phones. They're offering up some very helpful information. Sloppy work again on your part, I'm afraid. But worse for you is the fact that I believe I have a pretty good idea of the identity of the person who did contract your services. That's a huge advantage for me, don't you agree? But even worse than that, is the very real possibility of you being considered an accomplice to all these murders – Ingrid Bernard, her gardener and house-keeper, Frankie DuPont and Rahim Robba. Because if we don't catch Max, and Naida Horvat decides to say nothing, you'll be pretty vulnerable on that front. After all, up till now we've seen a lot more of you around the murder scenes than we have of them.'

Sullivan raised her shoulders and nodded her head.

'I'm just saying. So once again, my question is … will you talk to us?'

For the best part of a minute nobody spoke. Weber's mind was on fire. The pain in his mouth was intense and he was scared. Terrified.

'Okay,' he muttered at last, the muscles of his face straining with the pain of forming words. 'I'll talk.'

———

'I've seen it all now,' Broderick said, as the detectives took the stairs to the hospital reception below. 'A little unorthodox to say the least.'

'I had to go for it, sir. In pain, in despair and hand-cuffed to a hospital bed. A bit like shooting fish in a barrel.'

'I didn't know you had it in you.'

'Neither did I.'

'So, where are we?'

'For starters, we now know what he *doesn't* know. Plus, he's given us his real name. Alex Weber. That'll help.

'You said up there you'd a pretty good idea who sent him over here,' Broderick said, pausing to catch his breath. 'I hope it's the same person I'm thinking it might be, Tamara.'

'Me too, sir,' Sullivan replied, carrying on down the stairs. 'Me too.'

Chapter 54
TWO DAYS LATER, WASHINGTON D.C.

FOR THE SECOND time in a week, Congressman Richard Tremain sat at the head of a table in the Palladin Room in Marcel's Restaurant on Pennsylvania Ave. On this occasion, the twenty guests invited for the private supper were of an even higher calibre of political influencer than before. Each esteemed guest knew exactly why their invitation had been sent to them. In Washington there really is no such thing as a free dinner. The champagne and fine food would be given in return for their support for Richard Tremain's political ambitions through the coming months and years. If successful, Tremain would then use his influence to enhance his guests' agendas in business and government. It was the way of all things in the capital. The swamp remained – as it always would – undrained.

James Leamore-Adair leaned across from his position at Tremain's side.

'All present and correct. Nobody's let us down. Believe me, that's a very good sign.'

'Thank you, Jim. Quite a table you've convened here. The great and the good.'

'Well, the *great* certainly.'

'I have to admit I'm feeling a little daunted at this moment in time.'

'That won't get you to the White House, my friend. Remember, you're here because you deserve to be.'

'I'll drink to that,' Tremain said, raising his glass to salute his friend.

Things had moved swiftly over the last few days, and the clock was ticking fast in political circles. Tremain wasn't a big-name candidate. The press had already speculated on his potential bid for the top job, but the congressman was an under-supported outside candidate, and nobody knew that fact better than himself.

Leamore-Adair advocated that as a smaller player, Tremain had to announce his intentions soon. This was in order to build a following to take on some of the big hitters who'd already thrown their hats into the ring. One in particular was already keeping an over-close eye on any moves the congressman made. Timing was all.

Tremain had been in initial discussions at a low level for months, but tonight he would tell the small gathering of interested backers at the table of his decision to run for President. He would ask for candour from all present, but knew and hoped that he would not get it. That was part of the plan too.

'Throw the gossip mill one more piece of steak before we go for the real thing in a month's time,' Leamore-Adair had counselled.

Tremain had dreamed about this moment for years: the time when he would begin, in earnest, the journey to the job he had always believed could be his. Before him sat the people who could and would help him achieve his ambitions. They all understood what was about to happen and the work they would have to do to make Tremain's campaign a successful one.

Leamore-Adair reached over and touched the congressman's forearm. The time had come. Taking to his feet – glass and spoon in hand ready to tap for attention – Tremain allowed himself the indulgence of relishing his moment of power and hope.

Clearing his throat, he tapped on the side of the glass to call order. To his astonishment, instead of the respectful attention he had expected, his fellow diners had mostly turned away from him, many now staring towards the other end of the room. At the main door, two men in dark grey suits had entered the Palladin Room, and a slight altercation was taking place with one of Tremain's security men. The two newcomers flipped their identity badges in the man's face and moved on into the room. To everyone's surprise they walked quickly to the head of the table and showed their FBI badges once again, this time to the dumbfounded Tremain.

'Congressman Tremain,' the first man said. 'I am Special Agent Morgan and my colleague here is Special Agent Lipski. We need you to come with us, please, sir.'

'In connection with what, for God's sake?' Tremain spluttered, his face red with barely suppressed rage.

'We just need you to come with us, sir,' Morgan said. 'Now, please.'

Chapter 55
THREE WEEKS LATER, GAUCÍN, SPAIN

TURNING off the main Gaucín road and onto the track leading up to the Danaher farmhouse, Consuela glanced across to her father in the passenger seat and felt a sense of well-being. She'd not had that feeling as a child, growing up in a separate country from him and making do with his sporadic visits. Ric's decision to come and live in Spain had changed things. It had not been easy at first – for either of them – but they'd worked at it and Consuela's mother had wholeheartedly encouraged them to do so.

Ric's flight from the UK had come in on time, and the drive from Málaga airport had been an easy one. As the Mitsubishi climbed the hill in the early Sunday evening sunshine, the first thing both father and daughter could hear as they approached home was the distant sound of Leggo barking.

Coming to a halt between the farmhouse and its annexe, Ric jumped from the vehicle to greet his ancient hound.

'Pleased to see me, are you? That's a boy,' he said,

allowing Leggo full rein to jump up and enthusiastically lick his returning master.

'And he's not the only one looking forward to seeing you,' Consuela called out from the other side of the jeep.

Right on cue, the farmhouse door flew open and out onto the yard came Tamara Sullivan, Gus Broderick, Penny, Daisy and Cath, all whooping and holding glasses full of deliciously chilled cava, one of which Broderick handed to his old friend.

'Surprise, surprise, Ric. Hope it's a good one for you.'

'They don't come much better,' Ric laughed, raising his glass. 'Here's to all of you. And I hope you've had a nice little holiday up here, Tamara.'

Sullivan looked to Consuela.

'You haven't mentioned anything to your dad?'

'I thought I'd save it till we were all together,' Consuela said, smiling at her mischief.

Ric raised an eyebrow in mock alarm.

'What? Earthquake? Hurricane? Military coup? You haven't sold the goat, have you?'

'No, Ric,' Sullivan said, laughing at the thought. 'Just a little bit of police work. A little bit of *cross-border* police work, actually.'

They spent the next few hours eating, drinking and sitting outside the farmhouse talking and laughing. Sullivan and Consuela brought Ric up to date with everything while Broderick chipped in with his usual dry observations. When they finally finished, Ric Danaher sat back in his cane chair and pronounced his judgement.

'Well, that's the last time I do Airbnb for a copper. More trouble than you're bloody worth.'

As the party went on, Daisy sang a song and Penny

showed everyone an app on her phone that gave them all big ears and a red nose when their picture was taken. Cath couldn't help remarking that her brother's adjusted features were a huge improvement on his usual ones.

With night approaching from the east, everyone watched the late summer sun disappear in a blaze of orange and red light across the distant Straits and the Spanish coastline. Alone and monumental in the centre of the horizon stood the Rock.

'There's no other view like it,' Ric said. 'Thank you all for my homecoming.'

An hour later, everyone had happily moved indoors. With the wine still flowing, Ric and Cath sat chatting at the kitchen table, while Penny and Daisy helped Consuela make up the spare beds for the Brodericks to sleep in.

Stepping outside once more, Sullivan walked to the middle of the yard and looked up at the cloudless night sky. Here in the hills, with little ambient light, the Milky Way stretched from one side of the heavens to the other. Thousands upon thousands of stars hung like a never-ending cascade of diamonds above the darkened Spanish hillside. All Sullivan could do was stand and stare, her breath taken by the night's magnificence.

'Room for one more,' a voice said behind her.

It was Broderick, wine glass in hand and a rare smile on his face.

'You bet,' Sullivan said. 'Pick a star. Any star. Make your wish.'

'I've already done it. Now it's just a waiting game.'

Sullivan didn't have to ask what the wish was. She was certain she already knew. For a moment they both stood and stared upwards to the sky. There was a lot to reflect upon.

Broderick's thoughts were drawn to Loisa Robba, and not only because she was someone who had briefly known his wife, Helen. Loisa's story concerning the last days of Max Tremain's commune had stayed with him. She had told of how things had fallen apart after Gabby Johnson had fled and Max's relationship with his mother had become strained. His volatile nature and controlling ways had gone beyond a point where the group felt comfortable. Ingrid Bernard had been the first to go. She had made contact with her estranged husband and young daughter in Banús, and one morning she left the commune and did not return. Max had exploded in rage at what he saw as another act of gross disloyalty, and from that moment onwards had kept a sharp eye on the rest of them. Then the morning came when Max had discovered his mother dead in the swimming pool. His screams of pain had brought them all running to see the dreadful sight of Von floating face down in the still waters of the pool. Max had wanted to keep the death quiet, but the group had somehow insisted that the police be called. The investigation that followed concluded that Von had suffered death by misadventure. During this time, Max's tantrums and bullying increased dramatically.

Rahim had been the next to suggest going. He'd become a good friend of Loisa's, and over several days he persuaded her to run away with him to the Rock. He was a native of Gibraltar and he promised that his parents would help them both start a new life there. On the day they left, they found they were not alone. Frankie DuPont, Jana Kasoulidis, Domonique Taylor and Susannah Jackson left with them. The last of the commune members walked to the nearest town, four kilometres away, and got transport to Algeciras. They had split up there and gone their own way. The only exceptions were Rahim and Loisa, who had fallen in love and would later marry. Leaving the commune had been the last Loisa had heard of Max until the day he'd turned up on the Rock to kill both her and Rahim.

The horrifying legacy of it all led Loisa to leave both her job and the Rock. Daisy Broderick was heartbroken. Loisa told Broderick that she wanted to be alone, to escape to a new place and all further knowledge of the investigation. She left Gibraltar early one autumn morning to travel to the south-west of France. And that was that.

Sullivan, too, was considering the events of the last few weeks. Naida Horvat had been charged with the murders she had carried out with Max Tremain. Since her slow recovery from the shooting, she had said not one word. Her apparent vow of silence included no communication with the police or her legal representatives. Her face remained a blank, expressionless barrier to her thoughts and words. Whatever knowledge she had of her lover or his possible whereabouts would stay locked up in her poisoned mind.

Alex Weber had proved a far more malleable proposition. His testimony had immediately sealed the fate of Max's uncle, congressman Richard Tremain. The would-be contract killer's incompetence was explained by the history of falsehoods and fake representations he'd made in setting himself up as an expensive killer for hire. Weber had been a low-level CIA operative but was dismissed for moonlighting as a private investigator. Continuing his work as an investigator, he discovered that an efficient contract killer could easily command handsome fees for their work. Using friendly contacts on the dark net, Weber passed himself off as an executioner with far more experience and discretion than he actually possessed. It had been Richard Tremain's bad fortune to have entrusted his malevolent plans to such a preposterous fake. Weber would be charged with three counts of attempted murder. In the States, Tremain had been charged with conspiracy to commit murder. The FBI were also considering other charges based on information given to them by the Royal Gibraltar Police Force of his facilitating the rape of his late sister, Yvonne Tremain, in 1968. Needless to say, his political career had come to a very public and humiliating end.

Alberto Amigo was not charged with the murder or manslaughter of Gabby Johnson. He would finally receive a suspended sentence for preventing the lawful burial of a body. Cath Broderick had quickly taken the man under her wing, visiting him and offering to support him in any way she could.

All in all, the investigations had been hailed a huge success. Consuela too had benefitted. Chief Super Massetti had called her opposite number in Málaga to commend the Cuerpo officer's work. The Commissioner of Police had done the same. The only person who had been unhappy with Consuela was Pizarro. He'd travelled all the way to Cyprus only to find that the case had been solved at home in his absence. Upon his return, the praise he had discovered for his junior officer had angered him beyond words. Within days he'd packed his bags and taken his obnoxious working manners back with him to Cádiz.

The one loose end had been the fate of the American

commune member Savannah Jackson. FBI investigators finally traced her to Colorado. Sadly, they were four months too late to save her life. Savannah had been found dead at home in her hot tub in May. It was thought she had died of natural causes. A new post mortem subsequently found differently. They now deemed Savannah Jackson to be Max Tremain and Naida Horvat's first murder victim, her death, like that of the others, echoing the miserable end of Max's mother, Von.

'It's been a strange few weeks,' Sullivan said, her eyes still staring skywards.

'Funny few months, if you ask me,' Broderick replied.

'This one's been different, though. Things coming from everywhere at once. And the main man is still out there. A lunatic who thinks he's a god and still believes his father was Charles Manson.'

'*They fuck you up, your mum and dad.*'

'They certainly do. It's a wonder any of us survive, really.'

'I always think an investigation is like one of those domino stunts you see on the internet,' Broderick said. 'Where they line up thousands of individual dominoes with a tiny space between each. Then someone flicks the first domino down and the rest just fall in rapid succession one after the other till the whole line has collapsed. The only difference is that in an investigation the dominoes are facts and they get flicked in several places along the line. Dominoes falling, or facts connecting, here, there and everywhere. It all looks out of control and not as it should be. But in the end, it all comes together. All the facts joined up in one continuous line. Job done.'

'Except not on this one. We didn't get Max Tremain.'

'The dominoes are still falling on that, Tamara. They'll connect up one day. They always do.'

'And you? How do you feel?'

'A bit raw, but I'll take out of this what I can. Helen was smiling in that picture. She looked happy. In spite of everything, I still love her enough to find solace in that. It's enough to give me hope.'

'And the dominoes are still falling on that too, Guv. I hope they connect one day.'

Gus Broderick and Tamara Sullivan stood in silence for a few minutes more. At last they broke their gaze from the stars and turned to move indoors. In the warmth and glow of the farmhouse, friends and family were waiting for them.

Epilogue
CHRISTMAS, CAMBODIA

MAX HAD SPENT an hour in downtown Sihanoukville, checking out the morning tourist buses as they arrived from Phnom Penh. They were always full of the young and hopeful, and he had trained his eyes to search out the lonely and vulnerable amongst them. With Christmas Day less than a week away, the bustling coastal city was heaving with holiday visitors and the usual large influx of back-packers and dyed in the wool local expats. Although down-town was full of shops, bars, bakeries, guesthouses and busy markets, most newcomers fell from the buses and launched themselves towards the beaches straight away, unable to relax until they had confirmed that the golden sands and crystal-clear waters they had travelled so far to see were an actual reality.

Today Max had seen one or two possible 'family' members arrive in the town. Two girls and one man – all alone. Each had that look in their eyes that Max had come to recognise as the mask of the impressionable: an over-smiling, slightly desperate aura of hopefulness that fooled

Max not at all. Normally he would attempt contact with at least one of them, but today he had something else on his mind.

An appointment on Otres beach.

Ten weeks had passed since Max had arrived in Sihanoukville, and he'd filled them with busy days. Travelling out to the countryside, he had come across the perfect place to found his new commune: the ex-country retreat of a recently deceased Australian businessman. Standing in countryside just six kilometres from the coast and built in the French Colonial style, its seclusion and faded grandeur would provide an ideal environment for Max's new family to be born again. Max had already persuaded five new members to stay there, and their grateful natures and willing ways were the perfect qualities required of his new acolytes.

Now, as he walked on the long, soft-sanded beach of Otres 1, passing myriad bars offering cocktails, free wi-fi and British roast dinners, Max wondered if his planned meeting had been an entirely wise decision. Stopping to pick up water, he continued towards the quieter sands of Otres 2. Between these beaches lay a natural stretch without development. Much favoured by locals, many Khmer could be found relaxing there – often swimming in the ocean with their clothes on. Finding a spot on the beach line beneath the shade of the copious number of Tamarisk and Casuarina trees, Max sat down to wait and meditate.

Just after midday, he spied her, walking from the southern end of the beach. Despite the large sun hat covering her face, Max recognised her immediately. Her walk was distinctive, her bearing also. Dressed in a simple white cotton blouse and trousers rolled up to her knees to allow the lapping waves to cover her feet, the woman moved effortlessly towards him.

Max stood and walked slowly to meet her at the water's edge. At first, they stood in silence, as if greetings were unnecessary. The woman could see that Max was different. His hair and beard were shaved clean from his head. It was unsettling. At last he spoke.

'Thank you for coming. I wasn't sure you would.'

'Neither was I.'

'I'm sorry for all the pain. I hope you understand.'

'I do.'

'I promise you all the love I have.'

I know, but I'm scared.'

'You know that *fear* is *love*. You'll be safe here, I promise.'

Slowly Max reached out to take the woman's hand.

'You said that I would share your secret,' she said. 'What is that?'

'It was my mother's secret and then it became mine. It's simple. I am the *Son* of *Man*.'

'What does that mean?'

'I will teach you and everything will be just as it once was for us.'

Turning towards the casuarina trees and the shade of their tender branches and leaves, Max led the woman from the shore.

Helen Broderick walked with him across the white sands – her heart full of all the love she had.

About the author

As an actor, Robert has appeared in leading roles in a number of award-winning and long-running British television series, including *Jeeves and Wooster*, *Casualty*, *The House of Eliott* and Richard Harris's *Outside Edge*, for which he was nominated best actor in the British Comedy awards. Other series in which he has played major roles include John Sullivan's *Roger, Roger* and *Rock and Chips*, *Holby City*, *Doc Martin*, *New Tricks*, *Midsomer Murders*, *The Royal*, *Death in Paradise*, *Father Brown* and *Agatha Raisin*. He has most recently appeared as Dr Thomas Choake in *Poldark* for the BBC and as the psychotic drugs baron Shank, in Sky's black comedy *Sick Note*.

For the stage his work includes Michael Frayn's *Alarms and Excursions* and David Harrower's *Blackbird* – nominated Best Actor in the Manchester Evening News Drama Awards. In the West End he has appeared as Dr John Watson in *The Secret of Sherlock Holmes*, as Geoffrey Hammond in *Public Property* and as Jim Hacker in *Yes, Prime Minister*. He has also portrayed Victor Smiley in *The Perfect Murder* by bestselling crime writer Peter James, and John Betjeman in Christopher Matthew's *Summoned by Betjeman*. He has recently appeared in the first production of Bill Kenwright's Classic Comedy Company in Sir Alan Aykbourn's *Ten Times Table* and *How the Other Half Loves*. He will shortly be appearing as P.G. Wodehouse in the premiere of William Humble's *Wodehouse In Wonderland*.

His many BBC radio portrayals include Arthur Lowe in *Dear Arthur, Love John*, Ronnie Barker in *Goodnight from Him*, John Betjeman in *New Fame, New Love*, Nigel Breezer in the comedy *Celebrity Plumber* and Chief Inspector Trueman in *Trueman and Riley*, the long-running police detective series he co-created with writer Brian B. Thompson.

He currently co-presents, along with bestselling author Adam Croft, the popular crime fiction podcast *Partners in Crime* – partnersincrime.online, @CrimeFicPodcast on Twitter or www.facebook.com/partnersincrimepodcast on Facebook.

This book is the third in the Sullivan and Broderick murder mystery series following *The Rock* and *Poisoned Rock*. Robert's next novel will be *Blood Rock*, the fourth in the Sullivan and Broderick series. *Blood Rock* will be published by Hobeck Books in 2021. The ghost story, *Echo Rock*, also set in Gibraltar, has previously been an Amazon No. 1 bestseller and is available for free to Hobeck Books subscribers.

For more information and special offers go to Robert's website: www.robertdaws.com.

Acknowledgments

I have been a yearly visitor to Gibraltar for some twenty-five years. The warmth and spirit of its people, together with the wonder and magnitude of the Rock on which they live, have never ceased to amaze me. Even as I write, I am looking forward to my next visit.

I would like to thank those within London's Metropolitan Police Service and the Royal Gibraltar Police who have given their time to offer help and guidance. It has been invaluable. Thanks also to Nicky Guerrero, Peter Canessa, Stuart Green and to my friends at the marvellous Gibraltar Tourist Service and Gibraltar Literary Festival – Sally Dunsmore and Tony Byrne.

I hope I will be forgiven for having played hard and fast with the internal geography of the Gibraltar police head-quarters, as well as Gibraltar's main general hospital, St Bernard's. I have also changed the names of several places and establishments. Other than that, I have tried to be as accurate as possible with situation and location.

Huge thanks to my agents at Independent, Paul Stevens

and Will Peterson, for years and years of help, energy and kindness.

To Rebecca Collins and Adrian Hobart at the new and incredibly supportive publishing house Hobeck Books. 'Trad values. Indie spirit'.

To my lovely editors, John Appleton, Nancy Duin, Jenny Parrot and Sue Davison.

To the writer Jeff Guinn, for a spark to lead the way.

To Mr and Mrs James, for their invaluable support, friendship and encouragement.

To Adam Croft, pal and fellow podcaster on Partners in Crime.

To Katie, Jo, Mike, Emma, Jane, Steve, Kate, Ted and Judy for help in tough times.

To all the wonderful nieces and the nephews. Legends, all.

For Ben, Betsy and May for being lovely, hilarious and remaining only mildly interested in what I do.

Last, but not least, to my wife Amy, for her wisdom, patience and wonderfully creative mind. A dear writer friend, Christopher Matthew, once wrote, 'Eighty-five percent of a writer's life is spent thinking and thinking *very hard*. Unfortunately for writers, unless they are seen to be pounding away at a laptop keyboard, nobody really thinks they are working at all.' Amy has always understood this strange process, even when my 'thinking' has drifted into a pleasant little afternoon siesta.

Hobeck Books - the home of great stories

We hope you've enjoyed reading this book by the brilliant Robert Daws. We're proud to have Robert as part of our growing family of authors at Hobeck Books. If you would like to find out more about Robert and his work, please visit his website **www.robertdaws.com**.

If you enjoyed this book, you may be interested to know that if you subscribe to Hobeck Books you can download a selection of free short stories and novellas:

- *Echo Rock* by Robert Daws
- *Old Dogs, Old Tricks* by A B Morgan
- *The Silence of the Rabbit* by Wendy Turbin
- *Never Mind the Baubles: An Anthology of Twisted Winter Tales* by the Hobeck Team (including all the current Hobeck authors and Hobeck's two publishers)
- *The Clarice Cliff Vase* by Linda Huber

Also please visit the Hobeck Books website for details

of our other superb authors and their books, and if you would like to get in touch, we would love to hear from you.

Hobeck Books also presents a weekly podcast, the Hobcast, where founders Adrian Hobart and Rebecca Collins discuss all things book related, key issues from each week, including the ups and downs of running a creative business. Each episode includes an interview with one of the people who make Hobeck possible: the editors, the authors, the cover designers. These are the people who help Hobeck bring great stories to life. Without them, Hobeck wouldn't exist. The Hobcast can be listened to from all the usual platforms but it can also be found on the Hobeck website: **www.hobeck.net/hobcast**.

Finally, if you enjoyed this book, please also leave a review on the site you bought it from and spread the word. Reviews are hugely important to writers and they help other readers also.

Praise for *Killing Rock*

'A top crime thriller.'
Adam Croft, crime writer

'wonderful…this one I have been
unable to put down!'
Pat McDonald, crime writer

'A brilliant book that I cannot
recommend enough!'
Books From Dust Till Dawn

'…a book of style and substance…'
Bookmarks and Stages

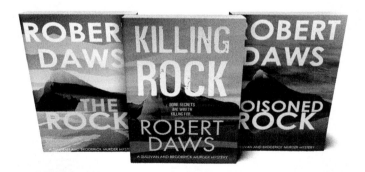

Printed in Great Britain
by Amazon